Ann Cleeves

Ann Cleeves is the author behind ITV's VERA and BBC One's SHETLAND. She has written over twenty-five novels, and is the creator of detectives Vera Stanhope and Jimmy Perez – characters loved both on screen and in print. Her books have now sold over one million copies worldwide.

Ann worked as a probation officer, bird observatory cook and auxiliary coastguard before she started writing. She is a member of 'Murder Squad', working with other British northern writers to promote crime fiction. In 2006 Ann was awarded the Duncan Lawrie Dagger (CWA Gold Dagger) for Best Crime Novel, for *Raven Black*, the first book in her Shetland series. In 2012 she was inducted into the CWA Crime Thriller Awards Hall of Fame. Ann lives in North Tyneside.

Bello:

hidden talent rediscovered

Bello is a digital-only imprint of Pan Macmillan,
established to breathe new life into previously published,
classic books.

At Bello we believe in the timeless power of the imagination,
of a good story, narrative and entertainment, and we want to
use digital technology to ensure that many more readers
can enjoy these books into the future.

We publish in ebook and print-on-demand formats
to bring these wonderful books to new audiences.

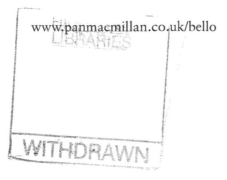

www.panmacmillan.co.uk/bello

B E L L

Ann Cleeves

HIGH ISLAND
BLUES

BELL◉

First published in 1996 by Macmillan

This edition published 2014 by Bello
an imprint of Pan Macmillan, a division of Macmillan Publishers Limited
Pan Macmillan, 20 New Wharf Road, London N1 9RR
Basingstoke and Oxford
Associated companies throughout the world

www.panmacmillan.co.uk/bello

ISBN 978-1-4472-5028-9 EPUB
ISBN 978-1-4472-8903-6 POD

Visit www.panmacmillan.com to read more about all our books
and to buy them. You will also find features, author interviews and
news of any author events, and you can sign up for e-newsletters
so that you're always first to hear about our new releases.

Author's Note

There is a small town on the Upper Texas Coast called High Island. The Houston Audubon Society has two sanctuaries and birdwatchers visit the area from all over the world. There is no Oaklands Hotel and all the characters in the book are fictitious.

Chapter One

Cecily had wanted George there at nine, had insisted on it, so he had left home in the dark. It was impossible to argue with Cecily. In the end he had time to kill and he took the last ten miles slowly, driving down straight lanes between potato fields. Miles away across the flat land a line of poplars broke the horizon, shadows in the gloom. There was an icy drizzle. When he came to a village there were still lights on in the red brick houses and a group of children, shrouded in hoods and scarfs, waiting for the school bus stood miserably in the doorway of Fred's Mini Mart. He passed battery chicken sheds, an immense glasshouse, a sugar beet processing plant. The agricultural heart of England, he thought, with depression. The heart of the agricultural industry, at least.

There was a second, identical village. A bridge over the canal and then the turning so overgrown that he almost missed it. No sign. Lady Cecily Jessop did not need to advertise her presence. No gate. An attempt had been made to fill the pot-holes with gravel and he had an image of Cecily herself with a wheelbarrow and shovel doing the work. It wouldn't have surprised him. She had told him once that she disliked employing menials. This was not, he thought, through any liberal notion of social justice, but out of meanness. Why pay someone to perform a task one could easily perform oneself?

Why then, he wondered, is she prepared to pay me?

The summons had come two days before by fax. It was written in the third person as if she were royalty: 'Lady Cecily Jessop wishes to consult Mr Palmer-Jones professionally. She would be grateful if he could attend The Deuchars at 9 a.m. on March 5th.'

The formality had been broken by a handwritten note on the bottom: 'I'm bloody busy at the moment, so don't be late!'

He had tried to contact her for more details but she was too busy, it seemed, to answer the telephone.

Molly had been affronted by the rudeness of the fax and by the fact that she had not been invited.

'Ignore it,' she said. 'If she wants us to work for her badly enough she'll be in touch again. And you can tell her we're a partnership. We make joint decisions about the cases we take on!'

George, however, had been unable to ignore the fax. Since his retirement from the Home Office he had been asked to serve on environmental working parties and committees. He had met Cecily Jessop at these meetings and had been impressed by her tenacity and her ability to drink whisky by the tumblerful and still talk sense. She was a celebrity and he was flattered, despite himself, that she had called on him for help. He was curious to see what she wanted of him.

She called the house 'the mouldering heap', though he knew she felt an affection for it. Why else would she stay on? She had no close relatives and could have sold it without causing offence. She wasn't the type to feel any obligations to maintain the ancestral home. Maintenance came low on her list of priorities. 'It'll see me out,' she said as it crumbled about her. He had visited her there before and thought she was like a squatter, making the best of the discomfort. It was another example of her meanness. She was a wealthy woman but she preferred to camp out in one room, with a tin bucket to catch drips from the ceiling.

There was no reply from the grand door under the pillared portico, though he heard the bell echo inside. He had expected none. Cecily disliked casual callers. He found her in the kitchen drinking rum in hot milk and smoking a pipe. She had left her wellingtons at the door and wore hand-knitted woollen socks with holes in the toes, a pleated tweed skirt and a sweater with a Fair Isle pattern which George supposed had been knitted by Vanessa. Vanessa had been her friend and companion since they had met as girls during the war. Vanessa had stuck by Cecily through her two divorces and her drinking. It was Vanessa who brought a semblance of order to the house. 'My housekeeper' Cecily called her, and Vanessa accepted that without a fuss though George doubted that it was a paid position.

'Rum, George?' Cecily said. 'You need something to keep out the cold. It might be March but it's bloody freezing.'

'No thank you, Cecily,' George said politely. 'Coffee will be fine.'

'Oh, well,' she said. 'Suit yourself.' Then, with a sergeant major's roar, 'Nessie, come and make George a coffee.' There was a pause and she added, 'There's a dear.'

She was seventy, but fit and formidable. Very tall. Very thin. And still working, as she made clear to everyone she met. She might have left the university but there was no retirement for *her*. No sliding quietly into her grave while the bastards fucked up the planet. She'd been a delegate at the Rio summit meeting and she was still collating data for her work on bird migration and environmental damage. One room at the Deuchars had been made reliably waterproof and there she kept her computer. She had never learned to use it but employed a sixth-former, the son of one of her farm labourers, to come in every Sunday to work the magic. The figures which spilled from the printer she knew how to use and she still produced papers which made the scientific world take notice. The latest was on the decrease of bird migrants from sub-Saharan Africa.

'I'll have to go out again in a minute,' she said. 'I'm working a constant effort ringing site for the BTO. You've got to show willing, haven't you?' She raised her voice and shouted again: 'Come on Nessie, we haven't got all day.'

'Perhaps I could put the kettle on,' George said, 'while you tell me what this is all about.'

'Extortion, George,' she said darkly. 'That's what this is about.'

She got to her feet and padded across the tiled floor to a dresser so riddled with woodworm that it was surprising it stood up. From a china toast-rack she took a letter, still in its envelope, and set it on the table before him. It was addressed by printed label to Hubert

Warrender MP at his home address. George recognized the name. Warrender was a junior environment minister.

'Bertie's an old chum of mine,' Cecily said. 'He mentioned it in passing: "See you've got a finger in another pie, Cec. I can't even open my mail without bumping into you." I couldn't think what he was talking about so he passed the thing on.'

It was a letter soliciting support for a new charity – the Wildlife Partnership. The Partnership had worked successfully in the States for some time, buying land, especially in threatened areas of Central and South America. Now it was extending its operation to Europe. Many natural history groups in Britain and the United States had already made donations and famous British naturalists had added their support to the venture. There followed a list of names including that of Lady Cecily Jessop. Also in the envelope was a brochure with photos of the rain forest and of fetching Brazilian children.

'Bertie gave them a hundred quid,' she said. 'Soft bugger.'

'By cheque?' asked George. 'Made out to the Partnership?'

'No,' she said. 'He telephoned in a credit card donation. The only address is a Post Office box number.'

'I take it you hadn't given permission for your name to be used,' George said.

'I've never even heard of them.'

'Are you sure there wasn't a letter, asking perhaps for you to get in touch with them if you had any objection? It could have been overlooked as junk mail.'

'I'm not a fool George, and I read everything that comes to this house addressed to me.'

'Have you complained to the charity?'

'I've tried,' she said. 'But is doesn't seem that easy. I phoned the telephone number. It's answered by some inarticulate youth who only seems programmed to accept donations. I asked to speak to his employer but I was told he was on his own in the office. When I asked where the office *was* I was told he wasn't at liberty to say.' She mimicked a West Country accent: 'I'm sorry madam but we haven't got the facility to welcome personal callers,' and then continued, 'He'd obviously been told to say that. He was too dim to dream it up for himself.'

She looked at her watch.

'Sorry, George,' she said. 'You'll have to make that coffee later. Come into the garden with me to check the nets.'

Outside, the rain had stopped, but droplets of water still clung to the fine mesh net strung between two poles in the bushes. A song thrush was caught in one of the shelves in the net. She extracted it carefully and took it to a wooden shed where she kept her ringing pliers and scales.

'They probably think I'm dead,' she said, 'so there's no danger in using my name. Or so gaga that I won't complain.'

'I don't see,' George said, as she released the thrush and watched it fly away into the gloom, 'what you want me to do about it. I imagine that a solicitor's letter to the PO box the charity is using would stop it using your name again.'

'But that wouldn't stop them operating, George, would it? And I smell something fishy. Find out, for instance, if they're a real charity.'

'If they're not,' he said, 'that would be a serious fraud. A matter for the police.'

'Oh,' she said impatiently, 'I don't want the police involved at this stage. For all I know the Wildlife Partnership is well meaning but disorganized. Doing good work. I just want to find out who's behind it.'

'There's no hidden agenda here, is there?' he said suddenly, suspicious, 'something you're not telling me?'

'Of course not.' Her anger seemed real enough. 'I want to hire you George if that's not too much trouble for you. I understand that it's the sort of thing you do for a living.'

'I work with my wife,' he said. 'I'd have to consult her.'

'Nonsense,' she insisted. 'You wouldn't be here if you didn't intend to take the case.'

'It'll take time. It won't be cheap.'

'I can afford it,' she said extravagantly. 'Besides, we're friends, aren't we George? I'll expect a discount.'

It was late afternoon and the drizzle had turned to heavy rain. The office window was covered in condensation and the fumes from the portable Calor gas heater caught at Jason's throat. He was licking envelopes which made him feel sick and light-headed. The telephone rang.

'Good afternoon,' he said brightly. There had been training in telephone manner in the course he had taken at school, when they'd decided he wasn't clever enough for A levels. 'This is the Wildlife Partnership. How may I help you?'

'Hi, Jason!' He recognized the voice immediately. It was his boss. Unconsciously he slicked back the hair already thick with gel. He found the American drawl unbelievably romantic. He'd always liked the pictures. 'How's it going, hon?'

'Oh,' he said. 'You know.'

'A bit slow, huh?'

'A bit,' he admitted reluctantly. This was his first job. He wanted to make it a success and he wanted to please the caller. After all, promises had been made at his interview. 'You could be in at the start of something big Jason. Who knows? If our charity captures the imagination of the British people we might like you to come to our Houston headquarters for training. Even to visit our refuges in Central and South America. Would you be prepared to travel to Texas, Jason?'

So he had put up with the boredom. He had filled envelopes and answered the telephone. He had written down credit card numbers and answered the punters' queries, following the information his boss had written down for him. The questions seldom varied from the prepared script and now he had the answers off-pat: "We were founded in response to the Rio summit meeting and have the support of all the major environmental charities. At present we have two reserves, one in Brazil and one in Costa Rica. Plans are under way to purchase a third. We employ local staff wherever possible.'

'We've got a problem Jason.' The American voice was smooth, reassuring. He waited for it to continue.

'We'll have to close down the office for a while. I'd like to tell you Jason, just how much we've valued your work over the past couple of months. We'll be in touch when we need your help again.'

It was only after he replaced the receiver that he realized he'd been given the sack. And that he hadn't been paid for his last week's work.

Chapter Two

The three of them met at a Mexican place on Highway 290, the road west out of Houston. Mick had suggested it. He was the local. Rob had arrived in town that day. He worked for a travel company and had a group of British birdwatchers in tow. He'd dumped them at the Marriott Hotel, telling them they needed to rest after the flight. One night there then on to High Island for some serious birding. Oliver was the only one on holiday and he'd come over specially for this reunion.

The restaurant was a tin shack surrounded by seedy clapboard houses. It was busy and they waited on the porch for a table, drinking frozen margaritas, eyeing each other up. This was the first time they'd been together for twenty years.

There were just the three of them. That was what they had agreed. No wives. No kids. Not this first time. The place was noisy. Inside, about a dozen parties were going on. Conversation was difficult and not only because of the noise.

'So,' Oliver said, 'we made it. The great reunion. Really, I never thought we would. Not the three of us.'

He looked very cool in a white shirt and white linen trousers. Very much the Englishman on holiday. Middle age suited him though his hair was quite grey.

'If anyone was likely to dip out I'd have thought it would be you,' Rob said. He'd just come back from the Middle East, leading one of the first groups of tourists into Jordan from Israel. He'd picked up some bug and lost a lot of weight, so he looked thin and haunted, as brown and gaunt as a Bedouin. And that was the pattern of the relationship already established again. Rob and Oliver.

Antagonistic sparring partners, opposites in every way. But closer than brothers, Mick thought, with a trace of the old envy, when the chips were down.

It was Rob who'd sat up all night with Oliver twenty years ago, when the phone call came from Julia to the motel on the way to High Island. Rob who'd been almost weeping with frustration: 'For Christ's sake don't do it Ollie. Not for her. She's not worth it.'

And when that night was over and Oliver was determined to do the honourable thing it was Rob who supported him through it. He stood as the best man in the smart little church and kissed the bride affectionately for the photos. Mick hadn't been there – he'd already moved to Houston by then – but they'd sent him the photos. Julia wore white, a high-bodied, fall-skirted number which was fashionable at the time. It would have been appropriate even if she hadn't been five months' pregnant.

Rob's thoughts must have been drifting in the same direction because he asked suddenly: 'How is Julia?' It was a malicious question. He guessed that Julia was the last person Oliver wanted to talk about.

'Oh. Busy. You know.' Oliver stared out from the porch at a couple of kids playing in the darkening street. They had only managed one child, the important one, the one who had tied him to Julia. Sally, the love of his life, nineteen now and wanting to be an actress.

'I suppose Julia's working is she?' Rob persisted mischievously, 'now Sally's off your hands?'

'Not paid work,' Oliver admitted. 'Voluntary things. The Red Cross. . . WI. She's a magistrate. And music takes up a lot of her time. She sings in rather a good choir.'

And costs me a fortune, he thought with resignation, with her car and her dresses and her position in the village to keep up.

'I'm surprised she found time to come with you on this trip,' Rob said. Oliver looked at him steadily, recognizing the sarcasm, failing to rise to the bait.

'Oh, well,' he replied. 'She deserves a break, you know.'

The margaritas were served in glasses like goldfish bowls. After a month of abstinence in the Middle East and a long flight, Rob felt the alcohol kick into his system. It was like being a student again, pissed for the first time. He felt suddenly emotional. He wanted to tell Oliver he was a stupid bastard. It wasn't too late to leave Julia. He'd given her twenty years of his life and he could walk out at any time. Rob would stand by him. But he said nothing and they sat for a moment in silence.

'Do you guys see much of each other?' Mick asked at last. He had a peculiar hybrid accent, West Country English crossed with Texan twang, still hesitant. 'I mean, perhaps it's strange to have a reunion at all if you two spend every weekend birding together. I mean, I hope you're not here just because of me ...' His voice tailed off. Perhaps he realized that it sounded as if he were soliciting some declaration of friendship. He'd never been able to take that for granted.

'No,' Rob said. 'We don't meet. I live in Bristol now. That's where the travel agent I work for is based. And I'm abroad a lot, leading trips.'

He looked at Oliver, challenging him to give another explanation for their failure to keep in touch, but they were called through the tannoy system to eat: 'Brownscombe. Table for Brownscombe.'

They pushed past the crowd on the porch towards a waiter who led them into the building. Inside it was noisy and even hotter. Fans whirred on the ceiling but had little effect, except to add to the background sound. A teenage girl was celebrating her birthday. As they took their seats all the waiters and kitchen staff paraded to her table, banging pots and pans, singing and whooping.

Outside it started to rain. There was a crack of lightning. The lamps flickered then a white light shone briefly on the manic procession dancing back to the kitchen. The three men sat at a small table next to a window now streaming with rain water. They ordered fajitas because that was what Mick recommended, and while they waited they pulled tortilla chips covered in melted cheese from a pile and covered them in salsa. Rob asked for a Corona beer. Then there was a silence as they stared at each other again, saw each other for the first time as middle-aged men.

'And business is doing well for you, Mick?' Oliver asked politely. He might have been at one of Julia's charity cocktail parties. 'I must say you seem to have settled down out here. Environmental consultancy, is that it? That seems to be taking off in the UK, too. We're representing a firm involved in a wind farm in Northumberland. They've been hired to do the environmental impact assessment. Quite a lucrative contract actually.'

'We have some business in the UK,' Mick said. 'But Laurie looks after that. She's the driving force in the relationship.' He smiled sadly. 'I'm just her gofer.'

'Laurie should be here.' Rob spoke so sharply that they all looked up at him. 'She was there, at Oaklands, when we discussed it, wasn't she? It might even have been her idea. "A reunion in twenty years time," we said. "High Island in the spring with the migrants going through."'

Mick looked uncomfortable. 'I guess when we discussed it we never thought one of us would end up marrying her,' he said. 'Not really. She'll be at High Island tomorrow.'

I never imagined *Mick* would end up marrying Laurie, Rob thought. Mick, short and squat, dark as a tinker, and about as articulate. He pictured her the first time they'd seen her, walking down the straight road from Winnie, rice fields all around her. She was wearing a sleeveless vest, ripped jeans and scuffed boots. A stained leather cowboy hat hung by a thong round her neck and binoculars were slung over her shoulders like a cartridge case. She stuck out her thumb for a lift and the atmosphere in the clapped-out hire car changed. Each of them wanted her. This was what they'd hoped would happen all along. A real American adventure.

The fajitas came, with refried beans, more salsa and tortillas. They ate hungrily. Airline meals, Rob said, were always crap. He should know. He was an expert. He hadn't eaten anything decent since London the day before. He never ate on planes. They all relaxed. They talked about university, the paranoid Polish landlady in their first year digs.

'She could smell a girl in your room through two closed doors,' Oliver said.

'And it was always fish fingers for breakfast on Fridays,' Mick and Rob said together.

They laughed. It was a safe subject. They said they should have done this years ago.

When the meal was finished Rob and Oliver phoned for a cab to take them to their hotel. Oliver and Julia were spending the night at the Galleria Marriott too. Mick phoned for Laurie to collect him. She was in the office, he said. Working late. It was only round the corner. He didn't explain why he didn't have a car, or offer the others a lift.

Laurie's car arrived before the cab but it was still raining and she didn't get out. They had a tantalizing glimpse of her through the steamed-up window, a profile against the street light, a brief wave. Then she drove off very fast.

Laurie drove home in silence and Mick wondered if he had done something to upset her. He found it hard, these days, to judge her mood. It was still raining and already the flash flood-water was collecting in the playing fields by the side of the road.

The evening's reminiscences had triggered his memory of another rainy night. It was more than twenty years ago and he was driving down a Devon lane overgrown with campion and bramble and dripping cow parsley. The summer after university had been wet and business in the holiday trade had been bad. His father had taken the lack of bookings as a personal insult. He had blamed the charter operators with their cheap flights to the sun, the weather forecasters who prophesied gloom and his son for planning to run away to America.

In Wilf Brownscombe's eyes university had been bad enough, though he had taken some pride in seeing Mick's graduation picture in the *North Devon Journal Herald*. And why zoology, which was no use to man nor beast? Certainly not to an overworked businessman running a holiday complex. He'd been pleased when all that was over and Mick had come home to take some of the work off him. Then the boy had the nerve to say that he wanted three months off the following year to go bird watching in America. What sort of interest was that for a grown man anyway?

'It's before the season really starts Dad,' Mick had said. Wilf had thought it was pathetic really. Sometimes he wished his son would lose his temper, shout, behave like a real man. 'Easter's late next year.'

'Still busy though, isn't it? Still work to be done. Still your mother and me that'll have to do it all,' said his father.

So that summer and autumn, Mick had worked from dawn until the early hours of the following morning. He drove through the rain between the sites accumulated by his father: the new hotel which wouldn't have looked out of place in Torremolinos, the Marisco Tavern in the village by the sea, the caravan park on the headland. Supervising his father's empire, proving that he wasn't a waster, earning his three months leave without pay, his holiday with the only friends he'd made at university. He'd even given up birding that autumn. There'd been a red-eyed vireo in the churchyard at Lee. It had stayed for a week, even made the local paper. He'd not bothered going to see it.

He'd been on the plane though, with Rob and Oliver. He'd escaped in the end.

In the cab they hardly spoke. Oliver made a polite enquiry about Rob's trip to the Middle East. Rob answered shortly then sat back in silence, not sulking exactly but not prepared to make small talk either. He was too tired. What he'd really like was to go on to the hotel bar, have a bit of a session with Oliver, cut through all that politeness and reserve. In the air-conditioned iciness of the hotel lobby he was about to suggest it, but two members of his tour group had been waiting for him. They accosted him immediately. Oliver gave him an amused wave and sauntered off.

They were a couple, in their early sixties. They looked rather dowdy and out of place. Tiredness and anxiety had made the woman shrill and complaining.

'Where have you been then?' she demanded. She grabbed hold of Rob's arm, as if she were afraid he would run away and leave them again to the mercy of strangers. Suddenly embarrassed she let it go.

'I explained at the airport. I'd arranged to meet some friends for dinner.' He gave her his professional smile, though looking beyond her he watched Oliver disappear into a lift.

'Well really. I don't think that's on, do you Russ? Personally accompanied by expert staff, that's what the brochure says. I didn't fancy America anyway though Russ was keen when he got his early retirement. You see all those things on television. Riots and murders. I don't know how any of them sleep in their beds at night . . .'

She stopped abruptly. She had lost the point of her complaint. Her eyes were red and she looked exhausted. This would be a big trip for them. Perhaps they had never flown before. She'd probably not slept much in the week before leaving home.

'Russ is the birdwatcher,' she said. 'I'm only here for the trip.'

'We'll have to make sure you enjoy it then,' Rob said gently. 'What's the problem?'

The problem was the shower tap in their bathroom. They couldn't get it to work.

'You could have asked the hotel staff,' Rob said.

'I know, but I didn't like to. I'd have felt such a fool.' She was quite sheepish now, saw that she'd blown the thing out of all proportion, was prepared to laugh at herself.

He went with them to their room and showed them how to turn on the shower, watched their amazement at the power of the water jet.

'It's how the American's like it,' he said.

'Is it?' she said. 'Well, I can't say I'm surprised.'

'I'll see you at breakfast then,' he said.

'You *will* be at breakfast?' Her anxiety returned.

'Of course. Then the bus will take us to High Island.'

'I'm sorry,' she said, 'that I lost my temper.'

'That's all right,' he replied, smiling again. Some people thought West Country Wildlife Tours only kept him on because he could charm the old ladies.

'It's just that it means a lot to us, this trip. We've been waiting a long time for it,' she finished.

Chapter Three

Mick and Laurie Brownscombe lived very much like their neighbours. They had a large house set away from a wide road. There was a pool in the back garden and a garage with automatic doors and room enough for an Explorer and a little Toyota. None of this was considered excessive. Laurie might once have dropped out of school and made her living in ways she wouldn't want her kids to know about but now she was a regular mom in a regular neighbourhood. On the surface at least.

'Are you sure this is a good idea?' Mick said. He waited for Laurie to lock the house and set the alarm.

'Sure,' she said.

'What about the kids?'

'I've told you. The kids'll be fine. It's all arranged.'

She waited for him to get into the driver's seat of the Explorer. Two women in shorts, wearing towelling sweat-bands, walked down the street, arms swinging. Mick was distracted for a moment. It still seemed strange that in Texas walking was a form of exercise, not a means of getting where you wanted to go. For that you used the car. Reluctantly he returned his attention to Laurie.

'It seems kind of tacky,' he said. 'They're my friends.'

'Look,' she said. 'You got to hustle.' It was a joke between them, a catch-phrase, but he didn't laugh.

'Not my friends,' he said.

'All right,' she said, losing patience with him. 'I'll do the hustling. OK?'

He shrugged. He knew there was no point in arguing.

'Things aren't easy right now,' she said, 'and you wouldn't want to lose all this, would you?' The sweep of her head took in the house, the car, the yard.

'I guess not,' he said, 'but I'm not going to be popular.'

She grinned. 'You think you're popular now? You ended up with the girl didn't you? They're both as jealous as hell.'

'You like that don't you?'

She laughed again. 'Sure I like it. You watch. I'll have them eating out of my hand.'

He looked at her helplessly but there didn't seem to be anything else to say. He drove down the I10 past the glittering skyscrapers of Houston and through the flat land towards the coast.

Rob Earl stood at the front of the bus and spoke to the party. He used a microphone because he knew from experience that at least half of his audience would be hard of hearing. It was that sort of group. He'd led trips to High Island before, usually as part of a Texas package for keen birders, taking in the Big Bend and Laguna Atascosa at the same time. This was a new venture, a gentle introduction to the Upper Texas Coast based for ten days at High Island. There would be no long bus trips and no early starts unless the punters wanted to get up to make the most of the migration on the reserves.

The tour didn't come cheap because the accommodation was good, and Mary Ann could charge just about what she liked in the spring. Birders came from all over the world to the peninsula, and there weren't that many places to stay. The Gulfway Motel was booked from one year to the next. Besides, Oaklands was something special.

The party was much as he had expected considering the nature of the tour. There were a lot of retired people. Most came from the West Country where the independent travel agent for whom he worked was based. He recognized a few familiar faces, people who had travelled with him before. There were plenty of experienced birders, but few fanatics. He relaxed. This would be easy. They wouldn't be hard to please.

'High Island isn't an island at all, of course. It's a small town, close to the coast, raised slightly above the surrounding wetland. I believe it's all of thirty-nine feet above sea level. Hardly a mountain, of course, but distinctive enough to be attractive to birds.'

There was an appreciative, slightly superior chuckle from his audience.

'There are four main birdwatching areas on the Upper Texas Coast: Anahuac, a National Wildlife Refuge which has more than twenty-seven thousand acres of marsh, the Bolivar Flats, an area of saltmarsh and beach, and two Houston Audubon Society Sanctuaries in High Island itself – the famous Boy Scout and Smith Oaks woods. We'll spend time at each depending on the weather. What we need are strong, turbulent head winds to meet the migrants as they fly north from the Yucatan peninsula. That should result in what we call a fall and the Americans call a fall out. If that happens it'll be the most spectacular birding experience of your lives: thousands of tired migrants seeking shelter in the woodlands on the reserves. From a personal point of view I'll be watching the weather forecasts very carefully. I first visited High Island twenty years ago and I've never experienced the ideal conditions for a classic fall. Then on Sunday there's the Easter Bird Race or Birdathon which will benefit a number of environmental organizations. Oaklands has been asked to put up a team. I'll be around for volunteers later in the week.'

He sensed that the passengers' interest was wandering. They were tired and they wanted to see birds, not talk about them. He sat down. The group dozed.

The couple who had accosted Rob in the hotel the night before waved at him shyly to catch his attention. He walked up the swaying bus to sit beside them. After a night's sleep they were apologetic and wanted to chat. They needed to be reassured that he bore no hard feelings for the outburst of the night before. Their name was May. Russell had worked for the South West Electricity Board since he had left school and he had taken early retirement with quite a decent redundancy pay-out soon after the company was privatized.

'We couldn't have afforded it otherwise,' he said. 'Not a trip like this.'

He seemed dazed by his own good fortune. He'd watched all the slide shows of other chaps' travels. Never thought he'd actually see those American warblers for himself.

Connie had been a cook in a small private school. She retired with Russell so they could spend more time together. 'The boys bought me ever such a nice bunch of flowers when I left,' she said. 'But there was nothing from the school. Not even a thank you.'

This was what it was like at the beginning of a trip. Everyone wanted to tell Rob something about themselves. Each traveller wanted to be special, not just another anonymous tourist. Usually these confidences irritated him – he was paid to show them birds not listen to their life stories – but today he was feeling mellow, even sentimental. He asked the Mays if they had children. That was where these conversations usually led. To proud descriptions of offspring, their work and qualifications, to photographs of adored grandchildren. But Russell and Connie only looked at each other and he sensed a tragedy, a terrible gap in their lives. No, they said. No children.

'We've got friends in Houston,' Russell said as if that were some compensation. 'Old neighbours who moved out to work with British Gas. We thought we might hire a car, spend some time with them. Connie would like that. It would kill two birds with one stone you might say. A few ticks for me and some gossip for Con. That would be all right, wouldn't it? It wouldn't put you out?'

'Of course not.' Rob was expansive. 'It's very relaxed where we're staying. Just treat it like home.'

But he imagined that they lived in a tidy semi and thought that Oaklands wouldn't be much like home.

The bus drove east down the I10 past the urban sprawl which had developed along the freeway: motels, second-hand car lots decked out with shimmering bunting, huge concrete churches with extravagant names. They had no sense of any country beyond until they crossed the San Jacinto River and looked out at the forest of oil refineries towards the coast. Then there was the Trinity River and views of open countryside: the wide expanses of water of Galveston Bay, rice fields and cattle, and in the distance a water tower, shining like an alien space craft. Ahead of them, along the flat, straight road, they could see almost into Louisiana and watched the huge, chrome-plated trucks appear out of the heat haze.

They turned off the 110 before Winnic so that they could drive past the National Wildlife Refuge at Anahuac. There marsh and swamp stretched to a horizon which was as straight and even as if it was the sea. They got out briefly to see herons, stilts and wading birds. Some would have liked to stay longer but Rob herded them back onto the bus. Mary Ann would be waiting for them. She would be expecting them for lunch. He would have liked to stay too – he loved the sense of space and the rich smell of the swamp – but he knew better than to take liberties with Mary Ann.

At the I24 they turned south towards the coast. Two turkey vultures soared above the road. Russell May took out his check-list and ticked off the species. There were more rice fields, more cows.

Despite Rob's warning they had been expecting something more dramatic of High Island, perhaps a real hill rising out of the flat land. But as they approached the town all that broke the horizon was the steep, semi-circular bridge crossing the intra coastal canal. Beyond that they reached the town almost without noticing. They came to a field of nodding donkeys, part of the local oil industry, and then they were in High Island, which hadn't seemed to be a hill at all, just trees floating above the marsh.

Oaklands was to the north of the town. The bus turned off the highway just after the bridge and drove down a road of single-storey houses without boundary fences, mostly clapboard, some in need of repair.

Rob, directing the driver, saw the detail as if for the first time, the wooden swinging seat outside one house, basket-ball posts and a kids' climbing frame outside another. A dog chased out into the middle of the dusty road and barked at them. A woman flapped out in her slippers to call it back. She stopped to wave at the bus. High Island prided itself on being friendly to the birders.

They came to a gate, already open, and a cattle grid. A track led through huge magnolias with shiny leaves and oaks covered in lichen. The house was surrounded by trees so it seemed that if it let up guard for a moment the woodland would take it over again. Then they saw the house.

It was bigger and more ornate than any of them had expected, gloriously overdone, all turrets, and verandas and angled roofs. It was three-storeyed, L-shaped with a clock tower and pointed windows in the roof. On the inside of the L there was a magnificent wrought iron veranda and on the long side of the house a new wooden porch, with a view of a lawn which had been cleared from the woodland, and a pool.

'It was built in 1897,' Rob said, as proud as if he owned it himself. 'At one time a railway line brought visitors right up to the door. It was very grand. Miss Cleary has brought it back to its former glory. When I first came here it was very different. Falling to pieces. You wouldn't believe the change.'

But nobody was listening to him. They had had enough of travelling. They had climbed from the bus and were waiting in the heat to collect their luggage.

Chapter Four

When Rob had stayed in Oaklands twenty years ago it had looked like the set of a second rate horror movie. The paint had been peeling and the whole place smelled of decay. It had been run as a boarding house by a widow who had a child to support. Salesmen stayed there and student teachers at the High School, and a couple of elderly long term residents who should have been in a nursing home but couldn't afford to move.

It had been Laurie's idea to stay there, after they'd picked her up on the road from Winnie. They had seen her from a long way off, appearing out of the heat haze like a mirage, watched her hitch a lift, slowed down the car to stop beside her.

'Where are you heading for?' Rob had asked, trying to sound cool.

'Wherever you're going,' she'd said, corny as hell, but somehow carrying it off.

'We're making for the coast,' he'd said. 'High Island. We can take you there.'

'Why not? You got somewhere to stay?'

'Not yet.'

'We could stay at Oaklands. They're kind of family. It'll be cheap at least.'

So they'd stayed there for a week, the four of them. All the time his obsession for Laurie grew and they waited for the weather to change and the migrants to come. There had been plenty to see: egrets and ibises on the salt lagoons and coypu and alligator, but the humidity and the tension of waiting for a fall had made them as bad tempered and fractious as children. The weather was too still and warm and they had flown back to Britain without ever having seen the trees in Smith Oaks crawling with brightly coloured warblers. It was Laurie who said they should meet up in twenty years time. A reunion at the Oaklands Hotel, High Island. Something to look forward to. Something to blow away those High Island blues.

The woman who ran Oaklands then, Mrs Cleary, had been an aunt of Laurie's. There had been a tension in the relationship which was never explained. She had been surprised to see Laurie on her doorstep, not hostile but wary. And though she must have been related to the girl's parents she never asked about them. Laurie's life was never discussed.

Elsie Cleary had a twelve-year-old daughter named Mary Ann, who had taken a bit of a shine to Rob. When they left for home he promised to write to her. He had kept his word and sent her postcards from exotic places, funny notes about other birdwatchers, poems and limericks. She wrote back with news of the peninsula. After he'd been appointed leader with the tour company he wrote to Mary Ann to tell her. He still thought of her as a child although by then she'd been away to Business School. She wrote back on smart headed notepaper telling him that her mother had died and she'd taken on the running of Oaklands herself.

'I'd like to run it along the lines of an English country hotel,' she'd written, so he supposed she must have travelled to Britain, although she had never said. 'Kind of relaxed and homely. Would your company consider using it as a base for High Island? I'd give you a good discount for a regular booking.'

The first year he had gone there with some trepidation not knowing what to expect. It would be more convenient than the motel in Winnie where they usually stayed. Oaklands was within walking distance of the Audubon sanctuaries. But most of his customers considered travelling to Texas as adventure enough, and he did not think they would relish the Oaklands he remembered, with ants in the kitchen and lizards in the baths. In fact, the hotel had been transformed. It had been painted gleaming white, the timbers mended, the garden weeded. There were a couple of elderly residents rocking gently in chairs on the porch. Rob suspected that Mary Ann kept them on not out of sentiment but sound commercial judgement. They added to the atmosphere like the hand-sewn quilts on the beds and her grandmother's furniture. They shared iced tea with the English visitors and talked in soft Texan voices about the old times.

Mary Ann still managed Oaklands single-handed. There had never been a boyfriend so far as Rob knew, certainly not a husband. She was a slim, dark woman, very smart, never bare legged even in the hottest weather. She reminded Rob rather of some French women he had met – formidable, stylish, independent. He had kept on good terms with her but he would never have dared intimacy though he found her attractive, and he enjoyed a challenge. After all he could not afford to offend her. His clients liked staying at Oaklands. It had become a success. It was hard to get a room there even in the winter and the restaurant was full every night.

He watched her walk down the veranda steps to greet his group and thought that she was one of the most successful and contented people he knew.

Mary Ann was unusually agitated, though neither her guests nor the staff would have realized it. She had learned control from an early age. Her mother was a friendly and easy woman but Mary Ann had seen that she had more than enough to do in keeping the boarding house. She would not have the energy to deal with teenage traumas and tantrums besides. Living at Oaklands meant more to Mary Ann than anything, so she had stayed clear of unsuitable boyfriends and drugs, of mood swings and emotional demands which might have side-tracked her mother from the task of making just enough money to keep the hotel ticking over. And Mary Ann had worked hard at school and worked her way through college so she would learn how to do more than just keep the place solvent. She was determined to make it a success.

But throughout the morning, as she greeted other guests and waited for Rob Earl's party to arrive, she found herself distracted. Usually she looked forward to his group. They were undemanding, polite and grateful for the service provided. They weren't good tippers but the staff liked them. If there were any problems or misunderstandings, Rob was there to help. She'd always admired the British, since that first time when Rob and his friends had come to stay. They were the first foreigners she'd ever met. Later she'd had a vacation job in London, looking after the spoilt kids of a Houston businessman and his wife, and she'd taken to the English, to their coolness and reserve. Even the cold, grey weather had suited her.

She was grateful to Rob. In the early years of her running the hotel his parties had made all the difference financially. A big booking, right at the beginning of the season, proved to the bank that she was capable of running the place at a profit, that all the investment was worthwhile. And he had spread the word in England. Many of her British guests came there on his recommendation.

She still looked up to him a bit as she had when she was twelve. She looked forward to showing him the improvements she had made since his last visit and discussing with him her plans for the future. He made her laugh and she didn't do that very often. She had lots of plans. She wanted to establish a Wildlife Refuge right here in the grounds of the Oaklands Hotel. There was the Birdathon and the party she intended to throw for all the participants. She'd always been good at putting on a show and this would be special. All the Houston media would be there. She imagined the place full of lights and people and music, as it must have been when the hotel first opened.

Then she thought of Laurie, who seemed so respectable but who was still the street-fighter she'd always been. She thought of Mick and Laurie Brownscombe and wondered if she'd ever be free of them.

There was a knock at her office door to tell her that the English party had arrived. She straightened her skirt and went out to meet them. There would be iced lemonade and cookies set out on the porch for them and she liked to be available to answer any questions. She had learned that first impressions were important.

Esme and Joan had been quarrelling all the way from Houston. About the names of the rivers they crossed, the date Sam Houston set out on his march for freedom and whether McDonald's used the same quality of beef on both sides of the Atlantic. Neither lady had ever tasted a hamburger. They were sisters and they had always argued.

In childhood Joan had been considered the brainy one and Esme the pretty one and they continued to play those roles though both were now in their fifties. Joan was the older. She was large, big boned, with wild grey hair. She wore sensible Crimplene slacks and loose, brightly coloured patterned overshirts. She was a primary teacher and talked to Esme as if she were a wayward, slightly backward, eleven-year-old.

Esme was not much bigger than an eleven-year-old and still now there were traces of the prettiness. Her hair was carefully dyed and permed and she always wore make-up, which Joan considered an extravagance. It was something else to argue about. Esme worked in a tea shop in a smart market town in Somerset. She earned very little and Joan resented having to support her. Of the two, Esme was by far the happier.

Now she was delighted by the hotel. She pointed to the bluejays and to the hummingbird which came to a feeder to drink. She declared that the lemonade and biscuits were almost as good as those supplied by the Copper Kettle at home. Mary Ann accepted the compliments with a smile but as soon as it was polite she left her visitors chatting and went to join Rob who was standing on the grass, looking up into the canopy of the oaks.

After leaving the air-conditioned bus Rob found the heat intense. It was like stepping out of a plane in Bombay in the middle of the day. He walked over the coarse grass to the trees which marked the boundary of the hotel's land. He was listening to the unfamiliar bird calls, trying to get his ear in. Behind him he heard the murmuring of English voices, distracting and intrusive, and he wished that he'd been able to afford to take this as a real holiday. It would have been better if it could have been just him and Oliver and Mick.

Like in the old days. But he supposed it could never be like that now. There were Julia and Laurie to consider.

Mary Ann came up behind him, startling him. He stood awkwardly for a moment. He was never sure how to greet her, whether she expected him to kiss her or if she would think that was too forward. In the end he held out his hand, and *she* kissed him lightly on either cheek.

'Your English friends have arrived,' she said.

'The Adamsons? Did you recognize Oliver? I'm not sure I would have done.'

'Of course,' she said. 'I remember you all.'

'What about Mick and Laurie? Have you heard from them?'

He was still holding her hand and she withdrew it.

'No,' she said flatly. 'Not yet.'

'I think I explained when I booked. This is special. A kind of reunion. Twenty years after that first time. Though I'm not sure exactly what we're celebrating.'

'I know,' she said. 'I was expecting it almost. I was there. I heard you plan it.'

He looked at her.

'I don't remember that.'

'Well you wouldn't, would you? I was only a kid. Sitting outside an open door, listening to the grown-ups talking.'

He stood for a moment in silence then gave her one of his smiles.

'There you are then,' he said easily. 'It'll be a real reunion of everyone there. Just as it should be.'

But as she walked back to the hotel and her guests, he was frowning.

Chapter Five

Julia was feeling excluded and she thought, really, it was the height of rudeness. All the in-jokes. All that talk about twenty years ago. All the smutty laughter. It made one wonder what had gone on in that dreadful hire car, in this house. Having met Laurie at last she wouldn't have put it past her to have had sex with all three of them as a sort of dare. And *they* wouldn't have minded sharing. Not those three. One never expected men to be that close, Julia decided petulantly. They weren't supposed to be friends in the way women were. They were supposed to be more restrained.

Of course she had asked Oliver what had gone on in High Island that week before he had flown home to make an honest woman of her. She had brought up the subject again on the plane. What, she had demanded as he pretended to watch the movie, had been so important that they needed to get together to remember it?

But he had been as evasive as only Oliver could.

'Nothing,' he said in his best solicitor's voice. 'We were young and we were friends. That was all.'

It was too vexing. Julia sulked.

Laurie had made her appearance just before lunch, when most of the bird watching party had gone to their rooms. Rob and Oliver were chatting and Julia was wondering whether she should risk pulling a lounger into the sun. She had recently read an article on UV light and the premature ageing of the skin. She thought that Laurie couldn't have timed her arrival better if she'd tried. She was obviously a woman who needed an audience.

The Brownscombes had driven up in a big, boxy car like a Range Rover and Laurie had leapt out at once. She'd been wearing a denim skirt, calf length, but only half buttoned up the front. Then she'd put her arms around Oliver's neck and started kissing him! Not in a friendly, continental way, as even Julia was accustomed to do now that it had become fashionable. More like a long-lost lover, which perhaps she was. Then she had turned her attentions to Rob and if anything that embrace was even more pornographic. Julia had been forced to turn away through embarrassment.

They had spent all afternoon in reminiscence, sitting on the lawn with binoculars on the grass beside them, jumping up occasionally and exclaiming when they saw an interesting bird. At one point the woman who ran the hotel joined them and Julia was furious to discover that even she was a party to their secrets.

It was clear, throughout the afternoon, that Laurie had been doing her best to make a fool out of Oliver. At one point she kicked off her shoes and walked over the grass, her hips swaying, mimicking a woman who had tried to pick him up in a bar in Crystal Beach: 'Oh, I do *so* like little English boys. I eat them for my dinner.'

Now preparing for dinner and still sulking, Julia told herself that it was Laurie's husband she felt sorry for. She had met Mick Brownscombe before the three of them went off to America. Rob and Oliver had treated him as a bit of a clown, with his farmhand's accent and his stumbling shyness and she had dismissed him as insignificant. Now, she decided, insignificant or not, anyone who lived with Laurie deserved her pity.

She and Oliver had been given a large, rather dark room on the ground floor. The windows were covered with wire mesh to keep out the insects, and trees and shrubs grew close to the house. Heavy clouds were developing, covering the sun, but to Julia it still seemed unbearably hot. She suspected that she had brought the wrong sort of clothes and would make a spectacle of herself. Suddenly she felt homesick for an English April, for cool blustery showers, primroses in the hedgerows and daffodils.

She came out of the bathroom to choose a dress to wear. Oliver, standing by the window, turned to face her. Julia pulled her bath robe more closely around her body. Her attitude to love-making was much the same as to her weekly aerobics class. As soon as she started she wished it was over, but she supposed the exercise was good for her. Tonight, in this heat, she could not bear the thought of it. She snatched a dress from the wardrobe and returned to the bathroom, locking the door behind her. Oliver, saying nothing, turned back to the window and to his memories.

Texas had been the last stop on a three month trip. They had hit Houston after a two day drive from the Big Bend, via Aranzas, for the whooping cranes. Sci-fi City they'd called it, though the skyscrapers then had been nothing compared with the glittering towers which had been built more recently, and they'd moved on as soon as they could.

They had graduated the summer before then worked like lunatics until January to get together the money. Rob had put in eighteen-hour shifts at an all night filling station on the Great North Road, Mick had been general dogsbody at the holiday complex his parents ran and Oliver had been taken on as porter in the hospital where his father was a consultant surgeon.

His parents thought the trip to the States was a mistake, but they hadn't made a fuss. They could understand that he wanted to travel before he settled down. They weren't like Mick's parents who thought a trip to Barnstaple was an adventure.

Oliver had met Julia in the hospital. She was a student nurse though he realized now that she wasn't committed in any way to her work. She'd seen it as a stop gap between her undemanding girls' school and marriage. She'd never enjoyed nursing – it was too much like hard work – and she probably wouldn't have passed the exams. But she'd looked good in the part, he had to admit. It was the early seventies and she'd worn her uniform short. He'd fallen for the legs in black nylon and the neck with the hair scraped from it and the little white starched cap. He'd fallen for the flattery. Those days she'd listen to him talking for hours, her lips slightly parted, as if his opinions were the most important in the world.

She didn't live in the nurses' home, which from the beginning had seemed to him a good sign. Mummy and Daddy had bought her a flat which she shared with two other girls, picked by her parents from a list of applicants because they came from 'nice homes'. But although she had her own place she'd kept him hanging on, wanting some sort of commitment from him, driving him mad so in the end he'd have done anything to get inside the strait-jacket of her nurse's uniform: 'Of course I love you Julia. Of course I do.'

The first time had been on Christmas Eve. A Christmas present. She'd been round the wards in her cape, with her lantern, singing carols. Even then she'd been a member of the choir. He'd been working and he'd caught glimpses of her all evening – at the end of corridors, in the middle of a ward with her head thrown back to sing, her mouth wide open.

And in the flat she had let him do it. Of course he hadn't asked if she was on the pill. She was a nurse, wasn't she?

She wouldn't have been interested in him if he'd just been a hospital porter. He'd made the mistake of telling her who his father was. She'd have found out anyway. She still had a facility for finding out the details of other people's lives, hoarding them as if one day they might be of use to her.

Rob hadn't been able to stand her from the beginning. The 'Dumb Blonde' he called her, or, if he was feeling less charitable, the 'Snooty Bitch.' Oliver cared what Rob thought. He was pleased that his relationship with Julia would have a natural ending. By the end of January when they set off for America, he was beginning to be bored by her. He told himself it had been an amusing fling, something to fill in the time between university and the serious business of birding in the States.

The phone call had come while they were in Houston in a cheap motel on the way out of the city. They'd hoped to make it all the way to High Island but in the end they'd been too knackered and they'd holed up in a room next to the freeway with the noise of the traffic rumbling through the walls. On a whim he'd phoned home and got his father, unusually frosty, probably embarrassed, asking if there was a phone number which could reach him because Julia had something urgent to say to him.

'Julia?' Oliver had said, because he had almost forgotten about her. 'Oh, yes. Julia.'

And he had sat in the motel reception waiting for the phone to ring while the others went to buy food.

The call came much more quickly than he had expected. Julia was breathless, weepy, pleading but in a strange way jubilant. He didn't realize then that it was what she had planned all along.

She wouldn't have an abortion, she said, with a show of dignity. It was against her principles and anyway she *couldn't*. She wanted the baby. So it was up to him what happened next. She supposed she could manage with the child by herself though it would be a struggle and it would break her parents' hearts. Or they could get married.

By this point she was quite calm and business-like. Daddy would buy them a little house and give them an allowance until Oliver had qualified as a solicitor. Then she said she supposed he would want to think about it. She expected him to phone her the next day at her parents' home. She gave him the number slowly as if she were speaking to a child and replaced the receiver.

He had known at once that he was trapped without quite understanding why. Rob had said that he was being ridiculous. What did it matter what people might think? This was his life he was talking about. But Oliver could not see it like that. He thought marriage would give a point to a life, which had always frightened him with its aimlessness. With a wife and child to care for perhaps he would become decided and purposeful like his father.

Early the next morning Oliver had phoned Julia and formally asked her to marry him.

Then they had headed off down the road to High Island and Laurie and a week at Oaklands waiting for the weather to turn.

When Julia came out of the bathroom, dressed and made-up, ready for dinner, Oliver was sitting on the bed, still in his shorts and T-shirt watching the television.

'What *are* you doing?' she cried, taking out all her irritation and discomfort on him. 'Why aren't you ready?'

He seemed hardly to notice her presence. 'It's the weather forecast,' he said dreamily. 'Look at that cold front sweeping down from the Great Lakes.'

'What does that mean?' she asked, as if she knew how to be polite but she couldn't care less, actually.

'Migrants,' he said. 'Bucketfuls of migrants falling out of the sky and into the trees. Tanagers and vireos and bright, bright warblers.'

At dinner that was all the men talked about. Not the past – Julia was at least spared that – but the prospect of a fall. They sat together at a large round table in the corner of Mary Ann's restaurant, lingering long after the other residents had gone to bed.

Laurie did her best to change the subject. She broke into a discussion on the identification of Swainson's warbler and demanded their attention. Julia thought it was rather brave.

'Mick and I are doing some work for a new non-profit organization,' she said. 'It's a real exciting venture. It came out of the Rio summit, you know. A partnership between the West and the Third World. We were wondering if we might make a presentation to the English guests at the hotel. I know they'd be interested. Some of them might even want to be involved. You wouldn't mind that, would you Rob? Or you, Mary Ann?'

She looked around the table but the men seemed hardly to have been listening.

'Hey, Laurie,' Rob said. 'This really isn't a good time. I can't think about that today.'

She was about to persist but Mick caught her eye. She sat down. Only Julia saw how angry she was.

'What's the name of your charity?' Julia asked. Manners were important even out here and it pleased her to think that Laurie too was being ignored. Mary Ann had opened a door into the garden and the men stood on the threshold listening for the wind. The two women sat alone at the table.

'The Wildlife Partnership,' Laurie said. She brightened and seemed about to launch into her sales pitch. 'If you'd like more details I can take you through it.' She stretched under the table and like a magician brought out a glossy brochure.

Julia had experience of dealing with sales people and broke in: 'My husband specializes in charity law,' she added, rather cattily. 'But I expect you knew that.'

Chapter Six

In the morning it was cooler. Rob noticed the drop in temperature as soon as he woke. But the cloud was thin and it had not rained so he thought there was no hurry. Even if the cold front was on its way from Canada it had not yet arrived. He had time for a civilized breakfast.

In the dining-room a matronly waitress with flat feet asked him where he would like to sit. At a table by the window Russell and Connie May were watching him eagerly and he asked to join them. Since he had fixed their shower in Houston they had treated him like a hero. Now they poured him coffee. Connie still seemed tired and washed out but Russell couldn't keep still. He had finished his breakfast and he took up his binoculars and began to clean the lenses with a soft cloth and a photographer's brush. Rob thought he was as excited as a boy on his first bird club field trip.

'Well this is it, lover,' he said, over and again to his wife. 'After all this time we're here.'

Rob had decided to take them to Boy Scout Wood first. It was more organized than Smith Oaks Wood and more prepared for visitors. Although it was within walking distance he would borrow the hotel's mini bus. He didn't fancy the idea of shepherding his party down the 124 like a kindergarten group.

'We'll go then,' he said, 'as soon as everyone's ready. I'll meet you outside in twenty minutes. If you could tell the others . . .'

But Russell was already on his feet, rounding up the members of the party with the enthusiasm of a sheep dog, harrying them until they were all ready to go.

When Rob had come to High Island the year before there had

been a young woman in the group. He couldn't remember her name now. She hadn't been his type. But she had called Boy Scout Wood 'The Secret Garden' and for him the name had stuck. It was very small and compact, hardly more than a garden, so you could wander out of it quite easily and find yourself in the yard of a neighbouring house. And the tangle of trees came as a surprise. You turned off an ordinary street of tidy houses and found yourself in a wilderness.

The street was full of birders' cars. They were covered with stickers, some with distinctive birders' licence plates. Rob ignored the queue at the information booth and set his group up at Purkey's Pond, the only permanent surface water in the wooded part of the reserve. There was a gallery of tiered benches, overlooking the water. It was crammed with people leaning forward, binoculars focused. There were Dutch birders and Swedish birders and birders from all over the States. But most of all there were British birders and Rob waved to people he had last seen at Cley, in Norfolk, or shared a beer with in the observatory on Fair Isle.

'What have you got?' Rob asked an obese American. He had a backside which sagged either side of the bench.

The man chewed on a piece of gum. 'A couple of yellow billed cuckoos,' he said, then paused before adding, 'Nice enough, but I guess by the end of the day there'll be too many birds to count.'

Rob set up his telescope so he could show the more inexperienced members of the group the birds. He was beginning to know his party as individuals now. There were the dreadful Lovegroves, the middle-aged, spinster sisters, who bickered like a married couple on the brink of divorce. There was a seventy-five-year-old retired doctor from Inverness who had the build of a mountaineer and a bigger world list than Rob. And there was Ray, an ex-miner from Nottingham who was determined to see as many birds as he could until his redundancy money ran out.

Connie seemed worried about Ray. Although it hadn't started raining she was wearing a transparent plastic raincoat and a rainhood of a design Rob had not seen since his childhood. She might have been at a Mother's Union picnic at Weston-Super-Mare.

'Haven't you got family then, my dear?' she asked the miner.

'Bugger the family,' Ray said. 'They've lived off me long enough. I don't doubt they'll still be there when I get back.'

And Connie had given an odd little laugh as if she were not shocked, but confused.

All morning the sky grew darker. Still the rain did not come. Rob thought he would be let down again and prepared himself for another anti-climax. He became tense and anxious and bummed a cigarette, although he had given up smoking months before.

When Mick and Oliver didn't arrive, he worried that there was a rarity in Smith Oaks. He convinced himself that he was missing out. But when he asked the other birders who swept in a tide between the two reserves, they said no, it wasn't very different at Smith Oaks. It seemed that everyone was waiting for the migrants to fall from the sky.

Once he thought he saw Mick and Laurie standing hand in hand at the end of a trail but there were so many people that he could not be sure. There was no sign of Oliver.

The rain started when they were in a clearing in the woodland called the Cathedral, though it was more the size of a small chapel and not so much the shape of a nave but of a boat, with a wooden bench running around the edge as if round a deck rail. From the boardwalk it was possible to look right up into the tops of the trees.

The rain started slowly, with heavy individual drops, but then became a downpour. And with the rain came the birds. Suddenly there were twenty rose-breasted grosbeaks in the tree next to where Rob was standing and from the undergrowth all around came the mewing calls of the catbirds, competing with the sound of the rain.

In the roof of the Cathedral there were flashes of black and orange and Rob was calling to his group, 'Look! A flock of northern orioles!'

But in the excitement of the fall the group seemed to have scattered, responding to shouts from all over the reserve:

'Cerulean warbler. Down by the pool.'

'Who needs Blackburnian?'

So he was pointing out the orioles to strangers and when he turned to see who he was talking to, the wood was full of birders straining to see the forty red-eyed vireos on the willow by the pond, the black and white warblers against the trunk of an oak. In the end he gave up responsibility for showing the birds to his group and he went with the flow, along the boardwalks and the trails, taking care not to tread on the birds which had landed exhausted, at every step adding a new species to his day list. And all the time he was looking for the big one. Swainson's warbler which he had never seen in the world before, never even come close to. But while he was listening to the babble around him in case the shout went up that one had been seen, he was frustrated, thinking that half these birdwatchers wouldn't know a Swainson's warbler if it bit them.

He pushed his way down a narrow trail to the Prothonotory Pool, a lake of stagnant water with dead, silver trunked trees, emerging from it. There Oliver appeared. Out of nowhere like the migrants, the rainwater glistening in his face like tears. He came up to Rob, laughing, and threw his arms around him.

'Isn't it magnificent!' he yelled, and perhaps he was crying after all. Rob thought they had all gone crazy. 'Twenty years of waiting and it was all worth it.'

They took the trail back into the trees and still the birds were arriving. Now they could hardly hear each other speak above the mewing of the catbirds.

'Where's Mick?' Rob cried. 'And Laurie? The four of us should be together for this.'

'We came from Smith Oaks together. We knew you'd be here. But as soon as the rain started and things began happening we got separated. You can see what it's like.'

'We've got to find them. We'll never get a chance like this again.'

Rob saw that they were back by the entrance of the reserve, and that Oliver had reverted to type. The excitement had left him.

'I can't,' he said.

'What do you mean?'

'I can't come with you to look for Laurie and Mick,' Oliver spoke calmly. 'I promised Julia I'd see her at Oaklands.'

'Sod Julia!' Rob was furious. 'You said it yourself. This is what we came for.'

'It's not that easy.'

'We've dreamed of this for twenty years and now you're *leaving?*' Rob realized he was screaming. He tipped back his head so he was looking Oliver in the face and rain dripped down his neck.

'Tell me,' he said more quietly. 'What is it that Julia has on you Oliver? Why don't you just piss off and let her get on with it?'

'I've already told you,' Oliver said. 'It's not that easy.' In his lightweight Barbour jacket and his green wellies he looked like an English county gentleman out for a day's shooting. Rob looked more like a hunt saboteur.

'It can't just be the money,' Rob persisted. 'Tell me it's not just that.'

Oliver turned away and Rob could hardly make out his voice above the rain.

'It's important stuff, money,' he said lightly and he strode away into the street as if he had a spaniel at his heels.

Chapter Seven

When Oliver left, Rob supposed he should gather his group together but he could not face the chattering Lovegroves, even the good natured enthusiasm of the Mays. He realized that he had been expecting too much of this trip. He had thought they could recreate an old friendship which probably hadn't even been important to the others. He was a sad case. No wife or steady girlfriend. And all his real friends had been made twenty years before. But he wasn't so desperate, he thought, that he was going to brood about Oliver Adamson during the most brilliant fall in history. He looked about him to make sure none of his group was around, then took an overgrown path through water oak, willow oak and hackberry trees. Bird watching needed concentration and he preferred to be alone. In the distance he heard American voices calling to each other, but the trail he followed was narrow and empty.

The rain stopped and almost immediately afterwards the sun came out, slanting through the canopy on to the track ahead of him, the sudden heat making steam rise from the sodden undergrowth. In the sunshine the colours of the warblers were dazzlingly bright, the outlines sharp against the green of the spring leaves. It was like walking into the tropical house of a zoo. Or the Garden of Eden, he thought. All I need is Eve. And he wondered again where Mick and Laurie were and if they had been avoiding him.

He found a bench by the trail and he sat there while the sun dried his clothes, thinking how good it would be if Laurie came up the path so they could spend some time together, talk about the time they'd spent together. Then he thought again that he was turning into a sad old man.

He was aware of a shadow in the underbrush. Only a shadow, no colour. No bright yellow or scarlet. This was something brown and understated, more like a British bird than a neotropical warbler. He waited. All thoughts of Laurie were forgotten. There was another movement nearby but the bird disappeared too quickly for him to note any detail. He went through the possibilities. It was too big for a worm eating warbler, too drab for a yellow. And it was certainly behaving like a Swainson's, skulking at the bottom of the thorn bush. For five minutes nothing happened. Then Rob heard a rustling sound which might have been made by a small mammal rather than a bird.

Rob looked up the trail both ways. He was supposed to be a responsible tour leader and if he was going to break the rules of the sanctuary he didn't want anyone to see him. The trail was empty but he stayed where he was and made a 'pshhing' sound. Again he caught a brief glimpse of the warbler but it was an untickable view. It flew further away from the trail and into the underbrush.

'Sod it,' he muttered and he went in, off the trail, stepping over the rope strung between metal stakes which marked the boundary. He kicked at the bushes to flush the bird into the open, looking around him again to make sure that no one could see him.

The bird flew on to a low branch and sat there for five seconds. Rob was on to it immediately. He had to step back so he could focus his binoculars on it. Then he saw everything he needed – the cream eye stripe, the dagger-like bill, before it dropped down again into the tangle of thorn bushes.

'Got you!' he shouted out loud, punching the air with his fist 'Swainson's warbler. On my list!'

Then he heard voices approaching. Immediately he tried to scramble back on to the trail. He wanted to claim the glory for finding the bird but he didn't want to be caught out of bounds. The ground was swampy and as he turned back towards the path his boot caught in some twisted roots. He tripped and was so anxious to prevent damage to his binoculars and telescope that he fell flat on his face. Swearing furiously in a whisper, he decided it would be better to wait there until the walkers passed by than face the indignity of having to explain what he was doing away from the trail. He was afraid that the approaching walkers might be sanctuary volunteers. These were usually formidable southern ladies who terrified him.

As they came closer he could tell that the voices were female but not American. It was the Lovegrove sisters and they were still arguing.

'I'm sure that bird was a chestnut-sided warbler,' Joan said. 'I looked in the book.'

'I don't think it could have been, dear.' Esme was being sweetly patient. 'It didn't have chestnut sides.'

'Of course not!' Joan was triumphant. 'It was a female!'

Rob held his breath. He had already decided that the Lovegroves were his least favourite party members. Their ornithological experience seemed limited to feeding the garden birds which came to the table outside their kitchen window. That wouldn't have mattered if they realized how much they still had to learn, or if they kept quiet long enough to be told.

He had tried looking through the binoculars which they shared, a heavy pair of Ross which Joan said proudly had once belonged to an uncle who served in the navy. There had been a soup of algae behind the lens and he had not been able to see a thing. He found it hard to believe that the sisters were birdwatchers at all and for one fantastic moment had even thought they might be impostors, spies sent by his boss to make sure he was doing a good job.

He lay in the mud and kept quiet.

'Give me the binoculars now Esme,' Joan demanded. 'There's something I want to look at.'

There was a pause. 'Just as I thought. Look at that.'

Then he heard them walk on, their sensible shoes thudding on the path. The rainwater had already drained away. They were almost out of earshot when Esme said: 'I wonder what Mr Earl was *doing* lying behind that tree. You do suppose he was all right?'

'Don't be silly dear.' Joan was dismissive. 'It was field craft. I expect he was stalking something. That's why I didn't call out to him.'

'Well if you really think so . . .'

Rob got to his feet thinking that at least that would be a good story to tell at dinner. It would make Laurie laugh. He mimicked Joan's voice in his head to make sure that he remembered the words, then looked briefly around him through his binoculars. He was already covered in mud and while he was off limits it might be possible to get a longer view of the Swainson's warbler. He focused on the undergrowth where the bird had last disappeared. But all he could see was an old boot. A pair of old boots. And looking more closely he saw now that they were not so old. And about his size.

Treading very carefully he walked further into the undergrowth. He didn't make so much at this business that he could turn his back on an opportunity like this. If some rich birder had chucked away a perfectly good pair of walking boots he was prepared to do his bit by taking home the litter. The boots were leather, well made, American. But they were being worn and beyond the boots he saw a pair of grey trousers with big zipped patch pockets and a blue and white checked shirt and a thin, quilted body warmer. The sun had not reached these clothes and they were still wet from the rain.

The face was turned away from Rob. The wearer of the smart, outdoor clothes lay on his stomach. Rob was pleased about that because he thought if he had seen the face he might have been sick. The man hadn't tripped like him, and hit his head, though there was a wound of some sort on the back of the skull. Far more sinister was the hole in the quilted body warmer. It had not been made by a bullet, though there was something about the garment which reminded Rob of the bullet-proof vests the police sometimes wore on the television. This gash was too deep, he thought, to have been made by the blade of a knife. Then he thought that the coat had not been soaked only by rain but by blood.

He didn't need to see the face to know who was lying there. He recognized the clothes. He had seen them the afternoon before. Laurie had mentioned the trousers. They were real hard to get hold of in the States, she had said, and Mick liked to wear them for birding. Sometimes she did business trips to London and she always brought a pair back with her.

At the time Rob had been made jealous by this glimpse into their domestic life. Now he wondered how he would tell Laurie that Mick was dead. And what her reaction would be.

Chapter Eight

George involved Molly in his investigation for Cecily Jessop. As she never ceased to remind him, they were partners. Besides, he couldn't work up much interest in the case. He thought Cecily was making a fuss about nothing. What did it matter really, if an over-enthusiastic new charity had used her name without asking?

To his surprise Molly took the thing more seriously, became quite priggish on the subject. Before retirement she had worked as a social worker both for the local authority and in the voluntary field. If this was a con, she said, there was nothing more despicable. Anything which brought charities into disrepute affected the public's willingness to respond to good causes. It was the worst kind of theft.

She left the tedious business of contacting the Charity Commissioners to George. It was the sort of thing he was good at. He was used to dealing with sober men in grey suits. As a civil servant in the Home Office he'd worn a grey suit himself.

'I'll get in touch with the other celebrities in the brochure who are supposed to have endorsed the charity, shall I?' she asked. 'See if any of them actually gave permission for their name to be used.'

'If you can track them down.' George was beginning to wonder if any of this was worth the bother.

There were four other people listed with Cecily Jessop as supporters of the Wildlife Partnership: two academics, a famous explorer and the presenter of a children's television natural history show. Molly traced the academics through their universities. Neither had heard of the Wildlife Partnership. It seemed to Molly that both were flattered to have been chosen and would certainly have allowed their names to be listed in publicity material, had they been asked.

The explorer was away in eastern China, but her husband was charming and invited Molly to tea in his pretty little house in Kew. He was elderly, twice as old as his adventurous wife and obviously dazzled by her exploits.

'I was a businessman,' he said apologetically. 'At a conference in Lima. Louise walked into the hotel after one of her treks. Grimy and disheveled and rather sweaty actually. I fell for her straight away. Bullied her into marriage.' He paused, and added with astonishment, 'I don't think she's regretted it.'

'So South America was a special interest for her?'

'It was then,' he said. 'I suppose it was the book about her adventures in the rain forest which made her name. More recently she's become fascinated by China.'

'Do you know if the Wildlife Partnership approached her about supporting their projects in South and Central America?'

'I'm sure they didn't.' He spoke quite firmly.

'And you would know?'

'Oh, yes,' he said. 'Since I retired five years ago I've taken over all that side of things. I open any mail addressed to Louise and deal with it. Usually I can handle it without bothering her. She's a very special woman, you see. She shouldn't be troubled with trivia.'

Lucky old Louise, Molly thought, as she drove into Sainsbury's car-park to pick up some groceries for supper, knowing that George would complain if they had a takeaway meal again.

Sally Adamson, the presenter of *Wildside*, the children's programme, was more difficult to track down. First, Molly tried the BBC in Bristol, where the Natural History Unit was based. She was told that the latest series of *Wildside* had been completed almost a year before and that there were no plans to make any more. The team had been disbanded.

'I'm trying to trace Sally Adamson,' Molly persisted.

'I'm very sorry madam.' The voice at the end of the line was nasal and determinedly unhelpful. 'I've already explained that our contract with Miss Adamson has ended.'

'But you must still have her address on your file.'

'It's not our policy to give personal details of presenters to members of the public. I'm sure you can appreciate that.'

'What about her agent?' Molly spoke quickly, sensing that the woman was about to replace the receiver.

'I'm sorry?'

'I presume she *does* have an agent. To handle her contracts. You surely wouldn't have any objection to giving me her agent's name.'

There was a pause while the woman tried to invent one.

'I'm sure Miss Adamson would be very unhappy if she knew that the BBC had been obstructive, when there was the possibility of an offer of work.' Molly pressed home her advantage.

'I'll have to transfer you.'

Molly was passed on to a young man, whose voice seemed not quite to have broken. She was kept waiting for ten minutes, then he said, in a series of squeaks and growls: 'Miss Adamson is represented by Cyril Oxley.' He gave her an address in Kensington and a telephone number, speaking so quickly that she hardly had time to write it down.

'Thank you,' said Molly with only a hint of sarcasm. 'You've been very helpful.'

When Molly phoned Cyril Oxley about the possibility of Sally Adamson opening a school's new wildlife garden he was not at all suspicious. Molly sounded very like a headmistress and that sort of approach was made to Sally all the time. Less now, of course, that the programme was no longer on the air, but children, as he always said, were remarkably faithful.

'She couldn't do it for nothing,' he said. That was the problem. Schools and charities always expected actors to appear out of the kindness of their hearts. It was all very well for the rich and famous to give their time just for the glory but these poor kids had to survive on the dole.

'Of course not,' Molly assured him. 'We quite understand that.'

'It'll be a hundred pounds plus expenses,' he said. 'As it's a school.'

'That sounds very reasonable.'

'If you could give me the details . . .'

'I'd quite like to discuss the matter with Miss Adamson personally,' Molly said. 'I understand that you may not want to give out her telephone number, but if you could ask her to phone me.'

'A hundred pounds is the going rate. You won't persuade her to do it for less,' he said suspiciously.

'Of course not!' Molly was headmistressy and offended. 'St Ursula's isn't a *state* school, Mr Oxley. We don't quibble here about money.'

Sally phoned her back almost immediately. She said she'd be delighted to open the school's wildlife garden, and the expenses wouldn't be too horrendous actually, because although she lived in Bristol, at the moment her parents were in the States and she was looking after the house for them. Her mother was paranoid about security. Molly had to interrupt.

'I'm sorry,' she said. 'There isn't any school. I'm afraid I got you to ring under false pretences.'

'Is it real work?' Molly could hear the excitement. 'Acting?'

'I'm afraid not.'

'Oh.' Sally made no attempt to hide her disappointment.

'I'm a private investigator. Your name's come up in a case I'm working on.'

'That sounds intriguing.' At least she was not going to take out her disappointment on Molly.

'I wondered if I might buy you lunch.' Somewhere nice, Molly thought. Cecily could afford it and she had taken to this friendly girl. 'I'll come to you. I don't want to put you to any more inconvenience.'

'All right. I explained that I'm staying at my parents' house in Sussex.' She gave the address, directions.

'What about tomorrow?' Molly asked.

'Why not?' There was a pause and for the first time she sounded sorry for herself. 'After all, I'm not doing anything else.'

Sally's parents lived in a substantial house on the edge of a tidy village. There was no mud or cow muck in the main street and smart little cars were parked outside what had once been farm cottages. Molly was not invited into the house. Sally was waiting for her, and Molly sat in the car while she set an elaborate alarm system.

'What a fuss!' Sally said. 'Anyone with a screwdriver and a GCSE in woodwork could walk into my flat.'

She was tall, wide-mouthed, with dark hair cut very short.

They had lunch in a converted barn. Molly was afraid that the restaurant would be pretentious with fussy food and tiny portions, but the menu was English and limited enough for everything to be freshly cooked. The proprietor knew Sally.

'When are we going to see you on the telly again, Sal?'

'Oh, you know, Johnny. When they recognize what they're missing.' It was an answer she had given before.

They were shown to a table next to a long, arched window.

'I know people mean well,' Sally said, 'but I wish they'd stop asking.'

Molly did not know what to say.

'It was the same when I came out of drama school. They expected me to be playing Ophelia at the Royal Shakespeare a week later. My mother's the worst. She never took acting seriously anyway. She's waiting for me to find a husband and give up the whole crazy idea.'

'You didn't get the job on *Wildside* because of your interest in natural history then?'

'Not really. I mean I'm *interested*, committed to the Green cause. We all are, these days, aren't we? But they already had two scientists. They wanted someone young to act the scatty ignoramus, to ask the simple questions that kids might want to put. I thought it worked really well, but the ratings were never that good.' She paused, looked at the menu. 'Are you *really* a private investigator?'

'I'm not what you were expecting?' Molly saw herself through Sally's eyes: elderly, plump, a Billy Bunter haircut and round spectacles. Perhaps I should smarten myself up, she thought, then, robustly: No. Why should I?

'I don't know,' Sally said. 'I imagined someone tough, glamorous . . .' she paused again.

'Young?' Molly put in.

'Yes.' She laughed, slightly embarrassed. 'I suppose so. How can I help you?'

'Have you ever heard of the Wildlife Partnership?'

'The name's familiar. Is it something we covered on the show?'

'I don't think so.' Molly took out the brochure which had been sent to Cecily Jessop's friend. 'Your name's listed here as a supporter of the charity. I wondered if you'd given permission for it to be used.'

'No,' Sally said. 'I'm sure I've heard of it though.' She looked out of the window at a woman in a silk head scarf being dragged along by two dogs. 'I remember. It was at a party. It must have been more than a year ago because we'd just been told that the Beeb were considering axing the show. I'd never seen *Wildside* as a permanent thing, but I'd got used to the regular income. It would be one thing to leave because I'd been offered a proper acting job. Quite another to get the sack. I'm afraid I had too much to drink and a terrible head the day after.'

'Where was the party?'

'London. I'd come to stay with my parents again, and my father took me along to cheer me up. It was some sort of work's do, I think. I didn't feel much like partying and I spent most of the time with a big glass of wine sitting in a corner and talking about the Wildlife Partnership. Or listening. It was hard to get a word in. I did say that it sounded a marvellous idea and well worth supporting. It would have been courteous though if the organization had asked my permission before using my name on their literature.'

'Are you sure they didn't?'

'Quite sure.'

'Tell me about the person who told you about the Partnership.'

'It was a woman. Attractive, mid-thirties, blonde. More like a businesswoman, I thought, than someone involved in a charity.

Well groomed, slick, you know. She probably told me her name but I don't remember it now.'

'Anything else you recall about her?'

'Oh, yes,' Sally said. 'She was American. She had one of those southern, drawling American voices which are so hard for English actors to get right.'

'Was she living in England or on a visit?'

'I don't think she said. I'm not even sure what her role with the Wildlife Partnership was. What I remember most is her enthusiasm. She really wanted to get over her message. She said it was a revolutionary idea. The West and the Third World working as partners in conservation, taking joint decisions, listening to each other properly.'

'Did she ask you for a donation?'

'No, I didn't get the impression that she was soliciting money or trying to sign me up. I didn't feel that I was getting the hard sell. Not in that sense at least. Just that she was passionate about the idea and wanted to spread the word. She impressed me. There was something about her. That's why I remember her so well.' She paused, shrugged. 'If it was a con she was a better actress than I'll ever be.'

Chapter Nine

While Molly was eating roast lamb and Sussex pond pudding, George spent most of his day on the telephone. He tried the number given by the Wildlife Partnership to make credit card donations and found that it was unobtainable. He knew it would be a waste of time contacting British Telecom to find the office address. They would not give that sort of information to members of the public. But as Molly had said, he still had friends in high places, chums in the Home Office who owed him favours. An hour later he had an address. The Wildlife Partnership had been based in Filton, a suburb of Bristol.

The rest of the day he spent trying to track down who was behind the venture. He contacted the directors of other environmental organizations who might be expected to know. He spoke to the Charity Commission. By the time Molly arrived he felt less defeatist. There might be a way of getting to the bottom of this. Cecily Jessop might yet have reason to be grateful to him.

It was almost dark when Molly got home and as she drove down the lane towards the house she wondered again why they hadn't moved. Norton's Cross had been sensible when George had worked for the Home Office. Now, when neither of them needed to commute they could leave this benighted, congested corner of England and move somewhere with space and empty roads. She had been stuck for half an hour at the junction into the village.

But as she stopped the car to open the rotting wooden gate into the drive she knew they could not leave. They were too lazy, too settled and the place had too many memories. The house was a red brick Victorian vicarage. They had bought it in the early sixties when three parishes were amalgamated and it was no longer needed. Molly had made plans to renovate it but they had both been too busy. And neither of them cared, really, about the hideous paint which was still in the bathroom, the ugly gas fires, the draughts. The children had fretted when they were teenagers. Couldn't something, at least, be done about the kitchen? they had demanded. Didn't Molly know that Mark's mother had forbidden him ever to eat in the vicarage because it was unhygienic? Now the children were grown up and respectable but even they agreed that it wouldn't suit Molly and George to live somewhere smart.

George had seen the car lights and had a drink ready for her. There was a fire lit in the living-room and as she came in he was drawing the curtains against the gloom. She sensed that he was happier, that he had achieved something and she was relieved. Throughout their marriage he had suffered from bouts of depression. It wasn't a problem he would acknowledge, except by sometimes admitting to her that he felt a bit low, but she had shared it with him. Fighting the moods had worn her out. It had been harder than social work or bringing up the children. Sometimes it occurred to her that in retirement she deserved a rest.

'Well,' she said. 'How did you get on?' She spoke brightly and supposed that marriage must often be like this. Was there always one partner who provided the encouragement and support? And was it always the woman? Immediately she thought that wasn't fair. He hadn't demanded anything of her. She'd had a long day. That was all.

'I've traced the real Wildlife Partnership,' he said.

'There is one then?'

'It's an American non-profit organization based in Houston. They certainly seem to be legitimate. Small but efficient, though it's hard to find out where all their money comes from. A number of substantial anonymous donations. They've bought reserves in South and Central America, which certainly exist. One in Costa Rica and two in Brazil. I spoke to an RSPB reserves manager who visited one of them through Birdlife International. He seemed impressed by the management and what had been achieved.'

'But here?'

He shrugged.

'They're not registered. But the charity law's pretty complicated. Perhaps they thought they'd be able to operate here without registration.'

'Have you talked to anyone in Houston?'

'Not yet. The outfit seems to be run by volunteers but their PR is handled by a firm of environmental consultants called Brownscombe Associates. I'll phone them later. It'll be lunchtime in Texas now.'

'The American angle would fit,' Molly said.

'In what way?'

She told him about the conversation with Sally Adamson and the mysterious American woman who had accosted her at a party.

'What did you make of Ms Adamson?' George asked.

'She's an actress of course. Ambitious and trained to be charming. But I liked her.'

'I've traced the office which the Wildlife Partnership used in the UK,' George said. 'It's in Bristol.'

'That's where Sally Adamson lives. The BBC Natural History Unit is based there.'

'Do you think that's significant?' George asked. 'Do you think she knows more about it than she told you?'

'No,' Molly said. 'I believed her. Really, she was quite relaxed about the enquiry.' She paused, held out her glass for a refill. 'Will we go to Bristol? Look at the office?'

'I don't know. There may be no need. We might get all the answers from Brownscombe Associates.'

But later that evening, when he phoned Brownscombe Associates he gained little information. He spoke to Michael Brownscombe's personal assistant. She was pleasant and apologetic but she refused to pass on any information about clients' accounts. He would have to speak to Michael or Laurie, the partners, she said. He asked when it might be convenient to speak to Michael or Laurie and she was even more apologetic. They were both on vacation. For ten days. Perhaps he would like to phone back in about two weeks' time. She would notify them of his call.

'You must have a number for an emergency,' he persisted.

'Sure,' she said, as polite as ever. 'But excuse me, sir, this doesn't sound so urgent that I need to disturb them.' And she replaced the receiver.

'We'll go to Bristol then,' Molly said. 'We can track down what's been going on from this end.'

Reluctantly George agreed.

They left early the next morning. It meant a dreadful commuter train into town, then the InterCity from Paddington to Bristol. The address George had been given was in a busy street lined with shops, close to the British Aerospace factory. The taxi stopped outside a florist's shop. There were sad blooms in buckets on the pavement – daffodils and narcissi which had hardly opened but which were already turning brown – and in the window a display of wreaths. George and Molly looked out, confused.

'This is it,' the taxi driver said impatiently. 'This is the number you gave me.'

Then George saw that there was office space above the florist's shop and that a 'To Let' sign had been posted in the window. There was a separate door beside the shop which must have led upstairs, but it was locked. They looked through the letter-box but there was no mail on the floor. It must have been collected by the landlord or estate agent.

The florist was called Maggie. She was scrawny and middle-aged, a chain-smoker with nicotine coloured hair. They spoke to her for nearly an hour and in that time no customers came into the shop. She was glad to answer their questions. She enjoyed the company.

'It was a shame,' Maggie said. 'That poor babby up there all day by himself. A boy his age needs people around him.'

'What age are we talking about?'

'Seventeen, eighteen. But to look at him you wouldn't have thought he was more than fifteen. A nice kid. As proud as punch when he started. He said this was his first sniff at a job. I'd take him on here but you can see what it's like. I'll be lucky if I'm still here in twelve months' time.'

'Do you know anything about his employer?'

'I showed her round the office before she took it on. The landlord asked me. I keep a key.'

'What was she like?'

Maggie shrugged. 'One of those businesswomen. Too much lipstick and a jacket that a man should wear. Pushy, you know. Full of grand plans. She made out it would do until they got something better. I thought to myself: if you're that grand lady you wouldn't be looking at a place like this.'

'Local?' George asked.

'You joking? A voice like that? American, weren't she?'

'What was the name of the boy who worked here?' Molly asked.

'Jason. Jason Tucker.'

'You wouldn't happen to know where Jason lives?'

And Maggie gave them the address without question. It seemed she knew Jason's mum. They went to the bingo together.

When the couple turned up at Jason's home he was filling out forms. The Social Security didn't believe that he hadn't been paid for his last week at work. The man in the office had even implied that he had deliberately made himself unemployed. His mother was a care assistant in an old people's home and she couldn't afford to keep him. He didn't mention a father.

He was a child of the recession: respectable, insecure, desperate to please. It was clear that he had worked hard at school but nothing had come easily to him. He would have liked an office job. Filing, copying lists of numbers, one of the old, paper shuffling jobs which had all but disappeared. He said the Wildlife Partnership job had seemed a dream. Just right for him. And he liked the idea of helping animals.

'Did you get it through the Job Centre?' Molly asked.

'No. It was advertised in the local paper.'

'And there was an interview?'

'Not a real interview. Not formal. More of a chat like, with Miss Brown?'

'Miss Brown?'

'The American lady. From the Wildlife Partnership.'

'What did Miss Brown look like, Jason?'

He screwed up his face in concentration. He must have looked like that when he was taking his exams.

'Blonde hair tied back,' he said. 'Smart, you know. Well dressed. Kind of mysterious. She wore those tinted glasses. He paused and blushed. Perhaps the mysterious Miss Brown had figured in his fantasies. 'Her first name was Jessica. She told me to call her Jessica.'

'How old was she?' Molly asked.

That really threw him. 'I dunno,' he said.

'Younger than your mother?'

'Oh, yeah!'

'Thirty? Forty?'

'I suppose about thirty,' he said, but he still sounded uncertain.

'And she offered you the job?'

He nodded. 'She said it wouldn't be much fun.' He was defending her. 'She said I'd be stuck in the office, answering the phone. For the time being at least. I had to take down the details of the people who wanted to make credit card donations. Then there were the brochures to label and send out. Pretty boring it was really. Some days nothing happened at all. But I thought something might come of it. And it was a job, wasn't it? Better than nothing.'

He stared bleakly across the table at them.

'Weren't you ever tempted to stay at home?'

'No!' He pretended to be shocked, then added honestly: 'I never knew when she was going to phone, did I?'

'It was always Miss Brown who phoned? It was never somebody else from the organization. Michael? Laurie? Do those names mean anything to you?'

'No,' he said. 'It was always Jessica.'

'Did you meet anyone else?'

'No. She'd come in at the beginning of the month. Take away all the membership and donation details, give me my pay.'

'How were you paid?' Molly interrupted.

'Cash,' he said. 'Always cash.'

'Is there anything else you can think of, which might help us trace her?'

He shook his head sadly. They sat for a moment in silence.

'We've been authorized,' Molly said formally, 'by the person who's employing us, to pay your last week's wages and a small sum in compensation. Do you have a bank account?'

He nodded, not quite understanding, slow as ever to catch on.

She wrote a cheque for a hundred and fifty pounds and pushed it across the table towards him.

'We'll put it down to expenses,' she said to George in the street. 'Cecily Jessop can afford it.'

Chapter Ten

When they had returned from Bristol there had been a message from Cecily Jessop on the telephone answering machine. There had been none of the hesitation which was most people's response to the tape. Her voice echoed around their living-room as if she were yelling through a megaphone.

'What the hell are you up to George? Come and see me. Give me a progress report.'

So a month after the first time, he returned to the crumbling grandeur of The Deuchars. The sun was shining. Cecily was showing a group of school children round the garden, explaining the basic methodology of her common bird census. She wore a straw hat with a wide brim, which looked as if it had been nibbled by a goat, and a shapeless T-shirt under which her breasts sagged almost to her midriff. The outfit was completed by a pair of khaki army shorts and sand shoes. The teachers accompanying the party seemed surprised by her appearance and rather shocked by her language. Perhaps they expected something different from a Lady, but George was certain the children were learning nothing new.

'George!' Cecily shouted when she saw him walk through the trees towards her. 'And about time, too!'

They were working in woodland and there was a smell of wild garlic.

'Let me set these buggers something to occupy them and I'll be with you. We'll get Vanessa to make us some tea.'

They drank the tea sitting on the kitchen doorstep. There was the occasional shriek of a child's voice from the woods.

'It's nice to have kids about the place,' Cecily said. Then, complacently: 'I'm good with them you know, George. It's a gift. Perhaps I should have had a brood of my own. What do you think Vanessa? Do you see me as a mother?'

Vanessa was a small woman, still neatly attractive in a floral print frock and sandals. George could imagine that she had once been a force's sweetheart. At Cecily's question she looked up, but she did not answer. She had brought herself a chair from the kitchen so she was sitting a little apart. She was knitting very fast, looking absently about her as the needles flew. George had met her several times but couldn't remember ever having heard her speak. During the rest of the conversation Cecily ignored her.

'What have you found out for me, George?' Cecily demanded. Sitting close beside her he could still smell the garlic which must have been crushed by her sand shoes. Her knees were scratched and bruised like a boy's. 'How far have you got along the trail?'

'I believe I've reached a dead-end. For the moment at least. I'm sorry.'

'Nonsense George,' she said briskly. 'You can't have been trying.'

He summarized the investigation so far, the trip to Bristol, Molly's lunch with Sally.

'I was on that programme once,' she said. '*Wildside.*'

'Were you?'

'Don't sound so astonished George. I told you children liked me. It was after the Rio summit.'

'So you met Sally Adamson?'

'The girl who presents it? Yes. Pleasant enough. No science but what can you expect these days. I know her father of course.'

'Do you?'

'Oliver Adamson. He's a solicitor. Advised me on setting up the trust to run this place. A bit of a stuffed shirt but he seems to know his business. You must know Oliver, George. He's a birdwatcher. Or he was. Quite keen at one time.'

And George, dredging through his memory, realized that he did remember Oliver Adamson. But the birdwatching world was a small one, so that wasn't surprising.

'He dotes on that daughter of his,' Cecily was saying. 'I wouldn't be at all surprised if he hadn't pulled a few strings to get her that job. You can tell he'd do anything for her.'

'So you see,' George said, hoping to pull her attention back to the subject, 'I don't think there's very much more we can do for the moment.'

'What about the bank account? Those credit card donations must have been paid in somewhere. We could find out from the credit companies, trace what happened to the money after that.'

'We'd need to convince the police that a fraud had been committed before they'd be allowed access to any accounts. Until I've spoken to the American end of the operation I don't think I can do that. It certainly looks suspicious but its just possible that Jessica Brown was an agent of the Wildlife Partnership acting illegally but in good faith. The organization is doing valuable work. You wouldn't want to damage their reputation until we know what's going on.'

'So the answer lies with those Brownscombes,' she said.

'I'm afraid it does.'

'Oh, well,' she said graciously. 'I can wait for two weeks. Now the office in Bristol is shut no other mug is being ripped off. You can telephone the Brownscombes when they come back from holiday. I'm quite determined about this George. I want no defeatism. We'll get to the bottom of it.'

'Perhaps you'd like me to go over to the States,' George suggested hopefully. 'I could check out the Houston office in person. Make absolutely sure.'

'There'll be no need for that George. I told you I was prepared to pay reasonable expenses, not subsidize a birding holiday, so you can see the spring migration at High Island.'

'I suppose,' he said, 'there was no harm in trying.'

And at that she laughed like a clown, rocking backwards and forwards on the kitchen step, her hands clasped around her scabby knees. Vanessa stopped knitting briefly, looked indulgently at her friend and returned her attention to her clicking needles.

George watched Molly preparing supper. She was skinning chicken pieces with a sharp knife. While he'd been at The Deuchars she'd spent the day working in the garden. He wasn't sure her hands were entirely clean. He looked away.

The telephone rang. Molly straightened from the chicken. She wiped her hands across her forehead, leaving a streak of grease behind.

'It's all right,' George said. 'I'll get it.'

He recognized the voice at once. He'd bumped into Rob Earl at birdwatching sites since the younger man was a teenager and more recently they'd become good friends. They'd both been part of an expedition which had taken a Land Rover overland to India, birdwatching all the way. Despite the difference in their age and background they'd survived it pretty well.

'Back from your travels? Want a bed for the night?' They put Rob up often when he landed at Gatwick.

'No,' Rob said. 'I'm phoning from High Island.'

'Lucky bugger.' George was amused by the coincidence. 'I was just saying today that I wish I were in Texas. What have you had?'

'I can't talk about that now.'

'What's wrong?' George asked easily, not thinking that anything was really wrong, that it would be some scrape with a girl, some hassle with money. Rob was always in debt.

'I'm here leading a party for West Country Wildlife, but I arranged to meet up with a couple of old friends at the same time. We all arrived the day before yesterday. We're staying at the same place, the Oaklands Hotel. Do you know it?'

'I've heard of it. Never been lucky enough to stay there.'

'Well come and stay here now George. That's why I'm phoning. We need you here.'

'Seen something you can't identify?' As soon as he said it George knew the humour was misplaced.

Rob ignored it and continued in a clipped, shocked voice. 'There was a fall yesterday morning. Wonderful. Everything I'd ever imagined. Birds everywhere. It was predicted by the weather so the place was crawling with birders, too.' He paused. 'It was chaos George. You know what it's like. I went out with my party but people wandered off and in the excitement I didn't try to keep them together. It wasn't practical.'

He paused again and George realized that he wanted reassurance that he couldn't have acted differently.

'No,' George said. 'I can see that.'

'I was trying to get to grips with a Swainson's warbler. You know how difficult they can be, skulking at the back of a tangle of thorn bushes. I left the trail in the end and went in after it. Only I didn't just see the warbler George. There was a body, lying face down in the dead leaves. He'd been stabbed. No one will tell me anything but I know he was stabbed. There was a hole an inch thick in his back.'

There was a brief silence before he continued more quietly. 'It was an old mate of mine. One of my best mates. I was in Texas to see him. Please come, George. The sheriff in charge of the case seems to think he must have been killed by one of the British party. At the moment I'm the prime suspect because I was spotted near the body. West Country Wildlife will make the travel arrangements for you. There's a BA flight from Gatwick at ten in the morning. I've spoken to my boss and he's booked you on it. It's not good for business, you see, to have one of your leaders suspected of murder. He'll pay for the flight.'

He stopped, apparently waiting for a response. 'You will come George, won't you?'

'If this happened yesterday why didn't you phone before?'

'I thought they'd sort it out, catch whoever had done it straight away. This is a small town. You can't get away with anything. But they've decided it wasn't a local lunatic. They've decided it was me.'

'What was the name of the victim?' George asked.

'Mick Brownscombe. Perhaps you remember him. We were at college together. He was a good birder. One of the best.'

George did not reply. He was wondering why he was not more surprised.

'You will help, won't you?' Rob demanded, more desperately.

'Oh yes,' George said. 'I'll be there.'

Chapter Eleven

'The officer thinks I was hiding when the Lovegroves saw me,' Rob said. 'Well of course I was. But only because I didn't want to make a bloody fool of myself. Not because I'd just thrown Mick's body into the middle of a bush.'

George could tell that the flip talk was an act. Rob was rattled. They were sitting on the lawn outside Oaklands drinking cold beer. It was early evening and the place was quiet except for the noise of insects. Rob leaned forward, his elbows on his knees and talked to the grass.

'We were friends for Christ's sake. From university. We shared a flea infested lodging in Brighton and travelled into the campus every day on the same bus. Sussex University was a trendy place to be at then, George. You remember that. Full of the kids of politicians, actors and people who wrote columns for the Sunday papers. Oliver was there, too. You remember him, don't you George?'

George only nodded. There could be questions about Oliver later.

'He fitted in fine. He'd been to the right school. His parents had the right friends. But it wasn't so easy for me and Mick.'

'It was easier for you than Michael though.' George was guessing. Lack of confidence had never been one of Rob's problems. He was a show-off, an attention seeker. He wouldn't be intimidated by the smart young things with their rich parents and plummy accents.

'Yeah. I suppose so. At least I'd been around a bit.'

'And Michael hadn't?'

'No. A trip to Exeter for the Christmas shopping was a major event. It wasn't that he was poor. His folks probably had more dosh than Oliver's. They owned a holiday centre in North Devon and a couple of hotels. The Barnstaple Mafia he called them and he wasn't really joking. I think it was his dad who screwed him up. Mick was scared shitless of him. Scared of everything else as well when I first met him – foreign food, anyone who lived north of Bristol. And women. Boy was he scared of women!'

'He didn't have a girlfriend at university?'

'There was a girl he wrote to. Someone at home. He used to talk about her occasionally when he'd had a few beers. His one and only true love. You know what you're like when you're eighteen. She was younger than him. He waited for her all the way through college then something must have happened, just before he came with us to the States. I suppose she found someone else. I asked him about her, teasing: "How can you bear to leave her?" Something like that. He almost hit me. It was the only time I ever saw him lose his temper.'

'But there was no one at university?'

Rob shrugged. 'There might have been the occasional fumble at the back of a disco. And platonic friends he took on long walks across the Downs and poured out his soul to. But he was so slow. We were banging away like rattlesnakes and he was worshipping his little schoolgirl from afar.'

'Yes,' George said. 'I see.' His children had been young in the seventies. He remembered them in a perpetual state of exhaustion. 'And yet you brought him to the States with you after you had left college. If you had so little in common why did you choose him as a travelling companion?'

'He wanted to come,' Rob said. 'We needed someone else to share the car, share expenses, you know. We'd have taken a fourth if we could have found one.' He paused, realized he sounded heartless, looked up, 'I mean that wasn't the only reason. We were friends. He could be a bit intense but we liked him.'

And he would be an audience, George thought. As he remembered it Oliver and Rob had been a double act and they would want an audience.

'Besides,' Rob continued, 'we thought it would be good for him to travel.'

'And was it?' George asked.

'What do you mean?'

'Did America change him? Did being on the road with you and Oliver change him?'

'I hadn't thought so,' Rob said, 'until we got to High Island.'

'And then?'

'And then Mick shocked us all by getting the girl.' Rob looked up again and smiled but George could tell that it still rankled.

'Ah, yes,' George said. 'Laurie.'

'She's not here now. She went straight away. Back to Houston to be with her kids. They had two apparently. A boy and a girl. Teenagers. They'd been staying with friends. She wanted to be there to tell them . . .'

'Of course,' George said.

They sat for a moment in silence. Rob flapped away a mosquito.

'I had to tell her Mick was dead. She turned up at Boy Scout Wood that afternoon to look for him. Someone had gone to phone the sheriff's department but no one official had arrived. I didn't know what to say. I just wanted to hold her but that didn't seem right either.'

'How did she react to the news?'

'How do you suppose she reacted George? Someone had stuck a chisel through her husband's heart and he'd been thrown into the underbrush to rot. She was bloody upset.'

He drank from the beer bottle, wiped condensation from his hand on to his jeans.

George ignored the outburst. 'How do you know it was a chisel? Have they found the weapon?'

'No. It's something to do with the size of the wound. The wrong shape for a knife blade. That's what the news reports said this morning. They don't tell us anything.'

'Did Laurie ask to see the body?'

'Not then. Someone from the sheriff's department arranged for her to do that later.'

He hesitated. 'They took Mick to the county morgue in Texas City. I suppose someone will have told his parents. I don't even know if they're still alive. Mick didn't say. We really didn't have a chance to talk at all. I suppose we both thought there'd be plenty of time.'

There was a silence. From the house behind them came the clatter of crockery and cutlery as the tables were laid for dinner.

'Had you kept in touch with the Brownscombes?' George asked.

'Not really. A Christmas card the years I got round to sending Christmas cards. The odd postcard if I went anywhere special. Just to grip old Mick off. You know George. You can't resist a bit of gloating.'

'Did they write to you?'

'Laurie never did. Mick kept in touch in much the same way as me. I think there were notes when the kids were born. A couple of years ago he did a trip to Attu, that mind-blowing island off Alaska, and he wrote from there. But that was just a list of birds. There was never anything personal, which was odd really when he'd been so intense before.'

'Did you meet in that time?'

'Never. I've been to Texas of course with work since we were first here together. We usually fly into Houston if we're doing High Island and the coast. It would have been easy to fix up a meeting but I never did. I'm not sure why. I suppose I felt a bit awkward about it if I considered it at all. Mick and Laurie belonged to the past.'

'And they never visited you in the UK?'

'No. I didn't realize they had come back until Laurie mentioned visiting London on business.'

'Did she say what business?' George asked carefully.

'I don't think so. What relevance could that have?'

'Probably none,' he said. Unless it was to use her position as consultant for the Wildlife Partnership to set up a little enterprise of her own using the same name, he thought.

'Tell me,' he said. 'Whose idea was this reunion? Not the original plan. I understand that when you were first at Oaklands you all made a commitment to get together in twenty years' time. But who remembered about it? Who made all the arrangements?'

'I made the practical arrangements, booked the rooms with Mary Ann, decided on a date. I didn't see why I should have to pay for a flight when I was coming out this year anyway. But it wasn't my idea. It was Oliver. He wrote to me and to Mick and Laurie saying: What about it? Remember the pledge? I wasn't sure at first. I mean it's never the same is it, going back? Then the idea started to appeal. I was curious. I wanted to see how we'd get on, the four of us.'

'Were you surprised that Oliver suggested it?'

'No. He's always been the romantic one. He always had style. You know Oliver don't you, George? We went twitching together when we were at university. He stopped chasing rarities completely when he got married. Claims to be a local patch man now, though I don't remember him finding any good birds in Sussex. Never seen his name in the *British Birds Magazine Rarity Report!*

'Yes,' George said. 'I knew Oliver.'

Since Cecily had mentioned the name, memories of Oliver had become more focused. It was a sign of age, he supposed, that his long-term memory was clearer than his short. Besides, he had always had a detailed visual recall of rare birds and the events surrounding them.

He remembered a Ross's gull for example, which had turned up on the fish quay at North Shields the day before Christmas Eve. Oliver had been there then, with Rob. The bird had been found in the afternoon and by the time George had arrived in the north-east it had been dark. He had stayed in Newcastle and arrived at the quay just after dawn to find that Oliver and Rob had already refound it. He could picture the scene now: the rosy plumage of the gull caught in the bright, eastern light, the trawlers moving out of the Tyne with the tide, men muffled in heavy coats cycling to work in the shipyards.

It seemed that the boys had hitched up to North Shields the night before and had persuaded a pub landlady to let them sleep in her bar. Oliver would have charmed her with his politeness and his indolent good looks. She would have ended up thinking it was a privilege to have them to stay.

'I was surprised though,' Rob was saying, 'that Julia agreed to the reunion.'

'Why?'

'Julia never approved of Mick and me. We weren't in the right social league at all. Her father was a small-time businessman who made money and she had pretensions.' He paused. 'Julia is the reason I don't see much of Oliver, even when I'm in the UK. I can't stand what she's done to him. It's pitiful.' He leaned forward. 'For instance, the day of the fall, the day I found Mick's body, it was raining birds. Not just warblers, though you've never seen so many colours. They were everywhere. More like butterflies than birds. But there were tanagers, vireos, chats, thrushes. And Oliver just walked away from it. He said that Julia needed to see him, and he walked away.'

He looked at George, expecting a suitable reaction of horror. When none came he shook his head slightly to express his disbelief.

'What time would that have been?' George asked.

'I'm not sure. Half-past one. Two o'clock. About an hour before I found the body.'

'You can't be more precise?' George was disapproving.

'Are you joking? This was the biggest birding experience of my life. And you wonder why I didn't look at my watch?'

'I suppose you all made statements to the authorities?'

'Oliver and I have. The detective in charge of the case is a lieutenant based in the sheriff's department in Galveston, though we haven't met him yet. We spoke to an officer called Grant. He's the one who's decided I'm the murderer.'

'And Laurie?'

'A couple of deputies drove her home on Monday afternoon. I suppose they spoke to her then.'

'And you were only here for one night before Michael Brownscombe was killed?'

'Two, if you count the one in Houston. We met for a meal the evening I flew in. But we took it easy, you know. As I said before, we thought there would be plenty of time.'

'Did he tell you anything about his business?'

'Not much. I got the impression he was doing well.' He paused, then remembered. 'Oh, yes, the night before he died Laurie did try to interest us in one of their projects. She talked about some group they were representing which runs reserves in the Third World. I think she wanted a chance to sell it to my party. Get money out of them I suppose. Sign them up as supporters. I didn't really listen. We'd seen the weather forecast and we were talking about the fall.'

'Do you remember the name of the group the Brownscombes were representing?'

'I don't think I ever knew. Does it really matter George?'

George did not reply. Rob wondered if he had even heard. He was looking older than Rob remembered. Perhaps he'd been wrong to put so much faith in him. There seemed little point to these rambling questions.

They were sitting on white wooden chairs in the shade of the porch. George found his concentration wandering. In the gaps in conversation he had become aware of birdsong and tantalizing shadows in the distant trees. He felt a sudden excitement which had nothing to do with the tracking down of Mick Brownscombe's murderer.

'I wonder if you'd mind showing me where you found the body,' he said. 'Before it gets dark. That is if it wouldn't be too upsetting.'

Rob grinned. White teeth in a wolf's face. Unreliable, Molly had always called him. Unpredictable.

'I wouldn't find it too upsetting,' he said. 'But perhaps you'd better get your bins before we go. Just in case.'

Found out, George thought sheepishly, but he said nothing and he went into the house to fetch his binoculars.

Chapter Twelve

George realized that his questions to Rob had been ineffective. He had found it hard to take the initiative. He did not dislike air travel but it reminded him of a stay in hospital; all responsibility was given up to the experts in uniform. There was something restful about the enforced inactivity but now he still found it easier to go with the flow, to put off any decision about the case.

He drove to Boy Scout Wood. Soon it would be dusk and the light would go quickly. The birders were already leaving and the sanctuary was almost empty.

'You should have been here yesterday,' Rob was saying. 'What a circus! Teams from the local TV and radio stations tramping all over the place, buttonholing anyone willing to talk to them; sanctuary volunteers, birders, even some of my party. Not that they minded of course. They enjoyed being celebrities. I can't blame them. It's not as if any of them *knew* Mick.'

'Are you sure about that?'

'No. Not sure. But nobody claimed to know him, and he didn't seem to recognize anyone. He would have said, surely.'

'Perhaps.'

They sat on the tiered benches and looked down at the water. As the light faded the sound of birdsong grew louder.

'You can imagine what it was like, can't you George? These benches filled with people, all of them crazy with excitement. The rain and the noise and the smell.'

'Yes,' George said. 'I think I can imagine it. Is there anyone you can provide an alibi for during that day? Someone we can dismiss altogether?'

Rob shook his head. 'You would think, in a space this small, that would be easy. But it was madness. People rushing around. I bumped into people I knew, chatted for a moment, shared info, then moved on. Besides, you know what it's like using bins or a scope. The field of view's restricted. I was concentrating so much on the birds that Mick could have been killed ten yards away from me and I'd not have noticed.'

'In the same way I suppose it would have been easy for the killer to come up behind Mick. If he was using his scope he'd not see anything. Not so easy though, to stab him with a chisel and be sure of killing him.'

'I think he was hit on the head first,' Rob said.

'What do you mean?'

'When I found him, there was a head wound. Not serious perhaps. I don't know. That's what I noticed first.'

'That would make sense,' George said. 'It would be much easier to do the stabbing if the victim was lying face down on the ground, even if he were just winded. You could position the chisel properly, apply more force.'

'That makes it sound very calculating.'

'There was one stab wound,' George said. 'Not a frenzied attack. But I wondered why the murderer bothered. Why not hit him again on the head?'

Rob turned away. 'Come on,' he said. 'I'll show you where it happened.' He walked off quickly, his boots rattling the timbers of the boardwalk.

There were no boards on the trail he turned into. In places the ground was still muddy from the rainstorm. Elsewhere it was so overgrown that George wouldn't have realized it was a path if it hadn't been for the rope looped through metal stakes which marked it.

'I chose it because I thought it would be quiet,' Rob said. 'I wanted to get away from the crowd. I was just unlucky I suppose that the Lovegroves felt like a peaceful stroll too.'

'Just an unfortunate coincidence, you think?'

'What more could it be? Jesus, George, you don't think they

killed him? Those are two classic old biddies. You get women like them on every tour. I mean it's a right pain in the arse to have to share a five hour coach journey with them, but they're definitely not into contract killing.'

The police had removed all the debris of their presence and yet it was obvious where the body had been found. The underbrush was tramped down and flattened. Suddenly the wood seemed very quiet. The catbirds must have passed through.

'Sorry George,' Rob said. 'The Swainson's warbler's gone. I take it that you need it too.'

The attempt at humour was half-hearted. George did not respond. They stood on the trail and looked in.

'The authorities seem to think he was killed by the side of the path then pulled into the bushes,' Rob explained. He had turned away and George had to strain to hear him. 'He'd been dead for a couple of hours when I found him but the detective's theory is that I went back to make a better job of hiding the body.'

'It seems someone followed him down the trail or set up the meeting in advance. In either case it was premeditated. Are you sure you didn't see Michael in conversation with anyone that morning?'

'I didn't see him at all. At least I thought I caught a glimpse of him with Laurie at one point, but they were a long way off at the end of a trail. And we were all wearing waterproofs. It could have been anyone.' Rob looked at his watch. 'We should go back. I'm still supposed to be working and the punters like me to be there for dinner. Perhaps it's so they can sell their story to the tabloids when they get home: "How I shared a meal with the condemned man."'

George followed. At one point, close to where the trail joined the main boardwalk he paused. The rope there was dragging in the mud. One of the metal stakes had been removed. Rob crouched beside him as he looked at the hole where it had fitted, watched as George walked methodically backwards and forwards looking for it. He became impatient.

'That can't be the murder weapon,' he said. 'Even if the end were sharp enough it's not the right shape.'

'No,' George said. 'It would be sufficiently heavy though to cause a nasty head wound.' Heavy enough to kill, he thought. So why not? Why use the chisel at all? He gave up the search and walked on.

After the storms the weather had become humid again. The place smelled of wet vegetation. It was almost dark. Suddenly, through the trees came the sound of raised voices.

'Are you crazy?' In the steaming heat, surrounded by the foreign sounds of birds and insects, the English voice, educated and shrill, was shocking. 'Are you trying to ruin our lives?'

Rob and George paused. They had come once again to the clearing called the Cathedral. Hidden by trees they stood still and watched. The woman had taken up position at the centre of the deck in the last remaining light. Her companion was sitting in shadow so they could only make out a dark shape sprawled on one of the benches.

'I didn't know what she was planning,' he said reasonably. 'How could I? I wish you'd believe me. You can't think I had anything to do with that.'

'You didn't want to know. But you provoked it. It would never have happened if it hadn't been for you.'

'I didn't want to upset you. I only told you so you'd know to be careful.'

'Upset me!' The woman paused, then spat out, almost weeping with jealousy. 'You'd do anything for her, wouldn't you? It's a madness with you. It always had been. I should have realized. Don't you realize the danger you've put us in, you fool.'

Her voice soared to a screech, then she stopped and they were engulfed again by the sound of insects. She turned to her companion demanding some sign that her dramatics had had an effect. But the man remained quite still, merging into the woodland. He said nothing. The woman gulped a sob and ran off. She was not used to running and she scuttled, clumsily and breathlessly. The man waited until she had disappeared into the trees and then he walked slowly after her.

'Well,' George said. 'What a melodrama!' Because some comment had to be made and the display of emotion always embarrassed him. 'Were they members of your group?'

'Not exactly,' Rob said. 'Didn't you recognize him, George? That's my friend Oliver. The bitch in the flowery frock is Julia.'

Oliver walked slowly back to the hotel. They had driven to Boy Scout Wood but after her outburst Julia had taken the car. He thought that was just a gesture. She wouldn't have done anything silly. When he returned to Oaklands she would be ready for dinner, waiting for him. He wondered whether the certainty that she would still be there pleased or dismayed him, but found even that small decision impossible to make.

He walked through the grid of small streets, avoiding the main road. A boy on a bicycle drove frantically past him then pulled on his brakes outside a house. He had probably been told to be in before dark. There was an oblong of light as the front door opened then the street was quiet again.

As he turned in the gateway into Oaklands, Oliver wondered why he wasn't more sorry that Mick was dead. He had hardly thought about the murder all afternoon, except as an inconvenience. Perhaps more than an inconvenience. A risk.

It was probably because Mick had never given anything of himself away. He hadn't trusted them. Like me with Julia, he thought ruefully. And look what happened when I tried to confide in her!

Mick had opened up a bit at college but on that drive through the States he'd been as uptight as ever. Emotionally frozen, Sally might say. She was into psycho babble. Rob hadn't noticed. He wouldn't. And Oliver had forgotten how withdrawn Mick had been. Only now he had a picture of Mick in the hire car, always sitting in the back, never speaking, as they drove half-way across America. When they pointed things out to him – an eagle soaring over the red desert, a mountain ridge in the distance – he had turned his head, but he hadn't really looked.

Until they got to Oaklands and met Laurie, Oliver thought. Mick had looked at *her*. He had thawed out after that.

Oliver walked through the trees and saw the house. There were lights in every window and as he approached he heard the sound of voices and laughter.

He used the pay phone in the lobby to call his daughter. To put off the moment when he would have to face Julia. Then he went to their room prepared to apologize. Half an hour later, when he led his wife into dinner, no one would have believed that they had been rowing.

During the meal George was overtaken by a terrible weariness so he could not concentrate on any of the conversations going on around him. He had asked not to be introduced to the West Country Wildlife party and he sat, unnoticed, at the foot of the large table where most of them had been placed. Perhaps because of the contrast between Julia's exhibition in the wood and the polite and apparently amiable image the Adamsons now presented, it seemed to him that he could not trust any of the courteous exchanges which he overheard.

After coffee he closed his eyes and almost dropped off to sleep where he sat. When he woke with a start a moment later solicitous faces were turned towards him. As if in a nightmare the gentle profiles of elderly men and women spun around him. He saw them as mocking masks hiding passions of hatred and revenge. Time for bed, he thought. Obviously he was too old to survive jet lag and a carafe of Californian wine without ill effect.

When he had arrived at Oaklands the hotel had been full. As a favour to Rob, Mary Ann had offered to put him up in one of the staff rooms. These were in a new single-storey block built away from the house and he had to cross the garden to reach them.

As he walked round the house from the restaurant he saw Julia, sitting in one of the old people's rocking chairs on the porch. He saw her through a mesh screen which had been put up to keep out insects, but a light was on behind her and even in his befuddled state he thought she had been crying. He paused, wondering whether to approach her, but she fled, making no attempt to hide her escape, turning over the chair in her haste.

Chapter Thirteen

The next morning Mary Ann had a message for George. Joe had called. He usually dropped into the restaurant at the Gulfway motel at ten. Perhaps Mr Palmer-Jones would meet him there.

'Joe?' George asked.

'Joe Benson. The constable.' She smiled briefly. 'You'd better go. He's a big man round here.'

When he got to the restaurant he knew the constable was already there because his car was parked outside. His name was painted on it in big letters.

Benson was enormous. His face was brown and hard under a cream coloured stetson. He wore a denim shirt with mother-of-pearl buttons, his constable's badge, a gun in a holster. When George came in he stood up. George felt dwarfed. And Benson was hostile.

'Mr Palmer-Jones,' he said. 'Well I'm real glad you could call in.'

His voice mumbled somewhere deep in his stomach. The sarcasm was intentional.

'It was good of you to see me.'

Benson looked at him and considered how to deal with that politeness.

'You sit down and we'll get Miss Lily to bring us some coffee.'

The restaurant was empty. George thought he had probably arranged for it to be that way. They looked at each other until the coffee came and Miss Lily disappeared into the kitchen.

'I'm wondering why that boy felt he had to send for you,' Benson said.

'He's nearly forty. Hardly a boy.'

Benson shrugged and suddenly they had something in common. He wasn't many years younger than George. They were both of the generation which remembered the Second World War and the legacy of the depression. Compared with us, he seemed to be saying. Compared with our age and experience, Rob Earl's just a foolish lad.

'You understand what I'm saying.' The voice was still aggressive but he was prepared to listen.

George tried to sound conciliatory. 'His employers, West Country Wildlife Tours, asked me to come. To give reassurance to their customers and to provide support for Rob during this difficult time. Of course I have no intention of intruding on your investigation.'

Benson recognized the lie but ignored it.

'Well now, I wouldn't say it was *my* investigation. The sheriff of Galveston County is in charge. He has a team of detectives. They're good men and women. I think we can both leave things to them.' He paused. 'We don't like amateurs. They get in the way.'

'But you do have an interest in what goes on in High Island?'

'Sure I have an interest. Perhaps I should explain how things work here. I believe constable means something different to you. I'm an elected representative of this community, responsible for law enforcement on the peninsula. I have a deputy working for me. A sergeant. Of course we work closely with the sheriff's department in Galveston but we live here. We know these people. Sure we care what goes on.'

'Yes,' George said. 'I see.'

Benson looked up at the ceiling. 'You could say I'm a servant of the community,' he said. 'This isn't a wealthy town. Not any more. Maybe you wouldn't visit for the scenery. But we do have tourists and they bring thousands of dollars to this region every year. "Avi-tourists" they call them. You know what I'm talking about Mr Palmer-Jones?'

'Birders,' George said. 'You're talking about birders.'

'I've got a friend.' Benson's musings were still directed to the whirring fan above his head. 'He owns his own gas station. He showed me some figures some research guy had put together. It proved that without all those visitors to High Island and the coast small businesses like his could go bust.' He paused. 'Those businesses are concerned, Mr Palmer-Jones. The tourists come from overseas. Maybe they over-react to bad publicity. That's the way of the world. They hear there's been a murder on a sanctuary in Texas they decide to go somewhere else. So if the tour companies want to send over a Brit PI to keep their customers happy I've got to go along with it. Do you understand me?'

'I understand that I'm here under sufferance.'

Benson seemed not to hear him. 'It also means that I'm under pressure to clear the case up quickly. We make an arrest, lock someone up, it's not news any more. But we're going to do it right whatever the boy thinks.' He sat forward, looked straight at George. 'I'm not under *that* much pressure.'

'Mr Benson,' George said. 'I believe you.'

'Good.' He smiled. 'Well that's good. This might be a small town, sir, but I'd like you to know that we do things right here. You don't have to worry about that. When your friend died everything was done according to the proper procedure. Miss Cleary called me at home. I contacted the sheriff's office, then I came straight down. A sergeant from Galveston arrived soon after and we cleared the area. The Identification Unit came. You know they have specially trained officers to search the scene of the crime. The medical examiner took a while to get here because he's based at the county morgue in Texas City, but the IDU are glad sometimes to get in there first. And he's an experienced man.'

'Has he done a preliminary report?'

'He'd report directly to the sheriff.'

'But you would know, wouldn't you, what the initial findings were?'

'Have you ever been a cop, Mr Palmer-Jones?'

'Not exactly.'

'You don't operate like a cop.'

'The medical examiner's report?' George prompted.

'He was stabbed. The weapon was thick bladed, but sharp.'

'What about the head wounds?' George asked.

'You know about them?' Benson seemed surprised, impressed. 'They didn't kill him.'

'But he was knocked over first, then the assailant stood over him and stabbed him?'

'That's the theory.'

'And your IDU. I presume they found the instrument which caused the head wound? A heavy stake with an eye at one end through which the boundary rope had been threaded.'

It was a guess and he was showing off. He'd look a fool if he were wrong.

Benson scowled. 'Someone been talking to you?'

George shook his head. 'I noticed that it was missing yesterday. What about the murder weapon? The thick bladed instrument? Did they find that?'

'No, Mr Palmer-Jones, they didn't find that.' He called into the kitchen for more coffee. Outside in the road a car braked sharply. They heard high spirited men's voices, jeers and cat-calls. Then the engine revved up and the car drove quickly away.

George drank the strong black coffee.

'Rob Earl didn't do it, you know,' he said.

Benson said nothing. George thought he had gone too far but he persisted.

'Why would he? What was the motive?'

'As I understand it your friend was always jealous of Mr Brownscombe. He'd taken a fancy to his wife.'

'That was twenty years ago! Rob's had dozens of girlfriends since then.'

'It wasn't anyone from around here,' Benson said stubbornly. 'Like I said, I know these people. There are one or two who might kill a man in a fight in a bar. But not that sort of attack. Not a stranger from behind.'

They looked at each other in silence.

'Have the detectives looked into the Brownscombes' business dealings?' George asked.

'I don't know. You think that might be important?'

'There's a non-profit organization called the Wildlife Partnership. It's based in Houston and the Brownscombes have done some work for it. There's a possibility that in the UK it's been involved in a charity fraud. Perhaps it's not relevant but they might want to look into it.'

'Sure. I'll pass the information on. Did you discuss this with Mr Earl?'

'No.'

'Thank you, Mr Palmer-Jones. I appreciate that decision.'

'Rob isn't a murderer,' George said.

Benson took a deep breath. For a moment George thought the man would lose his temper. Instead he spoke quietly. 'Well if you tell me that, I'm inclined to believe you. But it's not me you have to convince.'

'No,' George said, 'but I'm grateful anyway.'

'Did you ever meet Mick Brownscombe?'

'A couple of times a long time ago.'

'I can't seem to get a handle on him. I mean what was the guy like?'

'He was quiet, self-effacing, nervous. A country boy who often seemed out of his depth.'

'Not the sort to get murdered then?'

'I'm not sure.' George paused. This was Molly's territory but he'd learned something from her over the years. 'The sort perhaps to be bullied and taken advantage of. A victim if you like.'

'You go in for all this psychology?'

'Like you, I think it's important to know who we're dealing with.'

'Maybe.' Benson yawned to show what he really thought of all that stuff. George took no notice and continued.

'For example, it would be interesting to meet his parents. Are they coming over for the funeral?'

'I don't think they are.'

'Doesn't that strike you as odd?'

'Not really. I guess they're old and they can't face the trip. I'm telling you,' Benson said. 'You're making it too complex. In my experience murder's the most simple of crimes. Money. Women. Revenge. What else is there?'

Families, George thought. Fear. Failure. 'I expect you're right,' he said.

'So you'll leave it to the sheriff's department?'

'I was wondering,' George spoke slowly, 'if I might visit Laurie Brownscombe.'

Benson looked at him, said nothing.

'I thought she might speak to me. After all, I knew her husband. We shared an interest.'

'Yeah. Birds.' The word was deliberately unemphatic but Benson made his opinion clear. Birds were for shooting. 'But you're not gonna talk to her about birds.'

'Probably not. At least not exclusively.'

'You're pushing your luck here Mr Palmer-Jones.'

George did not answer.

Benson shrugged.

'She agrees to see you, I can't stop you.'

'Thank you.'

'Mr Palmer-Jones?'

'Yes.'

'You find anything interesting, you come to tell me.'

'Of course.'

'And you're there as a friend of the family.'

'I understand.'

'Mr Palmer-Jones?'

'Yes?'

'You come to see me anyway.'

'I'd enjoy that.'

Benson suddenly beamed. He sat forward and set forearms, as wide as shovels, on the table in front of him. 'Tell me,' he said. 'Do you ever drink beer?'

George smiled back.

'At every opportunity.'

'That's settled then. When you get back from Houston you give

82

me a call. You come round to my house and we'll have a few beers. And you tell me everything that lady said to you.'

Chapter Fourteen

Laurie Brownscombe lived in a leafy satellite town to the west of Houston. George phoned her from Oaklands before setting off in the car he had hired from the airport on his arrival. She sounded dazed and confused but not too grief stricken to take hold of the situation.

'Who did you say you were?'

'A friend of Rob's. I'm staying at the Oakland's Hotel. He asked me to come out to represent his interests.'

'You're a lawyer then?'

'No. Not a lawyer. Would you mind if I visited you? The authorities have no objection.'

She hesitated and he thought she would refuse.

'Sure,' she said at last, 'why not?' And he thought that curiosity had got the better of her.

He had been expecting someone glamorous. Like the woman described by Jason and the florist. Too much make up and designer clothes. Laurie wore jeans and a T-shirt and her sandy hair was long like a girl's. She's in mourning, he thought. Did I really expect her to dress up for me. He remembered Julia screaming like a demon in the woods, then playing the part of affectionate wife in the restaurant, told himself that appearances were deceptive, but still he could not reconcile the two images of Laurie Brownscombe.

She let him into a spacious, air conditioned house. There were marble tiles on the floor. The living space was large, open plan, dotted with sofas and arm chairs. The effect was generally so bland and impersonal that it might have been an executive lounge in an airport. Only in the corner which had been turned into a study were there any individual touches: a Tucker print of a peregrine on the wall above the desk, a solid wood carving of a lapwing used as a book end on the shelf.

Laurie went up to the carving, stroked it.

'Besides his clothes and his optical gear this is the only thing Mick brought with him from England when we married,' she said.

'Who did it? It's very good.'

'I don't know. Some friend of his.' She turned back to face him. 'Palmer-Jones,' she said. 'That's a very *English* name.'

He felt apologetic, as he did every time the double barrelled name was mentioned. It had been a pretension of his father's. He had always hated it but hadn't had the courage to change it while the old man was still alive. When he died it was too late. By then to have dropped either side of the hyphen would have been a foolish gesture. But it wasn't something you could explain to strangers.

'I suppose it is,' he said.

'You knew Mick?'

'Not well. I think I met him when he was a student. At Cley. Dungeness. Birdwatching places.'

'With Rob and Oliver?'

'That's right.'

'The three of them were together when I first met them too. They were wild. I guess that's why we got along so well.'

But you're not wild now, George thought. The Laurie Rob described wouldn't have lived in this anonymous house in this respectable suburb.

She seemed to guess his thoughts. 'We were young then. Things have changed.'

'For the better?' he asked.

'Sure, for the better.' She paused. 'I know Rob thought of us as kindred spirits but I couldn't be like him. Travelling. Living out of a suitcase. Moving from one rented apartment to another. It is like that, isn't it?'

'Pretty much.' Though it would be more accurate, George

suspected, to say that Rob moved from one girlfriend's apartment to another.

'I had enough of that as a kid,' she said. 'I like security.'

'Mick gave you that?'

'Yes he did. It was important to him too. He had a lousy childhood. His parents are still bastards. You know they're not even coming over for the funeral? They wouldn't come to see us wed and they won't come to see him buried.'

They had settled at a table in the kitchen area. There was a coffee machine on the bench. She poured coffee into a mug and handed it to George. He took it and sat down.

'Do you know why I'm here?' he asked.

'You said on the telephone to represent Rob's interests. I don't know why.'

'The detective in charge of the case thinks he killed your husband.'

She set her mug carefully on the table.

'I didn't know that.'

'They didn't tell you?'

She shook her head. 'I didn't give them any reason to think that,' she said. 'I wouldn't have done.'

'Are you sure?' George spoke sharply. 'It's not a motive they could have conjured up for themselves.'

'Of course I'm sure.'

'Apparently the detective thinks Rob has been infatuated with you for twenty years and when he met you again he couldn't contain his passion.'

'That ridiculous!' But she hadn't noticed the irony. She liked the idea. She hadn't been so devoted to her husband that she wouldn't have welcomed another man's attention.

'I know it's ridiculous. That's why I'm here.'

She stood looking down at him, considering.

'Why don't we go outside,' she said. 'Sit by the pool. There's some shade. The kids are upstairs. They couldn't face school this week. I don't want them listening in to this.'

The back garden was tidy, pleasant enough, uninspiring. George thought they probably had someone to look after it.

'Tell me about your marriage,' he said.

'Why?' She was startled but not offended. She's as hard as nails he thought suddenly. I wonder what made her like that. She might have confided in Molly but she'll never tell me.

'Because Mr Benson might have the wrong suspect but the right motive,' George said, 'and I've no time for subtleties. I need to prove Rob's innocence before his group fly back to Britain.'

'What do you want to know?' She was sitting in a swinging chair made out of floral canvas, curled like a cat, her hair striped with the shadow of the awning above her.

'If you were having an affair?'

'No,' she said. 'Never.'

'What about Mick?'

'I can't be certain about that, but I wouldn't have thought so. It wouldn't be his style. Besides, it wouldn't have been part of the deal.'

'What deal?'

'Marriage,' she said. 'That deal.'

'Is that how you saw it?'

She pushed against the ground with her foot so the chair rocked slightly and leant back against the padded cushion.

'I'm not sure what other way there is to see it.'

George said nothing.

'It worked OK,' she said. 'Really it did.'

A hummingbird came to a water bottle hung on a tree. It hovered, caught in the sunlight. They watched it until it flew away and then she started to talk. Her chair swung lazily backwards and forwards as she told her story. George listened, his eyes half shut.

'I was on the road to Winnie,' she said. 'It could have been anywhere. I just wanted to get out of town and I had relatives round there, thought someone would put me up. Besides, it was April, and I was a bit of a birder then, though it wouldn't have been cool to admit it. There were no sanctuaries on High Island at that time but I knew it could be good.

'I was waiting for a ride, thinking it would be just my luck if the first thing that stopped was a truck with a family man inside.

A good man. The sort that tells you he's worried about you and how you shouldn't be hitchhiking, and why don't you just go home. Then this car stopped. I saw three guys and at first I thought: No way. Not with three guys. I mean I was pretty wild in those days but not crazy. But they were young, you know, and English and I thought: What the hell! Why not? And they were birders too, so it seemed OK.

'They wanted somewhere to stay in High Island. They'd heard of it. Someone they'd met on the trip had told them about the spring warblers. You know. They didn't have much money but they had some, so I thought of the place my aunt had and took them there. It was run-down, not grand like it is today. She was glad of the custom. And she liked them, you know. It would have been hard not to like them.'

She stopped swinging and sat upright. Her feet were firmly planted on the paving stones.

'I could have had any of them,' she said. 'Even Ollie. I know he'd promised to go home to marry that girl he'd got pregnant but if I'd said to him: "Stay here with me," he'd have done it. No question. I could have had any one of them.'

She closed her eyes against the sun, leaned back again.

'But you chose Mick,' George said.

'Yes. I chose him.'

'He wasn't the obvious choice,' George said. 'Was he? Why Mick?'

He thought she wasn't going to answer and was about to repeat the question, when she said: 'I knew we were two of a kind and we'd get on just fine.' She smiled as if she realized this wasn't any sort of answer at all, challenging him to take the matter further.

'When did you set up the business?' George asked.

'About five years after we married. Mick had the skills. He'd done zoology at university. When he first got his Green Card he worked on the environmental team of an oil company based here in Houston. Then we decided to go it alone. We're small but we've done OK. We worked from home at first but more recently we've taken premises on a small business park not far from here. It was an expense, a risk I guess, but we've plans for expansion and it suits us fine.'

'What's your role in the business?'

'I'm a sort of general manager I suppose. I look for work, negotiate terms, do all the public relations things. Mick headed up the technical team. They do the surveying and prepare the reports. We employ young scientists on short-term contract when we need them.'

'Is your work mostly oil based?'

'It was at first. Surveying the route of new pipe-lines. You know the sort of thing?'

George nodded.

'We were small, no overheads. We could undercut most of the main players. And since then we've diversified. Now we do quite a lot of work for non-profit organizations.'

'Joined the side of the angels?'

'Yeah,' she said. 'You could say that. They didn't pay so well but Mick preferred it. And it was good for our image. Industrial companies could say: "You've heard of Brownscombe Associates. You know their environmental credentials. Now they're working for us." We all benefited.'

'What sort of work do you do for them?'

'A lot of it's data collection. But there's other stuff too. Fund-raising. Grant applications. I enjoy all that. A born saleswoman I guess.'

'Have you heard of an organization called the Wildlife Partnership?'

'Sure. We represent them. They're a small outfit working mostly in Central and South America. They wanted advice on promotion, how to get their message across more effectively. They could have employed a public relations firm but they wanted someone who understood the science, and Mick had done work on the ground for them. They couldn't afford much but we put together a package. It was based on the idea of shares. Getting people to invest in the future of the planet. Corny, I guess, but effective. I was going to try it out on Rob's group but I never got the chance . . .'

'Does the Wildlife Partnership operate in the UK?'

'No. We looked into it but there were too many legal problems. In the end it wouldn't have been worth the effort.' She looked at him, flashed a smile. 'You know George, there just aren't enough rich people in Britain.'

It would have been possible then to confront her with the Wildlife Partnership advertising material which had used Cecily Jessop's name, but he did not think it wise to show his hand so soon.

'I'd like to ask you about the time you spent together at Oaklands, leading up to the morning Mick died,' he said. 'It wouldn't upset you?'

He asked the question through habitual good manners. He did not think much would upset her.

'I told the deputies who drove me home,' she said.

'I'd find it helpful.'

'We'd arrived at Oaklands the afternoon before. Mary Ann threw a kind of party for us that night. Mary Ann Cleary. I explained she's a cousin. We had dinner and drinks and the boys were just talking about the weather and how amazing it would be for birds the next day. Of course it wasn't so exciting for Mick. But he was pleased for them. He wanted it to be special. He hoped it would be good.

'The next morning Rob took his party to Boy Scout Wood but we went to Smith Oaks first. There's a shop by the entrance where you can buy the patches which allowed you into the sanctuaries. I thought you could probably pay a fee at Boy Scout too, but Mick wasn't sure. He was always cautious. Always played by the rules.'

'Were Mr and Mrs Adamson with you?'

'Oliver was. Not Julia. He said she hadn't slept well and she'd decided to stay in bed. I wasn't sorry.'

'You didn't like her?'

'I only met her that first night, but no, I didn't like her.'

'Did you stay at Smith Oaks?'

'No. We had a quick look but Mick and Oliver wanted to find Rob, so we went back to Boy Scout.'

'You walked?'

'Are you joking? Americans never walk anywhere. Unless it's

with knapsacks and boots in the National Park. We took our car. Parked it in the street outside the sanctuary.'

'Did you find Rob?'

Laurie shook her head. 'Not while I was there but I didn't stay long. As soon as it started raining I gave up.'

George raised his eyebrows. 'The best fall in years and you gave up? I thought you were a "bit of a birder".''

'Only in good weather. Not seriously. I took the Explorer. The boys would be wet anyway so I thought they could walk back to Oaklands.'

'What did you do?'

She paused. 'I had lunch with Mary Ann. Like I said, we're distant family. We had things to talk about.'

'Was Julia there?'

'I didn't see her at lunch but I guess she was around. I remember Oliver turning up sometime looking for her. The rain stopped so I went back to Boy Scout. Rob was there, waiting by the information stand at the entrance to the wood. At first I couldn't understand what was wrong with him. He could hardly speak. I thought he was ill. He told me that Mick was dead. Then someone from the sheriff's office turned up and they took me home.'

She sat very still.

'Had Mick made any enemies through the business?' George asked. 'Had he stepped on any toes?'

'No. That wasn't Mick's way. He wasn't tough enough to be in business at all. If anyone made an enemy it was me.'

'Who?' George asked sharply.

She shook her head. 'I'm not talking about anyone specific. I've a more abrasive style. I won't be walked over.'

George let that go, though he wasn't sure he believed her. 'What will you do now?'

'What do you mean?' She looked up at him, putting her hand to her eyes to shade the sunlight reflected from the water.

'With the business?'

'I'll run it myself,' she said. 'I'll take on a graduate to do the surveys and write the reports. There are lots of unemployed environmental scientists out there. It won't be a problem.'

No, George thought, as he drove back down the I10 towards the coast. I don't suppose it will.

Chapter Fifteen

When George returned to the Oaklands Hotel the Mays were waiting for him. They had been waiting for most of the afternoon, had even decided against going on the trip Rob had organized to the wildlife refuge at Anahuac, although he had promised them alligators and that the wet prairie would hold birds they still needed for their list. The Mays were beside themselves. After their first encounter with Rob in the Marriott Hotel in Houston when they had been so critical, so – they realized it now – unreasonable, he had become a hero for them.

George recognized them, standing on the veranda looking out for his car. They had been sitting at his table on the night of his arrival; it had been their kind faces which had turned towards him when he was feeling unwell. They had not known then the purpose of his visit. Now rumours about him had spread and they considered him an ally.

When he climbed the steps on to the veranda they blocked his path. They were not used to making a fuss and were embarrassed about accosting him but quite determined.

Russell held out his hand, partly in greeting, partly to stop George's progress into the house.

'Mr Palmer-Jones,' he said. 'We need to speak to you.'

George stopped. He was tired. He wanted a bath and dinner.

'You have information about Mr Brownscombe's murder?' he asked.

'Not exactly information. But we think we can help.'

They were desperate to be taken seriously.

'Of course we can talk. But after I've had dinner? Perhaps I could come to your room. Then we won't be overheard.'

It was just the right response. They went away gratefully to prepare for him.

The Mays' room was pleasantly proportioned but small. They gave him the only chair – a rocker with a quilted cover thrown over the back – and sat on the bed. Connie's legs were too short to reach the floor. She had made instant coffee, spooning the powder from a jar she had brought with her from England, although sachets had been left on a tray in the room.

'We can't offer you anything stronger,' she said. 'Russell and I don't drink.'

There was nothing apologetic about the words. It was a statement of principle. She turned to her husband, encouraging him to explain their concern. He started hesitantly.

'I suppose we've had sheltered lives,' he said. 'I was a Special Constable when I was younger but you couldn't say I saw much active service. It was all routine. Now our social life revolves round the Natural History Society and the Bowls Club. Most of our friends are retired. Not having family we don't mix much with young people. But that doesn't mean we're narrow-minded. We might not come across folk like Rob Earl very often, but we can tell he's a *good* man, Mr Palmer-Jones. It's not possible that he committed murder.'

'He hasn't been arrested, you know,' George said. 'It was natural that the authorities would want to question him because he found the body. It would be just the same in Britain.'

'We thought you'd come out to stop him being arrested.' Connie had caught the sun. In the light of the bedside lamp her face was pink and earnest. 'That's what everyone's been saying.'

'Not quite.'

'But you are a private detective?'

'Of a sort.' He hated the description. 'Rob's employers hired me, but I'm here as his friend. Of course I'd like to find out what really happened. Not,' he added quickly, 'that I don't think the local agencies are competent to do that too.'

'I didn't take to that Mr Benson,' Connie said. 'He seems to be everywhere. And he carries a gun.'

'What we're really here to tell you,' Russell interrupted, 'is that we want to help. In any way we can. We don't think Rob would have killed anyone and we want to help you prove it.'

What did he imagine he could do? George wondered. Crawl around the underbrush of Boy Scout Wood looking for clues? Follow suspects down the main street of High Island? Or perjure himself by providing Rob with an alibi? Is that the sort of excitement he had hoped for when he joined the Specials?

'You could help by answering some questions,' George said carefully.

They were disappointed.

'Is that all?' After an afternoon of waiting it was an anti-climax.

'I need to piece together exactly what happened that morning.' He looked at Russell. 'I expect you know how tedious a painstaking investigation can be.'

'Well yes,' he said, flattered despite himself. 'Of course.'

'So if you could tell me what you did and saw that day. . .'

'We had breakfast. . .' Connie started. George felt a desire to yawn, stifled it. They would have to tell their story in their own way.

'Yes,' he prompted.

'Rob sat at our table, didn't he, Russ? And he was as relaxed as anything. He wouldn't have sat there, chatting away, if he was planning a murder, would he?'

'You went together as a group to Boy Scout Wood?'

'In the bus. Yes.'

'And did you stay as a group once you were inside the sanctuary?'

This time Russell answered. 'We did for a while. Rob was talking to us, telling us a bit of the history of the place. And some of the party were beginners. They needed Rob to tell them what they were seeing.'

'Those Lovegroves, for instance,' Connie said darkly. 'Never giving the man a minute's peace.'

'The Lovegroves aren't expert birdwatchers then?' George asked.

'They haven't got a clue!' George wondered how much of Connie's venom resulted from the fact that it was the Lovegroves' evidence which had landed Rob in trouble.

Russell spoke more reasonably. 'Everyone's got to start somewhere,' he said. 'But you'd think they'd try to get to grips with birds at home before attempting something as ambitious as Texas in the spring. It's just a waste of money, isn't it? They could be seeing anything.'

'Did the Lovegroves tell you why they decided to come on the West Country Wildlife trip in the first place?'

'No.' Russell smiled apologetically. 'To be truthful I try to avoid them. Once they get you in conversation they stick like limpets. But I get the feeling that it was all Esme's idea. Joan's just here to keep her company. That's the impression Joan likes to give anyway. That she's long suffering and hard done by.'

'Yes,' George said. 'I see.' He supposed he would have to speak to the Lovegroves. He wasn't looking forward to it. There was a moment's silence, then he asked: 'Can you tell me exactly what time it was when the party broke up?'

The Mays looked at each other. Connie answered: 'Not exactly. About midday I suppose. After the rain started. I turned round and saw crowds of people but no one I recognized.'

'And you didn't see Rob Earl after that?'

'No.' Russell replied sadly. 'I wish I could say that we had.'

'What about Mr Brownscombe? Did you see him at all?'

'Yes,' they chorused together.

'Could you tell me about that?'

'It was soon after we'd lost Mr Earl,' Russell said. 'We wandered back to the sanctuary entrance. There's a gallery there, looking down over a pool. Mr Brownscombe and Mr Adamson were on the bench next to us. We recognized them from the hotel and started chatting, comparing notes the way you do. He could tell from my accent that I came from the West Country and we talked a bit about the birdwatching sites at home. He still remembered them after all this time. I had the feeling, you know, that he might be homesick. He'd never gone back. It seemed very strange talking about Braunton Burrows and Fremington Creek with tanagers and vireos and orioles flying all around. Very strange.'

'So Mick Brownscombe grew up close to your home,' George said. 'Did you know him when he was a boy?'

'Not him. I suppose I might have come across him but I don't remember. Know his father of course. Everyone knows Wilf Brownscombe.'

'Oh.'

'Biggest crook in the county,' Russell May said. 'He's never been caught but that's what everyone says.'

'Does everyone say exactly what sort of crime he's involved in?'

'Mostly fraud I believe,' Russell said. 'He's very plausible. Persuaded a lot of people to invest in him. But he declared himself bankrupt a while back and they all lost money. He took local traders and suppliers down with him. Then he set up a new business in his wife's name. Not doing exactly the same thing as before – not enough profit in that for Wilf Brownscombe. Retirement homes he's into now. He can use the same hotels but charge twice as much. I don't know what else he's up to. He's got fingers in a lot of pies has Wilf Brownscombe. But if you met him you'd think he was a lovely fellow. He's famous for making big donations to charity.'

'Is he?' George said, and wondered if that was one coincidence too many.

George found it hard to sleep. At one-thirty he decided to phone Molly. She should just be waking up.

'I think you should take a trip to the seaside,' he said. 'You deserve a holiday. Go to Devon and find out all you can about Wilf Brownscombe, the father of the murdered man.'

Molly, who was never at her sweetest before breakfast, swore at him.

Chapter Sixteen

Early the next morning, George took Oliver to the coast. They walked along the beach to the Bolivar Flats.

It had been arranged the night before during dinner. Oliver had been on particularly good form. Perhaps he was a little high as if he had drunk too much but no one would have guessed that a good friend had died a few days before and another was suspected of murder. Then George had suggested the trip to Bolivar and he had fallen silent, looked helplessly at his wife.

'Of course you should go,' Julia had snapped. 'Why not? I should be used to your deserting me by now.'

'Why don't you come too?' George asked, but she had laughed at that.

'No thank you!' she had said. 'After all, I *am* on holiday.'

The day had started sunny but now there were sulphurous clouds which gave a vivid yellow light. They drove south until they hit the coast, then west along the Bolivar peninsula, a spit of sandy land with the Gulf of Mexico on one side of it and Galveston Bay on the other. The road was separated from the beach by dunes and scrub, and was so low that they could not see the ocean on the horizon, only the huge ships gliding down the Gulf. It was an optical illusion which made the boats seem to be sailing across land and with the odd yellow light gave the impression that this was a strange country where the normal rules of nature did not apply.

The road passed through the towns of Crystal Beach and Gilchrist. The wooden houses were built on stilts to protect them from floods and high tides. There were motels and shabby sea-food restaurants and small boats upturned on the sandy soil. At Rettilon Road, George turned off the highway to the beach. There they parked the car and walked along the shore to the marshland of the Bolivar Flats Sanctuary.

'It reminds me of East Anglia,' Oliver said. 'Something about the low horizon. Perhaps the light.'

'Do you get to Norfolk now? For the birding?'

'Hardly ever. I don't seem to have the time now with business, family commitments.'

'Of course,' George said, thinking that even when he had been busiest and the children were young he had found the time to drive to Cley in the autumn when the wind went easterly. But then Molly had understood, or he had always supposed that she had, how important it was to him to escape.

'I suppose you gave a statement to one of the sheriff's detectives,' George said.

'Yes,' Oliver said. 'That first afternoon.'

'Did you tell him that Rob was infatuated with Laurie?'

'Not exactly that.' Oliver gave an awkward giggle. 'He asked about the relationship. . .'

'And you told him that Rob was jealous of Mick Brownscombe.'

'Of course not. But I suppose it's possible that he jumped to that conclusion.'

You're a lawyer, George thought. You knew what you were doing. So why did you want to focus interest on Rob? But he let the answer go.

'Tell me about Mick Brownscombe,' he said. 'When did you last meet him?'

'You know that. Twenty years ago. That's why we're here.'

'But he came to London occasionally on business. He never phoned you up? He must have been lonely, stuck in a hotel room. He never suggested that you met for a boys' night out or a talk about the old times?'

'No,' Oliver said. 'Never. But then I would have been surprised if he had. He wasn't like that. He didn't find it easy to get on with people. He was shy, nervous. When we were travelling together sometimes he went days without speaking.'

'So he was rather unprepossessing,' George said. 'At least that's the impression I have. So why did Laurie choose him?'

'I don't know,' Oliver said. 'I've often wondered.' He gave a high-pitched laugh. George thought he had cultivated the image of a middle-aged buffer, elegant but rather stupid.

'What about Laurie?' George asked briskly. 'Did you ever meet her in the UK?'

Oliver paused, then seemed to decide to tell the truth.

'Yes,' he said. 'A couple of times. The first time it was much as you said. She was stuck in a hotel room after a meeting, bored. Too jet lagged to sleep properly. She phoned me at the office. Offered to buy me dinner. I was flattered I suppose. Curious. Anyway I agreed to meet her. We went to a French place in Covent Garden. It was hot. We sat outside. Isn't it strange, some things you remember really clearly? Nothing much happened. We talked. Mostly about our families. About work a bit. Then I dropped her back at her hotel and went home. I got a bollocking from Julia for working late again.'

'When was this?'

'About five years ago.'

'She hadn't tried to get in touch with Rob too?'

'She didn't say. Perhaps she had but he was away on his travels. I preferred to think that I was her first choice.' He gave another silly laugh.

'When did you meet her again?'

'More recently. Perhaps a year ago. But that was by chance.'

'You just bumped into her in the street?' George made his voice sceptical.

'Of course not. It was at a party. An oil company was launching a competition. It was offering a sponsorship deal to the charity which came up with the most imaginative scheme for reclaiming industrial wasteland. Laurie was in London for a meeting with the oil company and they invited her along.'

'Why were you there?'

'I specialize in environmental law, George. I'm often wheeled out at these dos. The groups think it makes up for my charging well below the market rate for my services. I didn't speak much to Laurie that night. I kept getting waylaid by eager young men from the county trusts wanting free advice. I hoped we might have a chance for a quiet drink later, but she just seemed to disappear. She had a long chat with Sally though.'

He broke off abruptly.

'Sally?'

'My daughter. Julia doesn't much enjoy these events so I'd taken Sally along. She was up from Bristol for the week and she'll do anything for a glass of free champagne.'

'Your daughter is the Sally Adamson who presented the children's natural history programme?'

'That's right!' Oliver was obviously delighted by the recognition. 'She was a bit depressed that night because the series had come to an end and they'd decided not to do another one. I brought her along to cheer her up. I knew she'd be the centre of attention. And I told her: "You're a real actress, my girl. You should be looking to the RSC or the National, not having to compete for an audience with monkeys and gerbils."'

'What did she and Laurie talk about?'

'I don't know. Work I suppose. Me.' He smiled but George did not respond. 'What is this all about?'

'Did Laurie talk to Sally about a charity called the Wildlife Partnership?'

'I don't know.'

'Did they ever meet again? Did Sally invite her down to Bristol?'

'I wouldn't have thought so. It was just a conversation at a party. Why?'

'Molly went to see your daughter, last week. Her name had been used in the advertising material of an organization called the Wildlife Partnership. Leaflets had been mailed soliciting donations. Famous people connected with natural history had been named as supporters without their permission. Sally was one of them. We were asked to look into it.'

Oliver was looking out over the Gulf of Mexico, concentrating very hard on a laughing gull, but George knew that he was listening.

'Sally told Molly that she *had* heard of the Wildlife Partnership. It had been mentioned by a woman at a party. The woman was American. This all seems to lead back, don't you think, to Laurie?'

Oliver lowered the binoculars.

'You think Laurie was behind some sort of scam?'

'I don't know. Somebody was.'

'Why would she bother? She can't need the money.'

'Do you know that?'

Oliver shrugged. 'I suppose not. She just gives the impression of a successful woman. But then she would. A confidence trickster would.' He turned away from the sea to face George. 'Do you think this has anything to do with Mick's murder?'

'I don't know. It's a possibility. If Laurie is involved in fraud it tells us at least that we can't take what she says about Mick for granted. She had things to hide.'

Oliver walked on. The sun came from behind a cloud and threw a brown shadow ahead of him. A flock of waders flew out of the saltmarsh. George stopped to identify them. Were they greater or lesser yellowlegs? Greater, he decided. He pulled out his notebook and wrote them down.

'I don't like Sally being mixed up in all this,' Oliver said and George remembered what Cecily had said about him: 'he dotes on that child.' 'Somehow it brings it all too close to home. She shouldn't have involved Sally.'

'Of course you wouldn't warn Laurie that she might be under suspicion?'

'No!' Oliver was impatient. 'Of course not.' He waited until George had caught him up, then he went on. 'She's reckless enough to do it. Not kill Mick. I don't mean that. But set up a false charity. Print the leaflets. Not even for the money. But just to see what happened, to see if she could get away with it. When we met that night in Covent Garden she said that she was bored: "There are times, Ollie, when I just want to go out and make something happen." Perhaps she did. Do you think so, George? Is that how it happened?'

George did not reply.

'This is horrible,' Oliver said. 'Julia was right. We should never have come.'

'Why *did* you come?' George asked. 'It was your idea, wasn't it, to keep everyone to the pledge you all made? To meet up again.'

'Sentiment,' Oliver said. 'To recreate that sense of friendship. Looking back nothing seems as important as that. I suppose it's just a part of getting old.' Then he gave another nervous laugh and took on the pose again of brainless fool. 'None of us is as sharp as we were George. We all look back to the good old days.'

'Was it age which made you decide to leave Boy Scout Wood in the middle of a fall?'

'Rob told you about that, did he? He seemed to think I was mad but I'd promised Julia I wouldn't be late.'

'I think if I'd been there,' George said, 'I'd have been tempted to stay.'

'Would you? Well you're not married to Julia.' He seemed to regret the retort and smiled to turn it into a joke. 'Rob caused rather a scene actually. He stood in the middle of the wood in the pouring rain and screamed like a maniac. I'd forgotten how mad he can be. He can't understand why I stay with Julia. He thinks it's her father's money which keeps me with her.'

'And is it?'

'Perhaps. Partly.' He was quite serious. 'It means I can take cases which other lawyers wouldn't touch with a barge pole. But it's not just that. She didn't get what she expected from the marriage either. She wanted someone ambitious and dynamic. I was a disappointment to her. It is important, isn't it, to be kind? Or does that sound pompous? It probably does. Rob always said I had a tendency to be pompous.'

'Where were Mick and Laurie when you two were rowing in Boy Scout Wood?'

'Laurie left when it started to rain. I suppose she'd seen falls like that before.'

'And Mick?'

'I lost him when he went off on his own to look for a Blackburnian warbler.'

'How did he seem to you that morning?'

'I don't think he had any premonition that someone would come up behind him and stick a chisel through his heart.' Oliver stopped. 'I'm sorry. That was crass. I think we're all feeling the strain. He didn't seem anxious or frightened but he did seem a bit low. Depressed even. All around us there was this buzz and he didn't seem affected by it. But that was the way Mick was, George. He was never an exhibitionist like Rob. And then I wondered if all the talk about Devon had made him homesick. We'd bumped into a couple who come from there and he was remembering places he'd gone birding as a kid.'

'Did he talk about them? His family?'

'No. It was just an impression I had. He was preoccupied. That was all.'

'After Rob had tried to persuade you to stay, when you were on your way out of the wood, did you meet anyone you recognized?'

'Only those sisters. The ones everyone tries to avoid. The Lovegroves. I think they called out to me. There was probably a bird they wanted me to identify. I just put up my hood and pretended not to hear.'

So, George thought, his kindness didn't extend to ageing spinsters.

'Where was Julia when you got back to Oaklands?'

'In our room. Waiting for me. Sulking, actually, because I was later than she'd expected.'

'She hadn't been out all morning?'

'Definitely not. Her clothes were dry, George. She's one suspect you can cross off your list.'

No, George thought. Not quite yet.

'You and Julia had lunch together. Did you invite Laurie to join you? I take it that she had returned to Oaklands by then.'

'You must be joking! Julia thinks Laurie's the original scarlet woman. Besides, Laurie was in a huddle with Mary Ann and she didn't even see us. It seemed a pretty heavy conversation and I wouldn't have wanted to interrupt.'

'In what way heavy? Acrimonious? Bad tempered?'

'Come off it, George! I mean I haven't known Mary Ann as an adult for very long, but can you imagine her losing her cool? It just looked as if they were in the middle of some serious negotiation.'

'Business then?'

'I don't know. I didn't try to overhear. Why don't you ask one of them?'

He seemed amused and spoke as if he were humouring a child. George realized that Oliver irritated him. It wasn't just his failure to take the investigation seriously. There was something of the martyr about him. He could understand Rob's urge to yell at Oliver and tell him to take a hold on his life. It was probably not kindness which kept him with Julia but laziness and the English cowardice which disliked above all things the creation of a scene. But would he murder to prevent a fuss or a scandal? The notion seemed ridiculous.

Without speaking they turned and began to walk back to the car. A peregrine flew over the marsh and suddenly the air was clouded by startled birds, calling and wheeling above them. Then the falcon disappeared inland and the herons and egrets settled back on to the pools like snow flakes.

Chapter Seventeen

It was late morning and Oaklands was quiet. George found Mary Ann in the restaurant. She was walking between the tables, checking the place settings. Every now and then she stopped to straighten a napkin or remove a dead flower. He stood at the door and watched. He imagined that she did this every day. It had the feel of a ritual, a celebration of her achievement.

'You like order,' he said.

She smiled. 'Above everything.'

'Perhaps it's a bad time to interrupt you.'

'No. I've done. How can I help you?' It was professional kindness. Even if she had hated the intrusion she wouldn't have said.

'Rob explained why I'm here?'

She nodded.

'Can we talk?'

'Of course. Let me make you tea. There's a British shop in Houston where you can buy leaf tea but no one here appreciates it. I'd love to share some with you.'

'We use tea-bags at home.'

'Do you?' There was an astonished pause and then she laughed. 'Have you ever been to Britain?'

'When I was a student I had a vacation job as a nanny. I've visited a few times since then.'

He hoped she would take him to her apartment. He was intrigued to see how she lived. He imagined somewhere cool and sparse. Instead she led him to her office. On a low table there was a kettle, and a tray with a teapot, caddy and strainer.

'I understand that you and Laurie Brownscombe are relatives,' he said.

'Kind of. Distant. Her dad was my mom's cousin. I think that was it. They were brought up in this house together when Mom's grandmother had the place. I never met him. Mom didn't approve. She always called him a drunk and a waster. He never could hold down a job. Not even then.'

'Oaklands wasn't a hotel at that time?'

'Oh, it's always been a hotel but it was pretty rundown. Mom took in boarders. Mostly old folks with a bit of money and no family. She loved the house and didn't want to lose it but she didn't have ambition.'

'And you did.'

'Sure. I could see its potential. I watched the people arriving every weekend to visit the sanctuaries, some of them in big, smart cars and I thought they might like a place to stay. An old-fashioned hotel with a bit of comfort and style. Perhaps it was having your friends turn up with Laurie all those years ago which gave me the idea. They seemed so exciting and I thought we could have people from all over the world stay with us.'

'Why did Laurie bring the boys here if relationships between your families were as poor as you say?'

'Mom felt sorry for her. She let her stay whenever things at home got too bad.'

'You and Laurie must be very close then? Almost sisters?'

Mary Ann hesitated and he expected another glib, polite answer.

'Laurie was older than me and she'd been allowed to run wild,' she said at last. 'We were never friends.'

'Not even when she married and settled down?'

'No.'

'Why?'

His persistence unsettled her. She gave her full attention to her own version of the tea ceremony, pouring boiling water on to leaves, stirring and covering the top with a tea-cosy emblazoned with Beefeaters. Another purchase, George supposed, from the British shop. Then she gave an answer which even she must have realized meant nothing:

'We were both too busy. We had our own lives to lead.'

George refused to leave it at that.

'But I presume you met up from time to time. At family occasions?'

'There's not much family left now.'

'She would have come to your mother's funeral for example.'

'Oh,' Mary Ann said bitterly. 'She wouldn't have missed that for the world.'

George looked at her, expecting some explanation, but it was clear that she already regretted the outburst and she continued in a more conciliatory tone:

'I did see Laurie and Mick occasionally. They came to the island sometimes in the spring if the weather looked good for migrants. If they were in the neighbourhood they would usually call.' It was clear that she viewed these visits with little enthusiasm.

'What were you and Laurie talking about on the day her husband died? You did have a discussion? She left Boy Scout Wood early to meet you.'

She had not expected the question, and was shocked by it.

'Did Laurie tell you that?'

'No.'

'We were discussing business,' she said.

'What sort of business?'

'I'm afraid that's confidential, Mr Palmer-Jones. I'm sure you understand.'

'I understand that a close friend is suspected of murder. Perhaps you'd be more prepared to discuss the matter with a detective.'

She faced him out for a moment, then she replied.

'We have a lot of land at Oaklands. At the moment we feel that it's wasted.'

'You don't plan to develop it?' He was horrified.

She laughed, relieving some of the tension between them. 'Not in the way you mean. But I see all the birders driving through town and paying to visit the Audubon sanctuaries. We couldn't accommodate more overnight guests without building and altering the atmosphere of the hotel, but we could welcome day visitors. If we had something to offer them.'

'A private nature reserve,' he said. 'In competition with Boy Scout and Smith Oaks.'

'Not in competition. People would still visit the Audubon sanctuaries, but they'd come to us, too. We own a small area of established woodland. We'd plant more, perhaps create a pool. And all the time we'd have the birds in mind. I think it's an exciting venture. Laurie thought so, too.'

'You gave Brownscombe Associates the contract for planning your new nature reserve?' He was surprised.

'Let's say we were in preliminary negotiations. I need advice about how to prepare the ground – and not just literally. I want to be sure it's worth doing. It was Laurie's idea to enter an Oaklands team in the Bolivar Birdathon. I've offered to host the reception which follows it. We'd hope to turn that into a tradition. It would all be good publicity.' She paused. 'Laurie did have some good ideas.' This was said so grudgingly that it was hardly a compliment.

'Who else knows about the plans?'

'No one except Laurie, so far. I'd like Rob's opinion but I've decided to keep the whole thing secret until I've cleared it with Houston Audubon. I think they'd approve – there's a lot of pressure on the existing sanctuaries – but the scheme would never work without their cooperation. And I don't want to start rumours. There are always rumours here in High Island. If news got out that I'm planning changes there'll be talk of high-rise condominiums or a retirement village and my life would be a misery.'

'Laurie didn't mention this to me.'

There was a brief pause before she answered. 'Of course not. I asked her to keep it confidential.'

'Can you think of anyone who would be opposed to your plans? If they really understood what you intended?'

She shook her head. 'Maybe a couple of old timers who've been here since my mother's time and who don't like change of any kind. But I don't think they'd put up any formal objection. What are you saying Mr Palmer-Jones? You don't believe my plans for a sanctuary at Oaklands can have anything to do with Mick's murder?'

'Probably not.'

But he thought the scheme was not as straightforward as Mary Ann pretended. She had been too reluctant to discuss it with him. And why had she asked Brownscombe Associates to advise her when there was clearly tension between her and Laurie? It seemed unlikely that she was acting simply out of a sense of family obligation.

'I'd be glad if you don't say anything about this until my plans are finalized,' she said. 'The publicity will be dependent on the announcement being a surprise.'

'No, I won't say anything.'

He wondered then if his judgement was wrong and he was making too much of the conversation between the cousins. They were probably two hard-headed businesswomen who put personal differences behind them to pursue the common goal of making money.

'Did Laurie ever talk to you about the Wildlife Partnership?' he asked. Mary Ann had admitted to taking trips in the UK, she had a Texan accent and to an adolescent like Jason, she might appear as glamorous. He thought there was no real possibility that she was behind the fraud – compared to running a business like Oaklands any profit would be negligible.

Mary Ann seemed surprised by the question but she answered without hesitation.

'Laurie mentioned it at the meeting we had the day Mick died. She showed me some of the publicity material she'd devised. She thought we might consider something similar for the expansion of Oaklands. The idea of partnership, you know. Private enterprise and non-profit organizations working together for the future of Texas. I thought it would work.'

She began to pile the cups and saucers together on the tray. It was clear that she wanted him to go. He asked one last question because he could see that the practicalities of running a business fascinated her, and he was interested in the detail, too.

'Tell me,' he said. 'How did you plan to pay the Brownscombes? By commission on the number of day passes sold for your sanctuary or one straight fee? I take it they weren't acting as your consultants without charging.'

Her hands seemed to tighten in an involuntary movement and a teaspoon slipped from her grasp and clattered on to the tray. George looked at her, waiting for an explanation for the panic, but she controlled herself and only answered the question.

'Well now, Mr Palmer-Jones, I don't think that had been entirely decided.'

'I remember him, you know.'

George was startled. He was standing in the lobby looking out into the garden, wondering if there would be time for a walk before lunch, thinking about what Mary Ann had told him. He thought he regretted the changes she was proposing. There surely *would* be changes – a bigger car-park, perhaps a visitor centre and coffee shop. It would be tastefully done, but would he enjoy seeing a night hawk flapping easily over the lawn at dusk if he had to share it with a crowd?

'I said I remember him.' The voice was quavery and impatient. It came from a small room used almost exclusively by the elderly residents. At first George could see nobody there. Then he walked in. The speaker had the shrivelled look of the very old and was so small that his chair hid him completely. He had been looking at George in a large framed mirror on the wall ahead of him and it was clear that the comment was directed at him.

'Who do you remember?' George asked.

'The one that died. You *are* interested in him, aren't you?'

'Very.'

'Well then.'

'You remember Mr Brownscombe coming to Oaklands with his wife to visit Miss Cleary?' So Mick *had* called in, George thought, when the weather was good for migrants just as Mary Ann had said.

'Not recently!' The old man was irritated by George's stupidity.

'No, no. I didn't mean that. Years ago. He came years ago with his friends. Miss Elsie was here then.'

'Elsie?'

'Yes. Elsie! Mary Ann's mother.'

'You were staying here twenty years ago?'

'I'd just arrived. Thought it would be for a week until my daughter made space for me. She never did.' He screwed up his eyes and George was afraid that he was going to cry but the gesture seemed to be an aid to concentration.

'I remember them driving up to the house that first time in their rental car, the girl and three boys. The radio blasting. They jumped out as if they owned the place. All talking at once. There was loud music all over the house the week they were here. No respect and I told them so. I wondered what I'd come to.'

'What else do you remember about that time?'

'Does it matter?' His eyes were hooded. He looked at George in the mirror.

'It might do.'

'I liked it better then,' he said. 'It felt more like family.'

George sat down in a high-backed chair too. He did not speak.

'They had time to talk to you,' the old man went on. He shot a glance at George to make it clear that he did not feel sorry for himself, he just wanted to explain.

'Who talked to you?'

'All of them. It was real friendly. The other people staying here. Elsie. She worked on her own in the kitchen then and she didn't mind us going in to sit with her. We're not allowed there now. They're all so busy. So I'd sit in her kitchen and we'd talk. She hadn't had it easy, she needed someone to listen to her. Lost her husband and her family were no use.'

'Did you ever meet Laurie's father? Elsie Cleary's cousin?'

'Nope. He weren't allowed near the place. I heard plenty about him though.'

'What did they say about him?'

'Nothing good.'

'Is Laurie's father still alive?'

The old man shrugged painfully. "'S far as I know. Sitting in a bar somewhere I expect.' He paused, then muttered to himself, slurring the words, mimicking a drunk: 'Dreaming of his inheritance.'

'What do you mean?'

'They say that's why Elsie didn't want him around the place. In case he took it into his head that Oaklands belonged to him.'

'Was there a chance that it did?'

He shrugged again. 'His mother and Elsie's mother were twin sisters. That's how I understand it. I'd have said he had a claim. He wasn't interested when he was young. He liked the city. That's what I heard. Off into Houston, leaving Elsie to run the place on her own. But now. . .'

He shut his eyes and seemed to doze for a while. In the distance there was the sound of voices. Rob Earl's party must have returned form their trip to the coast.

'I felt sorry for the one that died,' the old man said suddenly. His eyes were still closed. 'Brownscombe? Is that what they called him?'

'That's right. What do you mean?'

'When he was here that first time with the other kids I felt sorry for him.'

'Why?'

Slowly he turned and looked at George.

'Because he was burdened with trouble and worn down with care.'

That sounded to George like the first line of a hymn but he could not place it. He was not quite sure how to reply.

'We'd have shot them in my day,' the old man said, brightly and inconsequentially.

'Who?'

'All those people who come to look at the birds. Swarming round the town. Blocking the roads with their cars. Most of them foreigners.'

'The man who died was a birdwatcher,' George said.

'I know!' the old man said triumphantly. He shut his eyes again and began gently to snore.

Chapter Eighteen

For the members of Rob Earl's party it was a free afternoon. He had explained that he needed time to prepare for Sunday's Birdathon. He was determined that the Oaklands team would see more species in twenty-four hours than any other group. It seemed important to Mary Ann and he didn't want to let her down. If they were to compete successfully he'd have to stake out all the common birds in advance so they could concentrate on the more difficult stuff during the day. George thought that was an excuse, Rob was beginning to feel the strain of the investigation and needed time alone.

That afternoon Joan Lovegrove was thinking about the bird race too. She had aspirations to be in the team. She did not doubt her ability to get to grips with this birdwatching business, though she recognized her limitations. On their first day at Oaklands she had asked Rob Earl how long it would take her to be a competent birdwatcher. He'd said flippantly that he'd been at it for thirty years and he was still learning. There was something sarcastic about him which she had disliked from the beginning. In her thirty years as a teacher she had learned to recognize the cocky ones who thought it clever to answer back. There was a boy like Rob Earl in every class.

'I didn't mean *expert*,' she said, because sometimes flattery worked better with these boys than chiding. 'I meant competent.'

Rob had muttered something under his breath which she had not been able to catch. Obviously he was pretending the whole thing was more difficult than it really was. She supposed it was in his interest to make himself out to be indispensable.

Esme had taken up birdwatching first. Without consulting Joan she had enrolled in a Workers' Education Association class. There had been slide shows and once a month a field trip which had lasted all day. She had come back bragging about her newly acquired knowledge, pointing out common garden birds in the most irritating way. When Joan had suggested that she might enrol too – thinking only of Esme of course, it could not be much fun by herself – Esme had been strangely reluctant. Joan had wondered if there might be a man friend involved. Esme had been known in the past to make a fool of herself over a man. But there had been no obvious candidate for a suitor among the class members and Joan was forced to conclude that the interest in natural history was genuine.

It had been Esme's idea to come to Texas. Joan was not quite sure what had prompted the enthusiasm – some romantic picture perhaps of cowboys. Esme had never really grown up. It was impossible to think of her travelling alone. Anyone so helpless and scatter-brained would be a danger to herself and a nuisance to her companions. So Joan had decided to accompany her, and really had to admit that she was having an enjoyable time. Despite the murder. Or perhaps because of it.

It was a hot and sultry afternoon with shocking flashes of sunlight when the clouds parted. It had the humidity of a glasshouse. When George saw Joan Lovegrove he was at the back of the Smith Oaks sanctuary. There was an open meadow where cows grazed and a lake. Joan was standing by an old pumping station looking up into a tree. He was surprised to see her alone in an area not much visited by the birdwatchers. He would have thought the murder would have made her cautious.

Rob called the Lovegroves the 'ugly sisters,' which was unkind, but in Joan's case accurate. She was the large one, big boned with huge feet which made her seem to waddle when she walked like a diver in flippers. She must have heard George's footsteps because she turned round, not frightened but excited, and she called in a stage whisper:

'Mr Palmer-Jones! What luck! Do come quickly. I think I've spotted a black-billed cuckoo.'

George came quickly. Black-billed cuckoo was a rare bird. But he was disappointed. There was only one bird in the tree and it wasn't a cuckoo at all.

'I'm afraid,' he said, 'you're looking at a mourning dove. They're very common.'

'Ah!' She was quite unabashed. 'A modo. Isn't that what the Americans call them? An easy mistake, wouldn't you say?'

George wouldn't have said but he muttered politely. She paddled along beside him.

'I wonder,' she said, 'if I might join you on your walk. You can tell that I'm a beginner. It would be helpful to have some pointers to identification. I've read your articles, of course, in *Birdwatch* magazine. Most enlightening.'

'Thank you.'

He had intended to question the Lovegroves at some point and could hardly object to her company, but he had slipped away for a quiet hour's birding and felt resentful that his plans had been disturbed.

They walked through a small gate and back into the wood. Smith Oaks covered a bigger area than Boy Scout. The trees were taller, more widely spaced. It wasn't so intensively managed. There were fewer trails and fewer birders. It suited George better. He would have liked to have enjoyed it on his own.

'Your sister isn't with you today?' Although they bickered incessantly he had never before seen them apart.

'No. Esme feels the heat. This morning's expedition tired her out. She decided to take a nap after lunch. We've arranged that she'll join me here later.'

'The murder must have been upsetting for you.'

'Terrible! We were there, you know, when Mr Earl found the body.'

'Yes,' George said slowly. 'I hoped you might tell me about that.'

They came to a clearing off the main track with a picnic table and benches. They sat opposite to each other, strangely formal. It was as if, George thought, they were sitting at a table in an interview room. Apart from the mosquitoes, which seemed not to bother

Joan but which distracted him throughout the conversation so he worried at the end that he had missed something vital.

'We didn't see anything suspicious,' she said. 'Except for Mr Earl hiding.'

'Yes,' George said.

'And I know he's a friend of yours Mr Palmer-Jones, but that *did* seem suspicious.'

'I can see that it would.'

'It would have been wrong not to tell the detective what we saw.'

'Of course.' He wondered if Russell and Connie May had been giving her a hard time. 'Would you mind going through your movements that day Miss Lovegrove? You went in the bus with the others to Boy Scout Wood?'

'Yes.' She paused. 'It wasn't quite what I was expecting. It was much more confusing than my previous experiences. The birds weren't easy to see. And the noise! People shouting. Russell May became quite hysterical. I thought he'd have a heart attack. Mr Earl did his best to point things out to us but in the end he seemed to lose patience. It did say in the brochure that the trip was suitable for beginners!' Her voice was disapproving.

George said nothing. He was not there to defend Rob to his customers.

'So in the end Esme and I went for a walk by our selves.'

'And that's when you saw Mr Earl?'

'Well that was rather later. The hotel had provided a good packed lunch and we'd eaten that.'

'Did you meet anyone else you recognized during your walk?'

'I was looking at the birds, Mr Palmer-Jones, not the people. You should ask Esme about that. She's more easily distracted than I. There was certainly no one else on the trail by the body.'

She looked at her watch. Her wrist was unexpectedly thick, and George was reminded suddenly of a pantomime dame. The huge feet, the heavy features, the shock of grey hair which might have been a wig, made the dress she wore seem like a disguise and gave her a clownish quality.

'I must go,' she said. 'Esme will be waiting for me at the entrance to the reserve. That was the arrangement we made.'

But when they walked down the track there was no sign of Esme. Joan tutted theatrically, apologized as George waited with her. 'My sister has always been unreliable, Mr Palmer-Jones. As I said, easily distracted. She'll have attached herself to another party and forgotten about me.'

Quite unconcerned, she insisted that they return to the hotel.

When George returned to the hotel there was a message from Molly who was pursuing her own line of investigation. She had followed his instructions and was in Devon, in the village where Mick Brownscombe had been brought up. She had left a contact number and asked him to phone her. He called from his room.

'It's raining,' she said. 'I suppose you've spent all day sitting in the sun.'

After he'd made his peace with her and listened to her plans, he showered and changed for dinner, then sauntered across the grass to the main house. At the door to the bar he stopped. Inside Joan Lovegrove was making a scene.

'Well she must be somewhere,' Joan said. She looked around her as if she were accusing them all of conspiracy. She sounded irritated rather than anxious. Her audience were embarrassed by the scene, but also faintly amused. They were all there: Russell May dressed in the suit which he probably brought out each year for the Bowls Club dinner. Connie, dumpy and cheerful in a long floral frock like a Victorian nightdress. Julia and Oliver Adamson detached and above it all. And Rob Earl, still dressed in the jeans and T-shirt which he had been wearing all day, just back from the field, on his way to his room to change but attracted by the fuss in the bar.

'Well, mustn't she?' Joan Lovegrove demanded. 'I mean she just can't have disappeared into thin air.'

She too had changed for dinner and was wearing an unflattering creation in emerald green which in her youth could have been called a cocktail dress.

'Perhaps she went for a walk,' Rob said, adding in a perfectly audible whisper: 'To get some peace.'

There were stifled giggles. Joan looked at him furiously. It had the makings of a farce but George was uneasy. He walked into the room and they all looked at him. He felt like a stage detective making an entrance on one of those dreadful thrillers which were the staple of amateur theatre groups.

'Esme's disappeared!' Joan said, and she too could have been a middle-aged housewife, stage-struck and acting her heart out. Hamming it up for all she was worth.

If he were the producer he would tell them they needed to move more naturally. 'Darlings, I'm afraid that you're *terribly* wooden.' Instead he took a seat next to Joan and then the tableau was broken and they moved away in groups to chat or go for drinks, content to leave the matter to George. It was impossible, after all, to take either of the Lovegroves seriously.

'She wasn't here when you got back then?' he said.

'No.'

'When exactly did you last see her?'

'Just after lunch. In the morning there was an organized trip and of course we went along for that. Esme said that the heat was affecting her. She has rather a weak constitution. Or so she claims. I suppose it was about two o'clock when I left her. She was in our room then. When I first got back from Smith Oaks with you I wasn't concerned. Esme likes to play these little tricks. But after a while I began to worry. I spoke to Miss Cleary who was as pleasant as always but not terribly helpful. We talked to the girl at reception. She couldn't remember having seen Esme leave but she did seem rather vague . . .'

'I suppose,' George said, 'your sister could have left Oaklands without passing reception. Through one of the french doors on to the porch, for instance.'

'Well yes. So I thought I should ask all the guests if they'd seen her. And that's when you came in.'

The room had become quieter. People had moved from the bar into the restaurant.

'I know she's a grown woman, but I feel responsible for her. I always have.'

'I think perhaps we should alert the authorities,' George said gently.

'Do you? You don't think that would be an over-reaction? Esme has cried wolf before, Mr Palmer-Jones. She does enjoy a drama.'

'I think perhaps it's better to be safe than sorry.' George winced at the platitude but Joan seemed not to notice it.

'You do think she's all right, don't you?' For the first time it seemed to occur to her that her sister might be in danger. George tried to think of a reply that was honest and reassuring, but Joan did not wait for an answer. 'Of course she is. Of course. No harm ever comes to Esme.'

George phoned Joe Benson at home.

'Mr Palmer-Jones. I'm glad you called. You went to see Mrs Brownscombe?'

'I did. But that's not why I'm phoning.'

He explained that one of Rob Earl's party was missing.

'I thought you should know,' he said. 'Our concern might be unfounded. Miss Lovegrove doesn't seem to be a very sensible or thoughtful woman. It's quite possible that she wandered off without telling anyone. But all the same. . .'

'Well I do appreciate the communication Mr Palmer-Jones.' There was a pause and a sound which George took to be Benson gulping beer from a bottle. 'Now I'm reluctant to cause any panic here in High Island by drafting in people to start a full scale search right now.' He paused again, thinking perhaps of his friend who ran the gas station and the value to the local economy of wildlife tourism. 'I understand there's some sort of festival planned for the weekend. The Birdathon. We wouldn't want to spoil that. But you say none of the Brits has seen her all afternoon.'

'Apparently not.'

'And no one else is missing?'

'No.'

'Well maybe I'll come over to the Oaklands Hotel myself. And

I'll ask my deputy to make enquiries in the neighbourhood. Let's see if we can get her back to you before her disappearance hits the news.'

But in the end no discreet enquiries of Joe Benson's could prevent Esme Lovegrove's disappearance from hitting the news. George found her at midnight after an evening of waiting and increased tension. Joe Benson had sent him to bed. Throughout the evening any remaining hostility towards George had disappeared and he spoke like a kindly uncle, promising to wake him if Esme turned up. George walked across the lawn to the staff house where he was staying. The moon was covered by cloud. Esme's small body was lying across the doorway into the house. It was as if a faithful retriever had brought a gift for its master. But Esme's skull had been battered and she was dead.

Chapter Nineteen

Molly had followed George's advice and taken a trip to Devon. It went against the grain, but she knew he was right She accepted that the motive for Mick Brownscombe's murder lay somewhere in the past. It couldn't be a coincidence that Mick had been killed a couple of days after meeting up with his friends. She thought it had all started twenty years ago when they had travelled to the States together, before that even, when they were at university.

The character of Mick Brownscombe intrigued her. As a social worker she had often prepared social enquiry reports for the court on young offenders, explaining the influences in their family and surroundings which had made them turn to crime. She saw this as a similar exercise. What was there in Mick's background to make him a victim? Parents who had rejected him? A criminal father? Some other factor which had not yet come to light?

Molly was beginning her enquiries in a pub. Outside it was raining and the windows streamed with condensation. She was drinking cider, cloudy and rough and potent as hell. It was women's darts night and at the other end of the bar, gathered round the dart board there was a riotous assembly of women of all shapes and ages, cheering on their team. Here, near the fire, there was Molly and an old woman. It seemed that the men of the village had steered clear of the place for the night.

Molly had taken a room in the pub. There was plenty of space. The season hadn't properly started and the pub was on the edge of the village, a couple of miles inland, not quite on the tourist route. She had told the landlord that she was a writer. Not published yet but hopeful. He had accepted that without question. It was always possible to believe in failure.

The woman beside her was called Edie Gill. She drank whisky with ginger ale. To keep Molly company she said, though it was always Molly who went to the bar to buy the drinks. Edie knew she was doing her companion a favour.

Molly had tracked her down to a stone terraced house where she lived with her daughter. There she was unappreciated, an unpaid skivvy. When Molly had called she was in the scullery scrubbing her granddaughter's school shirts by hand because that was the only way you could really get them clean.

Molly asked how long she had lived there.

'Five years. Since my husband died.'

'Didn't you want to stay on in your own home?' Molly liked her daughter but could never live with her.

'No. I never could stand being on my own. Better to be useful and have a bit of company.' She was no fool. She understood the trade off.

Molly had told her the same story as the landlord. She was a writer, doing some research on the area for a book. Edie had lived and worked there all her life. Would she mind talking to Molly about the old times, answering a few questions?

Edie had rinsed out the last shirt and put it in the spinner with the others before answering. 'Not now. Come back later when I've cleared up the tea things. About seven.'

When Molly had arrived there had been a row of suspicious faces peering at her through the living-room window. She had realized it would be impossible to have a private conversation there. They stood together in the narrow hall.

'Would you mind if we talk in the Golden Fleece?' Molly asked. 'That's where I'm staying.'

She thought Edie might not like to be seen in a public house, but the old woman was already putting on her hat and coat.

'I'd like that,' she said. They stepped out into the street. 'I haven't had a night in the Fleece since Jack died.' She pulled a face. 'My daughter married a Methodist.' They laughed together.

And Edie Gill had sailed into the pub, waving to them all like royalty. The first drink for both of them had been on the house.

'Of course there have always been visitors,' Edie Gill said.

Molly had explained that she was writing a history of tourism. 'There were wealthy people who took houses for the summer and families staying in boarding houses, though that was mostly in Ilfracombe and there wasn't so much of that trade when they closed down the railway.' She paused, drained the glass of whisky. 'It was Wilf Brownscombe who brought the crowds to the village.'

'Wilf Brownscombe?' Molly asked, as if she'd never heard the name before.

'I went to school with his mother. She was a poor little thing. Pretty enough, but not much about her. And *my* daughter went to school with Wilf. They knocked about together for a while. There was nothing I could do about it. She was always a stubborn madam and if I'd put my foot down she'd have seen him all the more. She saw sense by herself. Better the Methodist than that'

'Why? What was wrong with Mr Brownscombe?'

She didn't answer and Molly thought she had not heard. The darts match members were becoming rowdy.

'Why do you want to know?' Edie demanded at last.

'Out of interest. It's general background for my book.'

Edie shook her head.

'You've been asking questions,' she said. 'You wanted to speak to someone who worked for the Brownscombes about twenty years ago. Do you think my friends would have given you my name without telling me? Do you think a stranger can come in nosing about without causing a stir? You're not writing a book. So who are you? Too old for the police, that's for certain.'

She paused briefly to take a breath but did not give Molly time to answer.

'Has he robbed you? Swindled you out of your savings? You wouldn't be the first one but he won't have done anything you can prove is illegal. He's too cunning for that. Or Viv is at least. And if it happened twenty years ago you've left it a bit late.'

'His son was murdered,' Molly said. 'In America.'

'I'd not heard.'

'Isn't that unusual? I'd have thought news like that would be common knowledge. Even if it didn't get into the papers.'

Edie shook her head. 'They're very close those two.'

'A friend of ours is suspected of the murder. We don't believe he's guilty. Nobody in America seems to have known Michael very well. I thought there might be some clue here to why someone should want to kill him. We even wondered if Michael might be mixed up with some fraud of his father's.'

'We?' Edie demanded. 'Who's we?'

'My husband and I. My husband's in America.'

'Michael won't be mixed up with any fraud of his father's, even if he was the type, which he wasn't. They haven't spoken for twenty years so far as I know. Michael hasn't been home at any rate and they haven't been out there to visit.'

'You were working for the Brownscombes when Michael went off?'

She nodded. 'Housekeeper at the White Gables Hotel. Wilf still owns it. He managed to keep it somehow when he went bust. It's full of old folks now like everywhere else they run.'

'And Michael was working there too, that summer before he went off to America?'

Edie moved her empty glass across the table and waited for Molly to go to the bar for another drink.

'Michael worked everywhere,' she said, then. 'You have to understand what it was like for the boy. Wilf Brownscombe's a bully. He always has been. He couldn't bully his wife so he bullied his son. And he bullied his workers so the business was always short-staffed. At one time the only employees left were the people he had a hold on: foreigners without the right papers and lads from the north on the run from the police. He never bullied me, mind. Jack sorted him out once when he was a boy and he never forgot it. Things changed a bit when jobs weren't so easy to find and some of the locals went back to work for him because they were desperate, but there were never enough staff to do the job properly.'

'So Michael filled in?'

Edie nodded but refused to be hurried. 'Michael was never much to look at. Short and round shouldered with a bit of a squint, which the doctors put right in the end but which the other kids never forgot, the cruel little monsters. He had to wear those round glasses with a sticking plaster over one lens. So his dad picked on him at home and the children picked on him at school. It's no wonder he grew up so nervy.'

She paused to take a drink but Molly knew better than to interrupt.

'He was bright though. He passed the 11-plus and got offered a place in Barnstaple. It was still the Grammar School in those days. Wilf threatened not to let him go. He said there was no point when he'd end up going into the business anyway but he was only tormenting. It was his idea of fun.

'I think things were easier for the boy then. He made new friends. I believe there was a teacher who took to him. Mick had always liked birdwatching and this teacher took him out, stuck up for him when he decided he wanted to go to college. Mind you, his dad still made him work. After school and at weekends trying to fit in his school work somehow. Even when he passed his exams and went away he was still back every holiday, filling in wherever he was needed, waiting on table, cleaning caravans, serving behind the bar. Some days he looked fit to drop but I never heard him complain.'

'Something must have happened then,' Molly said, 'to have made him break off relations completely.'

Edie Gill looked at her. 'Perhaps he just grew up. Perhaps he just decided he'd had enough. No one could blame him.'

'What was the name of the teacher who befriended him?'

'Oh, my dear, if I ever knew that I forgot it years ago.'

'What about a girlfriend?' Molly asked. 'I heard there was a girlfriend. Someone local, younger than him.'

'Where did you hear that?'

'From his friends at college. There was a schoolgirl he wrote to.'

'There was no one in the village,' Edie said. 'Not so far as I knew. Though I daresay he'd keep it quiet. Viv wouldn't like that at all. No one would be good enough for her Michael.'

'Do you remember the details of his leaving? Molly asked. 'It was the spring. This time of year. Exactly twenty years ago. Mick Brownscombe had been in America for a couple of months. He flew home to the UK with his friends. Almost immediately afterwards he went back to Texas to get married. With only his clothes and a few bits and pieces. Why the hurry? Did he come home in those couple of weeks?'

Edie shook her head. 'I didn't even know that he flew back with his friends. The way I heard it he met a girl out there and he stayed. I'm sure that's what we were told.'

'His parents didn't go out for the wedding?'

Edie shook her head again.

'Did they give any reason?'

'It was the start of the season, wasn't it? They were too busy.'

At the other end of the bar the match was finishing. There was a climax of applause as the last dart was thrown. Women gathered at the bar, hugging each other.

Edie Gill leaned forward across the table.

'You can't do any good for your friend here, my dear,' she said. 'I think you should go home. Save your time and your money.'

The playful tone of the beginning of the evening was gone and this was more like a threat.

'What happened, Edie?'

'Nothing at all happened, my dear.' They both knew it was a lie.

'I shan't give up,' Molly said.

'That's up to you, of course, but you'll find that most people's memories aren't as good as mine.' She paused. 'There's another thing you should consider.'

'Yes?'

'If I've heard that you're staying in the village asking questions, Mr Brownscombe will have heard too. And he's not a pleasant man when he's angry.' She shook her head to decline another drink and waited to be taken home. Molly did not move.

'And Mrs Brownscombe,' she asked. 'What's she like?'

'A hard case,' Edie said. 'Not a woman to cross.' It was another warning.

'Didn't she want to see her boy married? Won't she want to be there at his funeral? He *was* her only son?'

'And the love of her life, my dear. The apple of her eye.'

'Why didn't she stand up on his behalf to her husband?'

'She wanted what was best for Michael. She knew it would do no good to make a fuss.'

And you should know it too, Edie was saying.

Molly walked Edie home through the rain. She had drunk too much to drive. She held an umbrella over the old lady's head and stumbled with her up the path to the cottage door. The family must have been listening out because the door opened immediately and Edie was whisked away before Molly could thank her or say goodbye.

When she returned to the pub it was only nine o'clock. With the end of the darts match, men had begun to drift in and the place seemed less friendly. Perhaps because of what Edie had said she imagined the customers knew who she was and were talking about her. 'Daft old cow,' she imagined them saying. 'Why doesn't she mind her own business and piss off back to where she belongs?'

She walked up to the bar and ordered another glass of cider. The landlord raised his eyebrows but he poured it. She returned to her seat by the fire, determined to make the drink last. If she had any more she'd be ill in the morning but her room was cold and shabby and she did not feel ready for bed.

'Hey lady!' She hadn't seen him come in. He was a young man. Not local. A northern accent and a Newcastle United shirt, two earrings and a shaved head. Although it was a cool night and despite the rain he wore no jacket. He spoke conversationally, even softly, but the whole bar was listening.

'Yes?' Immediately she wished she had not drunk so much. Her glasses had steamed up and she took them off to wipe them. Then her vision was clearer but not her head.

'Mr Brownscombe would like a word.'

'Oh, good. I'd like a word with him.' It was her social worker's voice, bossy and educated. 'Perhaps you could ask him to phone me here and let me know when it would be convenient.'

The young Geordie was thrown off balance.

'No! He'd like a word now. He's sent me to fetch you.'

As she stood up to follow him she knew it was foolhardy. If she refused in front of all these people there would be nothing he could do. Partly it was bravado which got her to her feet – she refused to let these whispering men know she was nervous. Partly it was the knowledge that in the morning, when she was sober, she might not have the courage to face Wilf Brownscombe alone.

Chapter Twenty

There was a white house on a headland. When she got out of the car she could hear the waves on the rocks below. It was still raining and she had forgotten her umbrella. The young Geordie stayed in the car, a large, flashy machine which smelled of stale cigarette smoke. A pointed sign swinging like a pub sign in the wind said: White Gables Rest Home. The downstairs curtains had not been drawn and through two long windows she saw women in blue overalls hauling old people from chairs, set in a row. Presumably it was bedtime.

There was a glass door at the side of the house. It was unlocked and led into an overheated lobby. Molly stood for a moment shaking the rain from her hair. In the distance, through an open door, she could see a resident the care assistants had not reached. He sat in a high-backed chair, his face paralysed in a grimace. A towel had been tucked around his neck and he was dribbling.

'Can I help you?' Molly jumped. The woman had appeared behind her. She was not in uniform. A boss, Molly thought. One of the management. She looked at Molly, sizing her up. I'm probably as old as a lot of her residents, Molly thought. Perhaps she sees me as a potential client. She's put me down as a trouble-maker. I'd be offered one of the poky rooms at the back.

'I understand that Mr Brownscombe wants to see me,' she said.

The woman said nothing. She turned and expected Molly to follow. She wore a navy blue skirt and jacket and chunky jewellery which was probably gold. Her hair was pale apricot, permed and set like caramelized sugar. She looked to Molly like one of the fierce middle-aged women who run cosmetic counters in high-class department stores and gave Molly the same feeling of inadequacy. There was a thick carpet on the floor and her shoes made no sound.

'Excuse me,' Molly called after her. 'Are you Mrs Brownscombe?'

The woman stopped and turned. She wore glasses on a fine gold chain round her neck. She looked at her watch impatiently, nodded briefly as if she could not afford the time to speak and continued up the corridor. Molly scuttled after her.

'I'm so sorry about your son,' Molly said.

The woman stopped again.

'Who are you?' she demanded.

'Mrs Palmer-Jones,' Molly said. She was unusually grateful for the stupid name. Mrs Brownscombe seemed impressed. 'My husband's an ornithologist. He knew your son. He asked me to find you. To offer our condolences. He's already in Texas for the funeral.' It seemed important to tell Viv Brownscombe that she wasn't working alone. Even to Molly the story sounded unbelievable – condolences were sent by the post not delivered in person by scruffy old ladies.

'Michael has never mentioned you,' the woman said coldly.

'Would he have done? I understood that you weren't speaking.'

'What do you want? Money?' The woman's voice was dispassionate. 'You'll have to discuss that with me. Wilfred's an undischarged bankrupt. He has no assets.'

In her befuddled state it took Molly a while to realize she was being accused of blackmail. She was trying to put together an answer when a door into the corridor opened. A man appeared in front of them, blocking their path. Molly recognized him from the description of his son. They must have been very similar. He was small and dark and he even had a nervous tic which might have been the result of a lazy eye.

He was also, Molly saw, almost at once, very stupid. He might be a bully but he was the sort of bully who had started off as a victim. If Mick Brownscombe had not been bright enough to go to the Grammar School perhaps he would have ended up the same way.

'Where have you been?' He ignored Molly and spoke directly to his wife. 'There was a phone call for you. Some relative. I didn't know what to say.'

The nerve in his cheek twitched. He was very angry. He hated this place, these sick people, being dependent on his wife. Molly felt that at any moment he might lash out. Just throw a tantrum because he was miserable.

'This is Mrs Palmer-Jones. You were expecting her.' The conversation in the lobby, the oblique reference to blackmail, might never have taken place.

Brownscombe looked at Molly. Like a butcher at a fatstock market selecting a beast. Then he dismissed her as unimportant. She could tell exactly what he was thinking. He was not sufficiently clever to put on a show. Whatever the rumours going round the village this woman was no threat. He had been worrying about nothing. He smiled.

'You'd better come in,' Mrs Brownscombe said. 'Now that you're here.' The impulse to bring Molly to the nursing home had obviously been Wilf's. She had disapproved of it.

They had been standing in the corridor staring at each other. Wilf moved back through the door. The room was an office, rather overblown and grand. There was a large desk and a leather chair in one corner. Velvet curtains fell to the floor. A chintz sofa and armchair faced an ornate wood and marble fireplace. The gas fire had been lit. Mrs Brownscombe looked very much at home there. As if she had wandered down a floor in the department store from cosmetics to furniture.

'Perhaps you could ask Ingrid to bring us some tea,' she said to her husband, speaking slowly, as if he were one of her demented residents. Perhaps she was hoping to get rid of him so she and Molly could continue their conversation but he just went to the door and yelled the message to a woman in a blue uniform who was manoeuvring a drugs trolley down the corridor.

They sat on the sofa and looked at the fire.

'You wanted to see me,' Molly said.

'We'd heard you were asking after us.'

'As I explained to your wife I wanted to pass on our condolences.'

He accepted that without question. Molly looked at the woman. She hadn't been taken in but had decided to let Molly continue.

'You were a friend of Mickey's then?' he asked. He reached out to take a tumbler of whisky from the desk and she thought he was probably more drunk than she was. And that he was grieving. So much, she thought, for George's theory that Wilf was for some reason involved in his son's murder.

'My husband knew him. From the old days. You know, when he was at university and he used to go birdwatching with Rob Earl and Oliver Adamson.'

She expected recognition but the names seemed to mean nothing to him.

'I remember them,' Mrs Brownscombe said reluctantly. 'We never met them but Michael used to write home from Brighton every week. It was always Rob this and Oliver that.'

'Then he went to America with them.'

'And that was a bloody stupid idea.' Wilf could hardly contain himself. 'Three months in America. Just on holiday. I said to him: "Work thirty years without a break like me and then you'll deserve a holiday."'

'But he went anyway,' Molly said easily, not making too much of it. Kids, she seemed to be saying, they're all the same, aren't they? Do what they want. Don't even think of their parents.

Wilf Brownscombe was not listening. 'And now I'm on bloody perpetual holiday. Minder to a bunch of poor bastards who can't wipe their own arses. And not even trusted to do that. Living off a woman. Do you realize I've not even got a bank account of my own?' Molly was aware again of the anger, barely controlled, growing.

'You had a row then?' she said brightly. 'Before Mick went off.'

'Not in the end. In the end he went off with my blessing.' He looked up at her. 'Say what you like, I did my best for him.' He stared back into his glass.

'And then of course he got married,' Viv said chattily. It was so unlike her to volunteer information that Molly realized she was worried Wilf would give something away. Perhaps a confidence or confession which would explain her fear of blackmail. 'And he set up in business on his own. I understand he's done very well.'

'Yes,' Molly said. 'Did he tell you about his work?'

'Nothing,' Wilf answered angrily.

'He was working closely with a charity before he died. What they call in the States a non-profit organization. The Wildlife Partnership. Perhaps you've heard of it?'

Wilf shook his head.

'But I believe you're both very involved in charity work.'

He seemed confused. 'Before I was made bankrupt I was trustee of the hospice in town,' he said. 'We still support it when we can. And we give to the Donkey Sanctuary in Croyde.'

Unless they were magnificent actors, Molly thought, the Wildlife Partnership meant nothing to them. So that put paid to another of George's theories.

'Was Mick always interested in natural history?' she asked. 'Even before he went to university and met Rob and Oliver?'

'Oh, yes,' Viv Brownscombe said. 'He'd have turned the house into a zoo if we'd let him, wouldn't he, Wilf? We had seagulls with damaged wings, a hedgehog in a cardboard box and a sparrow that he'd rescued from the cat.' She seemed eager to remember him as a boy and Molly realized that in her own way she was grieving, too.

'We soon put paid to that,' Wilf said. 'We couldn't have vermin cluttering up the place. Not in a hotel. We'd have the health people down on us like a ton of bricks.'

'Wasn't there a teacher at the Grammar School who encouraged him?' Molly asked.

The couple looked at each other but she couldn't quite make out what they were thinking. Had they disliked the man, resented his influence on their son?

'That's right,' Wilf said. 'Butterworth. A weedy sort of chap. I could never make out what Michael saw in him.'

'Does he still live locally? He might be interested to hear of

Michael's death. They might even have been in touch over the years.'

'No.' Mr Brownscombe's answer was quite definite. 'They won't have written.'

'But he does still live in the area?'

'Well how would we know that? After all this time.' She turned away impatiently.

'Is there anyone else I should talk to? Perhaps an old girlfriend of Mick's?'

'No,' Viv snapped. 'There's no one left here who remembers him now.'

They sat for a moment.

'It must have been a shock when Michael married Laurie,' Molly said gently. 'And not very convenient for you, Mr Brownscombe. It left you without anyone to take on your business.'

She expected another outburst about Mick's ingratitude, but all Brownscombe said was: 'I daresay he did what he thought was right.'

'And how do you get on with your American daughter-in-law? I believe she's an attractive woman.' It was not the sort of comment she would usually have made but Wilf seemed convinced by it.

'So I hear,' he said resentfully.

'You've never met her?' She feigned surprise.

'Never got the chance,' he muttered.

'I don't think,' Mrs Brownscombe interrupted, 'that this is any of Mrs Palmer-Jones's business.'

But Wilf was too drunk or too lost in regret to take any notice of her.

'We didn't even get an invite to the wedding,' he said. 'After all we'd done for him. He sent a letter afterwards telling us they were married. It was the same when the children were born. A card with their names. Not even a photo.'

'Are you surprised, the way that you treated him?' Mrs Brownscombe spoke quietly. She had not lost her temper. It was a warning: keep your stupid mouth shut. Then she smiled and there was even gold in her teeth. 'As you'll have gathered, Mrs Palmer-Jones, Michael and my husband never really got on.'

'Will you get to the funeral?' Molly asked.

'No,' Mrs Brownscombe said. 'I don't think we could face it. We prefer to remember Michael as he was. Here, as a boy.'

The love of her life, Molly thought. The apple of her eye.

She was woken at seven the next morning by the landlord banging on the door to tell her that she had a telephone call. He seemed to take delight in waking her. There was no phone in her bedroom so she took the call in the bar, surrounded by dirty glasses and overflowing ashtrays.

She knew it would be George with more of his instructions. She started to complain. Her head was aching and she was not sure what to make of the Brownscombes. He cut her short.

'There's been another murder,' he said. 'I've just found the body.'

In Texas it would be one o'clock in the morning. Dark, but probably pleasantly warm. She had pulled a jersey over her winceyette pyjamas and still shivered. Rain lashed against the window.

'The victim was a middle-aged spinster. Ineffective. Slightly batty,' said George.

That would almost describe me, she thought.

'We believe she must have been a witness to the first murder. It's a distraction really.'

She could hear the impatience in his voice.

'I doubt if her relatives see it like that,' she said.

'Well of course not!' He hoped she was not going to be difficult. 'What are your plans now?'

'I thought I might try to trace a teacher of Michael's. Someone who took him birdwatching. The Brownscombes claim Mick never had a girlfriend. Perhaps he made her up to impress Rob and Oliver. If that's true this teacher is the only person he was close to before he left home.'

'Would that wait?' At least, she thought, he was asking her, not telling her.

'I suppose so.'

'You see this is all so *untidy*,' he went on. 'So many loose ends. So many distractions. I'd like at least to clear some of it up.'

And then, as she had expected, there came the list of instructions. She scribbled notes on the back of a beer mat.

'Well?' he demanded. 'What do you think?'

She said that she supposed it all made sense.

Chapter Twenty-One

George spoke to Molly on the phone in the hotel lobby. When the call was finished he stood on the veranda and looked over the garden to the block of staff houses. They were brightly lit by spotlights. The Identification Unit had already arrived from Galveston. The medical examiner would be there soon, but the body of Esme Lovegrove still lay where he had found it, like a rag doll tossed away by a playful dog.

The house was surprisingly quiet. Most of the guests were in bed when George had found the body and he had been discreet. He had walked quietly back to the house to speak to Joe Benson. There had been no drama, no screaming. Even Joan Lovegrove had accepted the news of her sister's death with very little fuss. The authorities had given her permission to fly home but she had rejected the idea. She would stay with her sister, she said, until they could both leave. George thought she would probably be less lonely here.

Joe Benson came up behind him and they leant over the veranda rail together.

'I left my room at seven o'clock,' George said. 'She wasn't there then.'

'So someone must have dumped the body, while you were at dinner. Or later while we were waiting to see if the lady showed up.'

'But she wasn't killed then,' George said. 'Was she? She'd been missing all afternoon. So why take the risk of moving her? It was as if someone wanted to be sure that she would be found.'

'Did you notice any of your party go missing during the evening?'

'No, but people were coming and going all the time. It's a big building and there wasn't an organized event. Sometimes Rob Earl gives a slide show or lecture. There was nothing like that tonight. It would have been easy to slip away for half an hour.'

'It might not even have taken that long if she was killed somewhere here in the woods. What about clothes? There might have been blood. Did anyone change their clothes during the course of the evening?'

George did not answer immediately.

'When I came into the bar at about seven o'clock Rob Earl was wearing jeans and a T-shirt. He'd just come in from a birdwatching trip. We discussed Esme's disappearance then he went up to his room to put on a shirt and tie. He was gone for about twenty minutes. We had dinner together. He wouldn't have had time to move the body, shower and change.'

'No,' Benson said. 'I guess not.'

'She must have seen something,' George said. 'Why else would anyone want to kill her? And if she did see something important on the day Mick Brownscombe died why didn't she tell the detective who questioned her?'

They stood for a moment in silence. A barn owl cried from the trees and George realized that he still needed the bird for his trip list.

'She wouldn't have been the sort to go in for blackmail?' Benson suggested tentatively. 'That's not the impression I got of her.'

'No,' George said, but he remembered Joan's words: Esme always enjoys a drama. He tried to picture Esme in conversation with the other party members. She had gone in for arch comments, teasing of a vaguely flirtatious nature, anything to draw attention to herself. She might have seen any information about the murder as too valuable to simply pass on to the detective. Then it would become common knowledge. Wouldn't she be tempted to save it so she could make some dramatic revelation? Without realizing that it actually gave away the identity of the murderer?

'I don't understand how Esme could have witnessed some

significant event without Joan seeing it too,' he said. 'They were always together.'

'But not this afternoon.'

'No. I wonder if she'd made an excuse about the heat having exhausted her. She just wanted her sister out of the way.'

'She'd arranged to meet someone?'

'It's possible,' George said. He thought of Esme, who had never grown up, with her floaty dresses, her powdered face and her hyacinth blue eye shadow. 'It would have been a man,' he said. 'If a man had flattered her, pretended to find her attractive, she'd have ignored any danger and gone with him.'

'So the killer's a man? Well, Sherlock. I didn't realize this business was so damn easy.'

George smiled, nodded across the garden to the team of detectives.

'Have they got a murder weapon?'

'Nope. But I guess it's more likely that'll be found where she was killed.'

'Any ideas?'

'What do they call it in those TV series you sell us? A blunt instrument. That's what they reckon it was.'

'But not the chisel,' George said, almost to himself. 'I wonder why.'

'You think there could be two separate killers?'

'I don't think anything at this stage.'

But in a sense there was too much to think about. Too many strands to the investigation. The case was messy and he hated untidiness. If he could clear up the minor mysteries, the distractions, then he might find out what lay behind the murders. He turned to Benson.

'Would you give me permission to leave High Island for a few hours? I realize I've not made a proper statement but I'll be back this afternoon.'

The constable rubbed his eyes with the back of his hand. It was the only sign that he might be tired.

'Well I told you, it's not my case. It's not my place to give permission for anything.'

'If I asked Detective Grant, do you think he would let me go?'

Benson considered. 'No,' he said at last. 'I don't think he would. He's an ambitious man and he plays by the rules.'

They stood for a moment in silence.

'I've just thought of something,' Benson said. 'Now you won't take this the wrong way, Mr Palmer-Jones? You won't take offence?'

'Of course not.'

'Well, you're not as young as you were.' He paused. 'What with the jet lag and all I'd say you were pretty tired by now.'

'Jet lag is a terrible thing,' George said.

'You can't sleep in your own bed. The IDU wouldn't want you going over there, disturbing their good work. We could ask Miss Cleary to find you somewhere in the main house but she's probably asleep by now and I wouldn't want to wake her. It can't have been an easy time for her. Two killings in a week.'

'No,' George said. 'We shouldn't disturb her.'

'What I suggest is that you find a motel room for the rest of the night. The Gulfway's full. Miss Lily told me that only today. But you should find something in Winnie. I don't think Detective Grant could object to that. You have a good sleep and be back here in the afternoon.'

'Thank you,' George said.

Benson looked at him. 'We old timers have to stick together.' He was only half joking. 'Now you take care, you hear.'

George's car was parked with all the others in a space which had probably once been a stable yard. It was at the back of the house close to the kitchen and there was no view from there of the spot-lit body and the IDU. The area was lit by a white security light. There were three big dustbins and he supposed that they would be searched by the detectives looking for the murder weapon and bloodstained clothing. It was unlikely that the murderer who had been so cool, slipping out from dinner to move the body, returning later to join the discussion about where Esme might be, would give himself away so easily.

He stood by his car and looked up at the dark silhouette of the house. There were lights at the windows on the ground floor, next to the kitchen. He guessed that was where Mary Ann Cleary had her apartment. Benson had been wrong then, to suppose that she was asleep.

Only one other window was lit. The house was so big and so dark that it would be impossible in the daylight to work out whose bedroom it was. Perhaps Joan Lovegrove was there, lying awake, despite the sedation she'd been given. Perhaps someone with a guilty conscience had left the light on in the hope of driving away nightmares.

He got into his car and drove slowly down the track, expecting at any moment to be stopped, but the detectives from Galveston had only just arrived and there was no one on the gate. As he passed through the quiet streets of the town he met a small convoy of cars. Reinforcements, he thought. And perhaps the medical examiner. He hoped that Esme's body would have been removed by the time it got light. Just before he joined the I10 at Winnie he saw a truck, with the logo of a television station on the side. Rob's punters would wake up to a circus of flashlights and fast-talking reporters.

The freeway into Houston was clear and he seemed to come to the dramatic skyline at once. It appeared so unexpectedly that he realized he could not have been concentrating on the road. He switched on the radio to keep himself awake and heard the first news report of Esme Lovegrove's death.

Chapter Twenty-Two

Although the business park where Brownscombe Associates had their office was marked on his road map, George had to drive round for a quarter of an hour before he found the actual building. The development was small-scale, providing accommodation for insurance offices, investment brokers and computer consultants, but the units – new brick and glass blocks – all looked similar. Brownscombe Associates was in a building at the edge of the park looking out over flat open space, which was probably a school sports ground.

It was 4 a.m. The door to the building which housed three other companies was locked. George parked in the shadow and dozed. At 6 a.m. a security guard turned up in a van. He unlocked the main door with a master key and drove away. As soon as his tail lights had disappeared George tried the door again but still it was impossible to get in. Access for employees was by a coded button press. He touched a few buttons hopefully but nothing happened. He returned to the car worried that if he made too many mistakes he might trigger an alarm system. As he had approached the entrance a bright security light had flashed on.

The first keen employee arrived at six-thirty. He carried a bundle of envelope files. From the car George had a good view of the button press but the man was so quick and deft that he could only make out the first figure. Two. Then two buttons pressed together. Then another single further down the pad. The man pushed the door open with his backside, his arms full of the files. George held his breath, hoping the door would just shut gently so the lock would not catch. But once inside the man pushed it tight again. A light went on in a second-floor office. Clarke Accountants. Brownscombe Associates was on the ground floor.

Five minutes later a pick-up truck drove down the road and stopped with a jerk outside the office block. George ducked down in his seat as it passed him. A heavy, middle-aged woman got out, and pulled a shopping bag after her. She shouted some words of Spanish at the driver, presumably her husband, and he drove away. She wore carpet slippers and a large overall tied at the back. The office cleaner.

It was obvious that she mistrusted the push button key. She set down her bag before tackling it. She fumbled in her overall pocket for a scrap of paper where the numbers had been written. Then she prodded the combination slowly and deliberately so George could see exactly what she was doing. Two, then four and six together, pressed with the index finger of each hand, then nine. The door clicked open. She turned her eyes skyward as if thanking heaven that the contraption had worked again.

She picked up her bag and let herself in, closing the door carefully behind her. After a moment the offices of Brownscombe Associates were flooded with light. There were three rooms in a row. Probably a reception area and individual work spaces for Michael and Laurie. All faced out to the car-park.

George climbed stiffly out of the car and pressed the buttons. The door unlocked and he let himself in. He saw then that he had only gained entry to a gloomy lobby, lit by shadowy emergency lights. There was a lift and a flight of stairs. Each of the businesses had its own separate security system.

The entrance to Brownscombe Associates was on his right. There was a heavy glass door with the firm's name in gold letters. A bunch of keys hung from the lock, but the cleaner was still inside. He could hear the sound of an industrial floor cleaner and her remarkably tuneful singing. He waited, aware that time was passing and soon other workers would be arriving.

Eventually it seemed that the cleaner had finished with the Brownscombes' offices and was prepared to move on elsewhere. She switched off the lights, wedged open the door and pulled through the floor polisher. George melted into the shadow by the stairwell. She pressed the lift button. George heard her pull the polisher into the lift and the machine move up to the next floor. The Brownscombes' door was still open and he slipped in. A few minutes later he heard the lift return and the cleaner close the door behind him.

He was in a reception area. There were two desks with computer screens and keyboards, a row of filing cabinets and in a corner easy chairs and a low table, where prospective clients would be given coffee and asked to wait. He found the current project files in the first cabinet he tried. It was locked but the keys were in the top drawer of one of the desks.

He found the Wildlife Partnership information immediately and he sat on one of the easy chairs to read it through. It was light enough now to see. He worked quickly and meticulously, reading every sheet, not skipping a word. It all suggested that the Wildlife Partnership was a legitimate account. There were copies of proposals made by the Brownscombes for work to be carried out. Mick had visited Central America several times to visit reserves and meet local workers but all the expenses were itemized and receipts provided. There was no indication that either of the Brownscombes had visited England on the organization's behalf, no copies of the mailshot sent to Cecily Jessop. George replaced the papers tidily. He was not disappointed.

He had achieved what he had come for and knew that he should leave. Even if Laurie had not yet returned to work he knew from his previous phone call that secretarial staff had been covering the Brownscombes' holiday and presumably they were continuing to hold the place together now. They could arrive at any moment. He had checked that the big glass door could be opened from the inside without a key.

But he did not leave. He realized with a shock that he was enjoying himself. The possibility that he might be caught only added to the exhilaration. He wondered how he would explain his rashness to Molly. She would say he was an old fool trying to recapture his youth.

He moved on to Laurie's office. At the window there were vertical blinds. He adjusted them so he could not be seen from outside but he still had sufficient light to read.

The room was business-like and uncluttered. The drawers of her desk were tidy. There was nothing personal. No photos of her children. Not even a box of Kleenex. The top of the desk was clear except for a computer terminal and a plastic tray marked FILING. He was grateful that the office system was so unsophisticated. In the tray were two slender files which must just have been opened. New business. One involved a shopping mall which had requested suggestions for landscaping. The other was labelled OAKLANDS and contained only a single sheet of paper.

This was a short letter from Mary Ann Cleary. It was formal, even hostile in tone. It asked Brownscombe Associates to draw up plans for the new wildlife sanctuary in the Oaklands grounds and confirmed a meeting between Mary Ann and Laurie to discuss the details. The final sentences read: 'I hope this settles the matter. I am prepared to co-operate with you over this project but have no desire to see you and Michael socially once it is completed, or to go over past history again.'

So, George thought, Mary Ann had been telling the truth about her meeting with Laurie, but as he had suspected, she had not told him everything.

George returned the files to the plastic tray and moved on to Michael's office. It was evident that Michael had worked in a less organized way than Laurie. A book shelf containing field guides, atlases, reports and a pile of large-scale maps stood against one wall. A plan had been laid out on the floor, presumably because there was no longer any room on the desk. This was covered with letters, data from field-workers and half-completed, hand written reports. George flicked through the chaos quickly. He saw nothing which might be relevant to Michael's murder.

The desk drawers seemed to be filled with junk chocolate bar wrappers, drawings which his children must have done when they were young. There was a crumpled fortieth birthday card from Laurie with a picture of an Indian elephant on the front. Inside she had written: 'Hope we make it to India before we're fifty. But you'll only do it if you learn to hustle!'

It was evidently a shared joke and George thought that despite her toughness Laurie would miss him.

In the bottom drawer, underneath a pile of computer paper used as scrap, there was a large brown envelope. It seemed to contain mementos of Michael's youth. Perhaps he had brought it with him from the UK with the carved lapwing and his binoculars and telescope.

George cleared a space on the desk and took out the contents, one at a time. There were photographs. One was of Michael as a child in his new Grammar School uniform. He stood in front of a holiday caravan and looked out at the camera sullenly. The other was of a girl. She was wearing the same brown and yellow tie but she was older, perhaps sixteen. Written on the back in round handwriting was: 'All my love. Nell.' Nell was round-faced and smiling, quite ordinary. Was she Michael's schoolgirl sweetheart? If so, why had Molly found no trace of her?

Next came a certificate, hand-written in flowery calligraphy which stated that Michael Brownscombe had been a member of the junior team which had won the North Devon Naturalists' Spring bird race in May 1970.

Then George brought out a letter which couldn't have come with the envelope when Michael moved to Texas. It was dated two years after his marriage. At the head of the paper a printed label with the writer's name and address had been stuck. The address was a village in North Devon which George did not recognize. The name was Paul Butterworth. He was the teacher who had encouraged Michael's birdwatching. So Molly's instinct was spot on again. The two men had kept in touch. George felt a mixture of admiration and resentment that she always seemed to get things right.

The letter contained descriptions for birdwatching trips, walks in places which he assumed Mick would remember, but after the details of badger watches and peregrines returning to breed on nearby cliffs there seemed to be a warning: 'They came to visit me again with more questions. Still flying kites, I think. Of course I said nothing. But I thought you should know that even after all this time they haven't given up.'

Last out of the envelope were some newspaper cuttings. They were clipped together with a rusting staple and so faded that they were hard to read in the half light coming through the blinds. They came from the *North Devon Journal Herald* and were dated just before Michael had made his trip to the States, with Rob and Oliver. George settled to read the substance of the text when he was startled by the sound of the door into reception being unlocked.

He froze, then replaced the contents into the envelope and put it back into the drawer. Later he would wonder why he hadn't taken the unread newspaper cuttings with him, but now he thought about nothing but making his escape. The only way out of Brownscombe Associates office was through reception. He closed the drawer silently, and began to make his way to the door to listen for movements in the outer office. But as he turned his elbow caught a wire basket overflowing with paper which sat on the edge of the desk. It fell and landed with a clatter on the floor. The noise seemed deafening.

A woman's voice, cheerful and unsuspicious sang out. 'Hi, Sandy! You're in early today, hon. Be an angel and cover the front office while I go upstairs to the restroom.'

There was the sound of a door closing. She must have been in too much of a hurry to wait for an answer.

George walked quickly to the reception and let himself into the lobby. By now it was crowded with people pushing their way up the stairs or waiting for the lift. A well dressed middle-aged man held the main door open for him and he left the building. It was eight-fifteen and the sun was shining. The day was already hot. He drove his car to another anonymous street in the business park and slept for an hour until the worst of the peak time traffic had passed. Then he made his way to High Island.

Chapter Twenty-Three

It was turning into the hottest day of the spring. George arrived back at the Oaklands Hotel in the early afternoon, still high after his successful raid into the office of Brownscombe Associates. Ex-senior civil servants didn't often get the opportunity to go breaking and entering. He was light-headed through lack of sleep and fizzing with ideas.

Despite the heat the place seemed powered by a manic energy. Competing radio and television reporters were camped out in the street by the gate into the hotel, prevented from entering by two impassive deputies. When George stopped to tell the deputy he was a resident, a young man jumped forward and stuck a microphone through the open window.

'This is Chuck Wendell. *Eye Witness News*. Could we have your reaction to this terrible tragedy. Do you still feel safe in there?'

George wound up the window and drove steadily through, but the television stations had found local people prepared to share their story. Along the street reporters with excited voices were talking to camera and encouraging their victims to give an opinion of the Oaklands Hotel and the visitors who chose to stay there.

Inside the hotel it was the same. Feverish discussion, rumour, complaint. At this time on a normal day residents would be lingering in the restaurant or drowsing in one of the air-conditioned lounges. It would be so quiet that you could hear lizards in the garden and the water sprinklers on the lawn. Instead there was a background noise of muttered conversations. But there seemed to be no movement yet to persuade the sheriff's department to let them all fly home. They were too involved in the drama for that. It was a soap opera being played out just for them and they didn't want to leave before the final episode.

Joe Benson was still in Mary Ann's office. There was a stubble of beard on his face and George thought he had probably been there all night. And that *he* must look equally disreputable. When he knocked on the door and walked in Benson did not seem surprised to see him.

'Coffee?' he asked. 'Or beer?'

'Coffee. Thanks.' Mary Ann's tea tray had been replaced by a coffee machine.

'You hear what they're saying out there?' Benson asked.

'Not in detail.'

'They don't seem to think very highly of us.' He turned his voice into a falsetto, parodied an upper-class English accent: 'I'm sure in Britain the police would have cleared it up by now.'

'Take no notice. Every community has its share of narrow-minded bigots.'

'Sure,' Benson said. 'I'm one myself. For instance I'm convinced that this killer's one of you Brits.'

'Why?'

He shrugged.

'You've heard the propaganda. We all carry guns and knives. We don't need to smash people's skulls in.' His voice was mocking but he seemed to be making a serious point.

'Is that what your detective thinks?'

'Ah, well now. I think the detective might just fall into that category we were discussing earlier.'

'Narrow-minded bigot?'

'Let's just say he hasn't formed a very favourable opinion of your friend Mr Earl.' He paused, leaned forward. 'The detective is a very upright man with strong traditional views. A family man. You know what I'm saying, Mr Palmer-Jones?'

George nodded.

'Your friend is single. He has an unconventional lifestyle. He travels to countries whose regimes we couldn't support. You know he's been to Cuba? Now that doesn't make him guilty. But it means our detective would *like* him to be guilty. I told you he's an upright man. He wouldn't rig the evidence. All the same he'll do his damnedest to find something.'

He sat for a moment in silence. 'There wouldn't be anything you want to discuss with me, Mr Palmer-Jones?'

'I don't think so. Not just yet.'

'You had a good night's sleep then?'

'Oh,' George said lightly. 'Not so bad.'

'I hope you don't intend to play this alone, sir. I reckon I've been very straight with you. I covered for you when the detectives asked where you were.'

'I'm waiting for a phone call from the UK,' George said. 'Then I'll have more idea.'

'And you'll tell me then what you've been up to? I tell you we could certainly use some movement.'

'There've been no developments this morning?'

'Nothing. Like I said. I don't think your compatriots *entirely* trust us. They haven't exactly been forthcoming. If they confide in you I can rely on you to pass the information on?'

'Oh, quite,' George said. 'Of course.'

And Benson beamed, almost as if he believed him.

George was looking for Oliver Adamson. He knocked at his bedroom door but there was no reply. He tried the restaurant and then the bar. There was no sign of Oliver but Rob Earl was there. He sat on a stool drinking beer. It looked as if he had been there for some time.

'George!' he said. 'Where the hell have you been?' He seemed to have been the only person to have noticed George's absence.

'Following the investigation on your behalf,' George replied pompously.

'I could have done with you here.' He sounded like a sulky child. 'You don't know what it's like George. All the whispering. It's one thing to have been accused of murdering Mick. He was a grown man, wasn't he, and should have been capable of looking after himself. Besides, they didn't really have the chance to get to know him. But Esme Lovegrove! Dear, sweet, dippy Esme. She irritated them to hell when she was alive but she's achieved sainthood in the last twenty-four hours.'

'Feeling sorry for yourself won't help.'

'I know. But I can't prove I didn't kill her and that makes me feel bloody helpless. And shit scared. You do realize they have the death penalty here George? It's not like at home where they can release you with a fat compensation cheque if they cock up, and you can make a fortune by selling your story to the papers.'

That was something George had tried not to think about. He ordered a beer. 'When did you last see her?' he asked.

'I've been through all that with the detective.'

'But perhaps you could tell *me*.' George allowed his impatience to show. Rob seemed not to notice.

'The Lovegroves came with me on the trip to the coast yesterday morning. They stuck to me like glue and they wouldn't stop talking. I'll admit that I was pissed off with them. You know what it's like, George, when you're trying to 'scope up a big flock of duck, get an accurate count and at the same time pick up anything out of the ordinary. You need to concentrate. And I was trying to suss things out for the Birdathon on Sunday.'

'You surely don't intend to go ahead with the bird race now?'

Rob seemed surprised. 'I think so. No one's said anything about cancelling. Why?'

'You don't think it's a little insensitive?'

'Because of the murders? No I don't. And I've already put a lot of work into it. I hope it goes ahead.'

'So you were with the Lovegroves all yesterday morning?'

'Yes. They wouldn't stop sniping at each other Talk about murderous.' He paused, then continued flippantly. 'That's a point George. Perhaps Joan took advantage of Mick's death to knock off her sister. It would be brilliant cover, wouldn't it? Everyone would assume both murders had been committed by the same person.'

'I take it you're not being serious.'

'Of course not. They were pains in the bum but I think they were fond of each other. The rowing had become a habit. It was just incredibly wearing to anyone who had to listen to it, and I don't suppose that's a real motive. We might all have felt like hitting Esme over the head to shut her up, but I can't see anyone actually doing it.'

He pushed an empty beer bottle away from him.

'Did you see Esme at lunch?'

'Yes. They sat at my table.' He paused, then went on, horrified. 'Did you know that they wanted to be part of the Birdathon team?'

'No,' George said. 'What did you say?'

'Well I could hardly say that we needed someone who could tell the difference between a robin and a rhinoceros. I said that I'd asked Russell May and he'd agreed to do it. Then Esme went all coy and reminded me that there had to be four team members. "There's you, Mr Adamson and Mr May. That leaves room for one more. Now who will you choose? Joannie or me?" I said I couldn't choose between them. It just wouldn't be gallant.'

'Then you escaped?'

'Yes. I said they could have a free afternoon.'

'Did you tell anyone where you were going?'

'No. The last thing I wanted was anyone tagging along. That's why I took the mini bus and went to Anahuac. I'd be less likely to bump into them there. Most of them haven't got transport. The Mays were talking about hiring a car for a few days but they haven't got round to it yet.'

'Did you meet anyone on the refuge?'

'Not to speak to. I think a car load registered after me, but I didn't see them again. It's such a huge space. The marsh goes on for miles. It was just what I needed. I went for a long walk and I was back later than I intended. When I arrived everyone was discussing Esme's disappearance.'

'Then you went straight upstairs to change? George asked.

'That's right'

'You didn't go outside first?'

'Of course not. The detective asked me that. What is this about George?'

'If Esme was murdered just before she was put by the staff house there would have been blood. Obviously they're interested in anyone who changed clothes during the evening.'

'Oh, Christ, George, they can check my things.'

'I think perhaps they'll already have done that.'

The barman brought them two more bottles of beer without their asking.

'Are you sure Mick had a girlfriend when he was at college?' George asked. 'He hadn't dreamed one up so as not to be different? It wasn't a figment of his imagination?'

'I don't think so. He was posting those letters to *someone*. And if he'd dreamed her up she wouldn't have been so ordinary. A schoolgirl, living at home with mummy and daddy. Not much of a fantasy, is it?'

'He must have spoken about her by name.'

'I suppose so, but I can't remember it now.'

'Could it have been Nell?'

'Yes!' He banged his fist on the counter so the beer bottles rattled. 'Little Nell. Like in Dickens. That's what he called her. Her proper name was Helen.'

'Does knowing the name make it easier to remember anything else about her?'

He shook his head. 'Sorry.'

But he seemed to consider the discovery of the girl's name as some sort of success and he added almost jauntily: 'What's the plan then George? How are you going to get me out of this mess?'

'I wish I knew,' George said. 'I've been looking for Oliver. Do you know where I can find him?'

'I expect he's with dear Julia. They seem to be spending a lot of time together lately. It's almost as if he *liked* her.' He put two fingers towards his mouth and made a face like someone being sick. The schoolboy again.

'I'll have a look in the garden.' George was almost out of the bar when he stopped and turned back.

'Does the name Paul Butterworth mean anything to you? He was a friend of Mick's. Before he went to university.'

Rob shook his head then said with stunning arrogance: 'I didn't think he had any real mates until he met us.'

Chapter Twenty-Four

In contrast to the other shocked and excitable hotel residents, Julia Adamson had become calm. She had even stopped worrying about the effects of the sun, and lay, a large white grub, on a lounger by the pool. She turned, intending to rub more oil on to her legs when she saw the old man who had flown out from Britain to save Rob Earl from arrest. At least that was what Oliver had told her though she could hardly believe it. He seemed too much of a gentleman to be a friend of Rob Earl's.

He walked across the lawn towards her and she felt an unfamiliar anxiety. It was the nervousness of a spoilt child, coming into conflict with authority for the first time. He sat beside her choosing one of the more upright chairs, so she felt at a disadvantage, sprawled. She turned on to her back and shut her eyes, refusing to acknowledge his presence. He said nothing. She lay for a few minutes waiting for him either to speak or to go away, feeling herself become more and more tense. When at last she opened her eyes he was looking into the distance but he must have heard her move because he spoke immediately.

'Mrs Adamson. I wonder if I might trouble you for a while?'

The voice was polite but quite firm. There was no question that he was begging for a favour. She got up and chose a chair like his. She was uncomfortably aware that her stomach, which was quite flat when she was lying on her back, sunbathing, now sagged slightly over the waistband of her bikini. Her clothes were folded in a neat pile on an empty chair. She fumbled for a shirt and pulled it on. He waited, politely, as if he had all the time in the world.

'I should have spoken to you before,' George said. 'To apologize for having intruded the other day in the wood. You and your husband were having something of an argument.'

She looked at him blankly.

'But perhaps you didn't realize I was there. It was the day I arrived.'

'No,' she said. 'I didn't realize.'

'Well I'm sorry anyway . . .'

There was a silence and she felt her flabby stomach contract with panic. It was none of his business and certainly she did not owe him an explanation but she found herself stuttering. 'It's the heat isn't it? Or the humidity. It seems to make us all short-tempered.'

She thought with anger of Oliver who had told her there was nothing to worry about.

'Oh, yes,' he agreed. 'It's very wearing.' But while she felt the perspiration on her forehead and running between her breasts he seemed to show no sign of being hot.

'Of course one must forgive your husband for being emotional,' he persisted. 'He had just lost one of his closest friends.'

'Not so close,' she snapped. 'They hadn't met for twenty years.'

She tried to remember exactly what they had shouted to each other in Boy Scout Wood. How much had Palmer-Jones overheard? Not much, she thought suddenly. He's fishing. The panic subsided and something of the old confidence returned.

'Mr and Mrs Brownscombe visited Britain occasionally on business.'

'Did they? Well they never got in touch with us. I suppose they might have contacted Oliver at work.'

'He didn't mention it to you?'

'No.'

'They might have met through his business,' George said. 'I understand that he specializes in charity law.'

'Yes.' Her monosyllabic answers made it clear that it was only good manners which kept her participating in the conversation.

'He represents wildlife charities?'

'Not exclusively,' she said haughtily. 'If he did he'd never make a living.'

'What about the Wildlife Partnership?' George asked. 'It's an American non-profit organization. Has Oliver had any dealings with them?'

'I wouldn't know,' Julia said.

'But Laurie Brownscombe mentioned the Partnership at dinner on your first night at Oaklands.'

'Did she? I remember her talking about some charity, giving us the hard sell actually. But she didn't mention a name. I would have remembered if she had.'

Why? George thought. Why would the Wildlife Partnership mean anything to you?

'Your daughter is one of its supporters,' George said.

'Is she? She tends to support all those causes. Whales, seals, bats. It was working on that television programme. I expect she'll grow out of it. They usually do, don't they?'

'Did your husband grow out of it?'

'Did he grow out of what?'

'A commitment to nature conservation.'

'Oh, that!' She leaned forward with her elbows on her pink, oily knees. 'I'll tell you one thing Mr Palmer-Jones. Oliver is a lot more interested in money than he pretends to be.'

'Does the name Cecily Jessop mean anything to you?'

'No,' she said. 'Should it do?'

She looked at him as if he were an idiot and he was quite convinced that with that reply, at least, she was telling the truth.

'Would you mind telling me what you and Oliver did yesterday?'

'I don't see why I should. I've already talked to that detective.'

'There's no reason, of course, why you should but I would find it very helpful. Did you go with Rob's party to the coast?'

'No!' She was horrified at the prospect. 'Actually we were out all day. We went to Galveston on the ferry, had lunch in rather a pleasant seafood restaurant in a converted warehouse by the docks. Did some shopping. You know, normal things. The things people do when they're on holiday.'

'So you wouldn't have seen Esme Lovegrove?'

'I saw her at breakfast. She was flirting dreadfully with Mr May. Poor man. He didn't know where to put himself.' She obviously had no qualms about speaking ill of the dead.

'What time did you arrive back at Oaklands?'

'In time to change for dinner. About six-thirty I suppose. We'd just got into the bar when Joan Lovegrove started making the scene about her sister. I'm afraid I didn't take much notice of her. One didn't take much notice of either of them.'

George sat for a moment in silence, then stood up.

'I was actually looking for Oliver,' he said. 'Do you know where he is?' She didn't answer immediately.

'He's botanizing,' she said. 'As if birds weren't enough! Miss Cleary apparently knew that he was interested in plants too. She wondered if there was anything special in the Oaklands woods. If you wait a moment I'll come with you, show you where he is.'

'No, no,' George said. 'Please don't trouble. I'll find him.' He very much wanted to talk to Oliver on his own.

And while Julia was still struggling into her sandals he had disappeared, moving remarkably quickly for an elderly man.

He found Oliver in the small patch of woodland which Mary Ann planned to turn into the wildlife refuge. He was wearing white trousers and a crumpled linen jacket. George thought the effect was supposed to be suave and colonial but it had not quite come off. He looked as if he were dressed in somebody else's clothes.

'Ah,' Oliver said. 'You've decided to avoid the madhouse too. I couldn't put up with it. All the false sentiment and gossip. Mary Ann asked me at the beginning of the week if it was worth doing a botanical survey of the wood. It gave me an excuse to escape.'

'Is it false sentiment?'

'Well I'm afraid I find it hard to get worked-up about the death of Esme Lovegrove. I hardly knew her. I wonder how many of those people felt any real sense of loss. On the whole we're really very selfish. Don't you think so George? We care about ourselves and our families. Beyond that the horror and the frenzy is a show.'

'What about our friends?' George asked. 'Do we care about them?'

'Well of course I'm sorry Mick was killed.' Oliver was almost dismissive.

'I went to Brownscombe Associates office this morning.'

'Oh?' Oliver was affable but still determinedly detached.

'I was interested to see if there was any evidence to support the view that Laurie might be behind the Wildlife Partnership fraud in the UK.'

'Oh, George really! Not that again! You must realize by now that Mick's death can't have had anything to do with some petty deception which took place thousands of miles away. If that were the case why is Esme Lovegrove dead? This is the work of a lunatic. I can't believe that the business with the Wildlife Partnership had any relevance at all.'

'You seem very certain,' George said. And it's odd, he thought, that you haven't asked what I found out at Brownscombe Associates. Aren't you interested in discovering if Laurie was involved? Or do you know already?'

'What do you mean?'

George paused then spoke deliberately, willing Oliver to understand. 'It's quite possible that the Wildlife Partnership is a distraction. If we could clear that matter up it would allow the officers to concentrate on more important areas of investigation.'

Sod the officers, he thought irreverently. If we could clear that up it would help *me* see the wood for the trees.

'Do the authorities know about the Wildlife Partnership?' For a moment Oliver lost his poise.

George did not answer the question. 'Why don't you just tell me what you know?' he said.

They stood for a moment in silence, staring at each other.

'You do understand what I'm saying,' George persisted. 'I want to keep the matter in perspective. If you tell me what you know it won't necessarily have to go any further.'

They were standing on the edge of the wood with a clear view of the house. Over Oliver's shoulder George could see Julia crossing the grass towards them. Oliver had his back to her. She had put on a long floral skirt over her bikini, and a big straw hat. She might have been the lady of the manor, dressed for opening a garden fête. She bore down on them. George knew he did not have much time.

'Well?' he demanded.

'I have already explained that I have no personal involvement in the Wildlife Partnership.' But the response was equivocal. It was a lawyer's answer.

'That doesn't mean you didn't know what was going on!' George almost shouted with impatience.

Oliver pulled at the waistband of his trousers, a nervous gesture. The knees were stained green. He must have been kneeling, taking his plant hunting seriously.

He seemed about to answer when he heard a movement behind him. He turned, saw Julia and greeted her with relief.

'Darling.' He touched her arm and George saw that his finger nails were dirty. It spoilt the effect of the white suit. 'George has some strange notion we can help him with information about the peculiar charity which Laurie was representing.' It was almost a question. He wanted her to make the decision about what should be told.

'Of course not,' she said. 'What nonsense! What on earth would we know about that?'

George let them walk back together across the grass, arm in arm in their fancy dress. He knew there would be no point in following them.

Chapter Twenty-Five

It was dusk. Heavy rain clouds to the north had cut the day short and there was a wind. The deputies still stood by the gate of the Oaklands Hotel but no one attempted to come in. The street outside was quiet. A couple of news people waited but the wind was cold and most had returned to the studio or to cover fresher stories – a stabbing in a High School in Galveston, new revelations about a senator's life.

Connie May sat on the Oaklands porch and wished the light was better. She'd brought her crochet, though Russell had laughed at her, had said this would be the trip of a lifetime and there would be no time for that. She was glad of it now. It had been a dreadful day. There had been enough gossip and rumour for her to imagine what Esme Lovegrove's body had looked like, dumped in the doorway like a bag of rubbish left out for the bin men. The thought of it made her feel sick. The same sort of sickness as when Russell had taken her on the steamer from Ilfracombe to Lundy Island and they'd anchored in the swell to let passengers off in little boats. It was only by concentrating on the crochet that she stopped herself throwing up.

When George came to sit beside her she knew at once that he wanted something. He was a pleasant man but not the sort to be sociable just for the sake of it. She finished her row, wound up her wool and waited for him to speak. He seemed very tired and she wondered if there was a wife somewhere, who should be looking after him.

'A couple of days ago you asked if you could help me,' he said.

'Yes.'

'Would you tell me about Esme? I never really got the chance to speak to her.'

He was surprised that she did not answer immediately. She had seemed eager to be part of the investigation.

'Could we go somewhere else?' she said. 'I mean right away from here. Just for a couple of hours. We were going to hire a car but we never got round to it. I mean it's a lovely hotel, but after all that's happened. . .'

She looked at him, hoping he would understand.

'Of course. Why don't I take you and Russell out to dinner? We'll take the ferry to Galveston. That's a city. There'll be more going on. Lots of people. And they won't all be talking about the murder.'

'Yes,' she said. 'I'd like that.'

It was the same road as he'd taken when he'd gone to the Bolivar Flats with Oliver. There were lights on in the bars in Crystal Beach and Gilchrist. The wind rattled the billboards and blew sand across the street. At Bolivar, at the end of the peninsula, they had to wait for a ferry. They watched it approaching, bobbing on the choppy water and Connie was reminded again of the Lundy steamer and hoped she would not make a spectacle of herself by being sick. They were first in and a small, hunched man waved them to park right in the bow. They spent the ten minute crossing sat in the car, and could see nothing. The water came over the side and drenched the windscreen with salt spray.

George found the restaurant where Oliver and Julia Adamson claimed to have had lunch the day before. It was the ground floor of a converted warehouse with a covered terrace which looked right out into the bay. Tonight everyone was eating in. The place was noisy and crowded and they had to wait for a table. It served seafood with a cajun flavour; blackened snapper and shrimp and dirty rice.

A waiter in a starched white shirt and tight black trousers led them to a table, handed them enormous laminated menus, began his spiel:

'Hi! my name's Carl. I'm your waiter for tonight. First off, can I get y' all a drink?'

'Orange juice,' Connie said firmly. 'That's all.'

'Yes ma'am. Hey! aren't you English?'

'Yes,' she said. 'From the West Country.'

'Isn't that something? I served two English people only yesterday.'

'At lunchtime?' George asked, not quite believing his luck.

'Yes, sir.'

'Perhaps they were friends of mine. A man and a woman? About forty? She's a blonde?'

'That's them!'

'I don't suppose you remember what time they were in. I'd arranged to meet them yesterday and I missed them.'

'Sure. It was early. The place was quiet. Must've been before twelve o'clock.'

'Thank you,' George said. So Oliver and Julia had been in Galveston as they'd said, but if they'd eaten at midday they would still have had time to return to the Oaklands Hotel to murder Esme Lovegrove.

Esme Lovegrove wasn't mentioned throughout the meal. They talked about the birding friends they had in common and Russell's preparations for Sunday's race. He seemed as determined as Rob that it should go ahead.

'I've always enjoyed a bird race,' he said. 'And I hear you're going to be a member of the team, too, George.'

'Oh, no,' George said. 'I don't think so. I haven't been asked.'

'I think you'll find Rob's counting on you.'

Over coffee Connie brought up the subject of Esme herself: 'She was a silly woman, though I dare say there was no harm to her.'

'In what way silly?'

'Spoilt. As if she'd never grown up. You could tell she was pretty when she was young. When you're young you can get away with things. Flirting, chatting up other people's husbands. When you get a bit older it's not very nice.'

'Did she chat up your husband?'

'Whenever she got the chance,' Connie said placidly. 'Though I don't suppose he noticed. Did you Russ?'

'No!' He seemed shocked, mildly flattered. 'To tell the truth I thought she was a bloody nuisance. Always wanting to look through the telescope. Always asking questions. That's what I thought she was after.'

He gave an embarrassed giggle as if he had made a particularly risqué joke. Connie gave him a disapproving stare and continued.

'I didn't mind for myself, George. We've been married for nearly forty years and I wouldn't have stayed with Russ if I couldn't trust him. But I didn't like the woman making a spectacle of herself. I thought she was an educated lady and she should have known better.'

'Was it just your husband she took a shine to?'

'Goodness me, no. Anything in trousers as we used to say when I was a girl.'

'Did you see her yesterday?'

'In the morning. We all went on a bus trip to the coast. Russell was keen and I thought I might as well. It wasn't much what I was expecting. A bit run down. I suppose when I think of the seaside I think of Weston. A prom and a cream tea after.' She laughed at her own silliness. 'I sat across the aisle from Esme on the coach.'

'Did you talk?'

'Well *she* talked,' Connie said. 'I didn't get much of a chance.'

'What did she talk about?'

'She talked about cream teas too. Perhaps that's what made me think of it. She runs a tea shop somewhere in the Cotswolds. She said that's what High Island needed. An old-fashioned tea shop. It would make a fortune. She said it was the most interesting job in the world because you got to hear everything that was going on. "You wouldn't believe some of the scandals I've overheard in my establishment." She went on like that all the way. Gossip and tittle tattle.' She paused. 'To be honest there wasn't much worth listening to. I didn't take it in. I pretended. Nodded in the right places. But I wasn't really listening.'

'You can't remember anything else she said? It might be helpful.'

'Well she talked about the murder. I don't suppose you can blame her. We were all doing that.'

'Did she have anything new to say? Any real information?'

Connie shook her head. 'I don't think so.'

'Did you have the impression that he was more than a chance acquaintance, that she had known Mick Brownscombe previously?'

'Oh, no. Nothing like that.'

The waiter in the tight trousers shimmied over to refill their coffee cups. George waited until he'd gone before speaking to Russell.

'You say that Esme followed you around when you were at Bolivar Flats. Did she talk to you?'

'Nothing sensible. She asked me to point out birds to her when all I wanted was to get to grips with them myself. Perhaps I was a bit short with her, but she did leave me alone and went off to pester someone else.'

'Rob Earl?'

'That's right. Poor chap. But at least he was being paid for it.'

'Did you talk to Miss Lovegrove after the coach trip?'

Connie replied. 'Not really. Russell asked them to join us for lunch. He was afraid he'd offended Esme and he wanted to be polite. But both sisters rushed off to sit with Mr Earl. We didn't mind of course. We'd just as soon be by ourselves.'

They smiled at each other. Russell reached over the table and patted her hand.

'You never saw her again?' George asked.

'No. Well, not exactly.' He waited for her to explain. She looked flustered and slightly embarrassed. 'I didn't say anything to the detective who talked to me this morning. I know I should have done but I wasn't *sure* you see and I don't find him very easy to talk to. He probably doesn't mean to bully but I find him quite frightening. And he asked about after lunch, and this happened before. Before we'd even asked Esme and Joan to sit with us.'

'What happened?'

'You know the little lounge, opposite reception?'

He nodded. It was the lounge used by the elderly residents, where he'd talked to the old man who remembered the Oaklands Hotel when it was run by Mary Ann's mother.

'I waited for Russell in there before lunch. I didn't fancy the bar. I just wanted somewhere quiet and cool to sit.'

'What did you see?'

'I didn't *see* anything but I heard. I didn't mean to listen but I couldn't help it, and it didn't seem important.'

He nodded, encouraging her to continue.

'I heard Esme out in the lobby. She just said: "About three-thirty then. I'll see you there." I didn't really think anything of it. I just wondered who she was chatting up this time.'

'And who was she chatting up?' he asked gently.

'I don't know,' she said. 'That's all I heard. From where I was sitting I couldn't see into the lobby. If anybody answered he must have spoken more quietly. And I wasn't really interested, George. I told you. She was just a silly woman.'

She took a handkerchief from her pocket and wiped her forehead, though the restaurant was air-conditioned and quite cool.

'I'm sorry she's dead,' she said. 'But I have to tell you how it was.'

'Of course.' He paused, tried to picture the room where he'd sat, chatting to the old Texan. 'I wonder if you noticed a large mirror,' he asked. 'It's on the wall above the mantelpiece. If you'd looked in there you'd have been able to see anyone in reception.'

She shook her head. 'I was sitting in the window,' she said, 'looking out over the garden, enjoying the view.'

Russell leaned forward, clasped both his wife's hands.

'You can't think Miss Lovegrove was arranging to meet the man who killed her, George. I thought she died much later. After seven o'clock.'

'Her body was moved after seven,' he said. 'It's more likely she was killed in the afternoon. That's when she disappeared.'

'We can't help you then,' Russell said. 'We had a walk through Boy Scout Wood. I wanted to get a clear picture of all the trails. You know, George. Ready for the bird race on Sunday.'

Oh, yes. George thought. The bloody bird race.

Chapter Twenty-Six

When the Mays had gone to bed he stood for a moment in the lobby. Mary Ann appeared from the bar. Her face was grey but she was as chic and well groomed as always. Her little black shoes tapped hurriedly across the tiled floor. He thought she had been waiting for him.

'I wondered if we could talk,' she said.

'Of course.' He was exhausted but she looked troubled. He could not ask her to wait until the morning. Always a soft touch for a pretty face, Molly would say.

'Come into my apartment.'

She led him down a corridor, past the kitchen, to a room at the back of the house, the room he had seen from the car-park the evening before. It was long and narrow, almost empty of furniture. There were wooden floors, a white sofa, a low, light wood table. Bookshelves covered one wall.

'A drink?' she asked. 'Scotch?'

'Absolutely.' After an evening of abstinence with the Mays he realized how much he needed a drink.

There must have been a small kitchen because she went out through a swing door and came back with glasses filled with ice, a bottle.

'What do you want to tell me?' he asked. He thought he knew.

She twisted the glass in her hand.

'It's probably not important,' she said. 'The storm brought it all back. A memory of something that happened twenty years ago. I'm not sure how accurate it is. It seems more like a dream after all this time.'

It was not what he had been expecting. He said nothing, waiting for her to continue.

'It was when Laurie and the boys came to stay, one night at the end of their visit. The noise of the wind in the trees reminded me because there'd been a storm that day too. It had brought the electricity cables down and there were no lights in the house. I think I was scared for some reason. Perhaps I still needed a lamp in my room to get me to sleep and I woke up in the dark. I went out on to the veranda. It had stopped raining and everything was wet, shining. There must have been a moon. The whole house was quiet apart from the water dripping from the roof and the trees.

'You remember it very well.'

'Yes,' she said. 'I can see it, you know, in flashes, like one of those jumpy early movies.'

'What happened?'

'I heard noises coming from the front room, the room where the Adamsons are staying now. There was a door then from the room right out on to the veranda and it was open a crack. It wasn't much of a room and my mother had put the boys in there. Sort of camping out. One of them had a mattress on the floor. Then they must have lit some candles because suddenly there was light from the window and when I looked I could see their faces. They were all gathered round one candle. Like kids trying to spook each other with ghost stories.'

'And it was just the boys who were there?'

'No, Laurie too. I remember her most. She had her hair loose and all frizzed out around her head. She was the centre of attention. The others were playing up to her. Trying to impress. Competitive. Even at my age I realized that.'

She sipped from her glass, returned to her memories.

'Like I said I thought they were telling ghost stories. They had that intense look. I'd been away at girl scout camp during the Easter vacation and that's how the girls had looked around the camp fire when they were trying to scare each other.'

'But they weren't telling stories?'

She shook her head. 'It was some sort of game. Laurie was in charge of it. You could tell it was her idea.'

'What sort of game?'

She seemed to sense disapproval in his voice, became suddenly a modern sophisticated woman instead of a twelve-year-old child.

'Not what you think. No undressing or groping in the dark. Nothing to shock or deprave.'

'It's not only nudity which can shock or deprave,' he said lightly.

'It was a truth game,' she said. 'Laurie was asking the questions.'

'Of course.'

'Perhaps it had been going on for a while, before I went out on to the porch, before they lit the candles.'

'But you heard some of it?'

She nodded. 'Laurie asked them how many women they'd made love to. That had me hooked. I was twelve years old. I mean sex was exciting, forbidden, never talked about. I couldn't move. Oliver went first. One too many, he said. They all laughed. I didn't understand the joke. Rob told a story. I think it was supposed to be funny but I was too innocent to know what it was all about.'

'And Mick?'

'He said he never had. Made it with a woman. As if it were a terrible admission, you know. As if it were the worst thing in the world.'

'What did Laurie say to that?'

'"Well, I think that's real sweet." I thought she was teasing him but he took her seriously. He was sort of grateful because she didn't laugh out loud.'

'Did the boys laugh out loud?'

'Not really. They couldn't after what Laurie had said.'

'Was that it? Was that the only question?'

She shook her head.

'Laurie asked what was the wickedest thing they'd ever done. She said that evil was far more interesting than sex. I thought that was so profound! She looked like a witch with her wild hair caught in the candle light, staring at each of them in turn, waiting for them to speak. I can't remember what Oliver said. Something flip, I expect.'

'But you remember the others?'

'Rob said he'd cheated at a Birdathon, though I don't think he called it that. Anyway, it was the sort of competition we plan to hold here on the peninsula on Sunday. Laurie told him that didn't count. It was like cheating at an exam. No one really got hurt. He said it felt wicked enough to him. A stringer was the lowest of the low. I'm sure that was the word he used. Stringer. Does that mean a cheat?'

George nodded. 'What did Mick say?'

'That once when he was drunk he'd stolen his father's car. Rob said that a father like his deserved to have his car stolen. If he wasn't such a mean bastard he'd have bought Mick a decent car of his own. "He didn't deserve to have it smashed up!" Mick said. They laughed but I thought at the time it must have been a bad accident because Mick looked all shaken just thinking about it.'

'Was that the end of the game?'

'No. The boys wouldn't leave it like that. Why should Laurie ask all the questions? Rob said it was her turn to answer. Which of the three of them did she like the best. She smiled, teasing, then said she liked them all. Rob said that was a cop out. It wouldn't do.

'"Well then," she said in a kind of drawl, stringing it out, making them wait for an answer, "it all depends what you mean, boys. Do you mean for a night, or a few days, or to spend the rest of my life with?"

'"The rest of your life," Rob said.

'"That's easy then," she said. "It would have to be Michael".'

'What was the others' reaction to that?'

'I don't know. Not now, thinking about it. Then I was a kid. There was a lot of joking and I took it at face value. But I guess she must have been serious.'

'Yes.' George stared into the whisky imagining the scene Mary Ann described. Four young people sitting in the dark, intensely connected through friendship and lust and jealousy. Had any of them realized that Laurie was making a real choice?

'Did the evening break up then?' he asked.

'No. Laurie asked what they all wanted to have achieved in twenty years' time. Rob said he wanted still to be travelling. Definitely *not* to have settled down. And I suppose he's achieved that. I admire him for not having given in.

'Oliver said: "A houseful of kids." There was a lot of laughing at that. It was another in-joke I didn't understand.

'Laurie said it was quite simple. She wanted to be rich. Oliver, sneered at her a bit for that, said something like: "I never took you for a bread-head Laurie." She answered very seriously: "Well, Oliver, you've never been poor."'

'And Mick? Did he say what he wanted out of the next twenty years?'

'Yes.' She paused. 'He said he wanted to be married to Laurie. The others groaned at that as if it was some kind of sick flattery. But I could tell that he was still playing the truth game. He really meant it.' She looked at George to see if he believed her.

'Then someone, Laurie I think. It would have been Laurie, said they would have to get together in twenty years' time to see how much they had achieved towards their goals. Here at the Oaklands Hotel, she said. And perhaps then the weather would be better. Perhaps then there would be a fall and they'd see all the warblers they wanted. The weather had been fine and clear until the storm and the birds hadn't stayed. They must have agreed, though I don't remember that. They must have agreed because they all came.'

'What happened next?' George asked, prompting her because she seemed lost in her daydream.

'They saw me. I guess I must have got too close to the door. Laurie suddenly shouted: "Jesus Christ there's a ghost on the veranda." And they brought me in and asked me how long I'd been out there. I didn't like to admit that I'd been snooping so I said just a few minutes, just long enough to hear them plan to come back to Oaklands. Rob told me he hoped I'd still be living here then and that I could be part of the reunion too. I said that was what I hoped would happen. In twenty years' time I wanted the Oaklands Hotel to be real smart and me to be here, running it. Then the lights came on suddenly. The room just looked a mess. It wasn't magic any more. I went to bed and by the time I'd got up in the morning they'd all gone. Laurie too.'

'Was that true?' George asked. 'Was that what you wanted even then?'

He knew the answer already. He thought that was why she remembered the evening so clearly. It wasn't only the strange light, and the storm and her fascination with adult conversation. She saw it as the beginning of her life's work. It was as important as that to her.

'Yes. You know I think it was. Even then.' She spoke casually, trying to make light of it.

'And I think you would have done anything to get what you wanted.'

'What do you mean?'

'Didn't Laurie believe that she was entitled to a share of the house?'

'Is that what she told you?'

He shook his head.

'She didn't believe that. She pretended she did though.'

'Your grandmother and Laurie's were sisters weren't they? Twins?'

'They were sisters but they weren't twins, though they looked as alike as peas in a pod as they grew older. My grandmother was the elder and Oaklands was left to her. Neither of the old ladies would have wanted Laurie's father to have it. Laurie knew that all along. She knew she had no real claim to the place and she didn't want to know until the hotel became successful. Like she said in the truth game she was always motivated by money. She was jealous that I was doing so well.'

'What did she do?'

'She started dropping in with Michael. Just to be neighbourly she said. She didn't come near the place when Mom was sick and I could have used the help. There were six old men here then, most of the rooms shut up and I was cleaning the bathrooms myself.

She didn't show an interest until I did the place up and she could see I was making a go of it. At first she just dropped hints. About how my grandmother would never have been able to keep the Oaklands Hotel going herself. About how the two sisters were partners. Not formal perhaps. Never written down. But they'd never think it would have to be. They'd think that the family would always stick together, always look after each other. That's what she'd say.'

Mary Ann swirled the remaining whisky in the bottom of her glass.

'It was her father's fault,' she said. 'He started it. According to Mom he was always going on about how the place should have been his. When he was sober enough to speak. Laurie took the idea from him.'

'That's why your mother didn't mix with that side of the family?'

She nodded.

'Things moved beyond hints, didn't they?'

She looked at him, weighing up what he knew, too tired perhaps to come to a judgement.

'I was at the Brownscombe offices this morning,' he said. 'I found a letter you'd sent to Laurie confirming the contract for the wildlife refuge.'

She continued to stare at him, then she drained the last of her whisky.

'I made a mistake,' she said. 'I talked to Laurie and Mick about my idea for the new refuge. They were in the business. I thought they could give me some advice. As they wanted to be neighbourly. Laurie began pushing straight away for Brownscombe Associates to be given the contract for surveying and planning it. I told her I hadn't reached that stage. She got mad, said that if I couldn't be reasonable she'd have to consult a lawyer about making a formal claim on the hotel. I was scared. I didn't think she'd win but if I had to defend that sort of action it could cripple me financially.'

'So you gave them the contract.'

'Yeah!' She got up and poured more whisky into both glasses. 'I was a coward. I wasn't prepared to take the risk. And as I said the other day she had some pretty good ideas. But then I thought. That's it. I'm never going to allow her to put pressure on me again. I put it in writing on the morning Michael died.'

'Why didn't you tell me all this when I asked you before?'

'Why do you think? What Laurie did amounted to blackmail. Suddenly her husband, a partner in the business and so also implicated in the blackmail, is found murdered. At the very least I'd be a suspect and hassled. I can't afford that kind of distraction. I need to run this hotel.'

'And how did the meeting go with Laurie last week?'

'Do you know, it's ironic. We got on better than we had for some years. She said that she hoped there were no hard feelings and I must understand her wanting to be involved in the place. As if the threats were a bluff or a joke. Of course I could understand. Look, Mr Palmer-Jones, if you think I had a motive for killing the man you're wrong. We ended up on good terms. I didn't think it would be so bad working with her. And I'd never had any quarrel with Mick.'

He left her then. He hoped she would sleep, that she would realize the hotel would function without her until morning. He walked through the windy night to his room.

Chapter Twenty-Seven

George had expected to sleep badly, but he woke early the next morning to squally sunshine and the surprised gratitude which always came after a full night's rest.

It had rained very heavily in the night. Surface water had gathered in a dip in the lawn. The restaurant had only just opened for breakfast and he ate alone.

From the phone in the lobby he used his charge-card to call the pub where Molly was staying in Devon. The landlord said she had gone away for a couple of days to research her book but she'd asked him to keep the room for her and he expected her back that evening.

'Any message?' the landlord asked, curious, shouting against the noise of the lunchtime drinkers.

'No,' George said. 'No message. I'll try again later.' He was disappointed, unreasonably cross with Molly because she was taking so long to get a result.

He phoned Laurie's house. The call was taken by a teenage girl, monosyllabic and sullen. He asked to speak to Laurie.

The girl was suspicious. 'Why? Who is it?' Perhaps they had been troubled by reporters, ghouls and cranks.

'A friend of your father's,' he said and gave his name.

Laurie seemed relaxed, almost cheerful.

'Hi, George! How can I help you?'

'I've a few more questions I'm afraid. I was wondering if I might come to see you.'

'Sure. But I was planning a trip into Houston today. Why don't you meet me there? We could have lunch. And it would save you a little travelling.'

'Why not?' he said, but he would have preferred a different arrangement. London was the only large city he'd ever felt comfortable in.

She suggested a place in the Galleria and gave him directions. He wrote them down then went to the reception desk to borrow a street map of the city centre. Connie May was on her way out of the restaurant.

'I'm going into Houston,' he said. 'You have friends there, don't you? Would you like a lift? Perhaps you could arrange to meet them.'

For a moment she seemed taken aback. 'That's very kind,' she said. 'But I'd rather stay here. Close to Russell. I know it's silly but I'd feel easier in my mind.' As if she could protect her husband.

'He could come too.'

'No. He wouldn't want to leave High Island. He thinks the rain might have brought some more birds.'

'I'll come with you!' It was Julia Adamson. He had not seen her. She must have been listening. She smiled at him. 'You will give me a lift Mr Palmer-Jones, won't you? I've been trying to persuade Oliver to take me all week.'

'I expect he had other things on his mind,' George murmured. He meant the murder of an old friend but she did not notice the sarcasm.

'Yes,' she said. 'This bloody bird race.'

'They still intend to go ahead with it?'

'Madness, isn't it? They seem keener than ever. You will take me Mr Palmer-Jones won't you? I could be ready in a moment.'

He paused. She took his hesitation as consent, thanked him and hurried away.

It took her half an hour to prepare for the trip. He waited with mounting impatience. He hated to be late. When Molly said she was almost ready it meant she had to grab a coat. Or change from the tennis shoes with the holes in to the new baseball boots their daughter had given her for Christmas. She seldom bothered to brush her hair. When Julia finally appeared she was very glossy. Very made up.

They walked round the house to the old stable yard where his car was parked. The drains were full and the trees were sodden. A mini bus drove down the drive and pulled up outside the kitchen door. A dozen officers, dressed in overalls and waterproof boots got out.

'My God!' Julia said. 'Do we get individual body guards now?'

'I think they're here to make a detailed search of the grounds.' He had expected it before.

'Isn't that a question of shutting the stable door once the horse has bolted?'

The flippant tone annoyed him. 'They haven't found either murder weapon yet. They searched the Boy Scout reserve after Michael died and found the iron post which caused the head wound but not the chisel which stabbed him. They'll be looking for the object used to kill Esme Lovegrove too.'

'Oh!' She put her hand to her mouth.

They drove to Houston in silence. The fields on either side of them were covered in the water which had drained from the road. The traffic was heavy and they sat in a queue on the outskirts of the city. At the Galleria, George chose an underground car-park. He and Julia took the lift together into the shopping centre.

'I'll meet you back at the car in three hours,' he said.

'Only three hours!' she exclaimed in mock horror.

'I'll have you know, Mr Palmer-Jones, that I'm a serious shopper.'

'If you're not there I'll go without you.' She began a little laugh, thinking that he was teasing, then saw that he was not.

The lift doors opened and they stepped out into a crowded mall.

'My wife's in Bristol today,' he said.

She turned sharply towards him but before she could ask what he meant he walked off. That would give her something to think about while she was shopping.

The Galleria complex was a tiered, covered amphitheatre built around an oval ice rink. Lines of children, holding hands, swooped and glided over the ice. The shops seemed expensive, the piped music generally discreet. There were occasional touches of Texan brashness to relieve the blandness: a small shop selling nothing but cowboy hats and boots, rows of denim skirts and blouses covered in diamante and coloured embroidery, stalls selling the biggest ice creams he had ever seen.

He saw Laurie from a distance. She did not notice him. She was sitting at a table outside a French café on the same level as the rink, watching the children. She wore jeans and boots and a white button-down shirt. No hat though. Not like the first time the boys had seen her walking down the road from Winnie. On the chair beside her were two shiny carrier bags with rope handles and gold lettering. She too had been shopping. It seemed an inappropriate occupation for a newly bereaved woman and he was oddly shocked.

When she saw him walk towards her she moved the bags from the chair so he could sit down. She must have sensed his disapproval because she said: 'I bought some treats for the kids. It's been a tough time for them and they've been great.' Her hair was loose and she pushed it away from her face with the palm of her hand. 'More questions, you said.'

'I've been talking to Mary Ann about Oaklands.'

'Ah.' It seemed almost like a sigh of relief.

'Why didn't you tell me?'

'It didn't seem right. If she hadn't told you first it would have been kind of snitching.'

'Why?'

'You work it out for yourself. She didn't exactly feel friendly to Brownscombe Associates, then Michael got murdered. People might take that the wrong way.'

'But you didn't? You didn't think Mary Ann killed Michael?'

'Of course not. She's family. I've known her since she was a kid.'

'But you made life awkward for her?'

'Nah!' A waitress came. They ordered coffee, savoury croissants. Laurie grinned. 'Well maybe a little awkward. I mean I'd been brought up to think of the Oaklands Hotel as my home too in a way. I didn't have anywhere else. I guess I thought I should have a stake in it. When I saw what she was making out of that place it made me mad. Michael thought I was crazy to mind so much. "Just let it go," he'd say. "We're doing all right." But I couldn't. I made him come with me to visit, just to let Mary Ann know that I was still interested.'

'What were you hoping for?'

'I don't know. Some way of being part of it I suppose. It wasn't just the money.' She paused. 'I went there when things were bad at my parents' place. It was always special for me.'

'Then she told you about the wildlife sanctuary?'

'Yes, and I suggested we could plan it and run it for her. It was just the sort of thing I was hoping for. You'd have thought she'd have jumped at the chance of giving us the contract. We'd have given her a good deal.'

'But she didn't jump at it?'

'No, she was real sniffy. At first anyway.'

'She thought you were blackmailing her.'

'No! It wasn't like that.'

'You told her you'd sue for a share in the hotel.'

'Hey, I say things when I get mad. Are you joking? Do you know how much it would cost to bring in the lawyers? I thought life was comfortable for her. Like you said, maybe I just wanted to be awkward.'

'And it worked didn't it? Mary Ann gave you the contract.'

'Yes, it worked. And though she might not admit it we work pretty well together. She liked some of my ideas.'

The waitress came up behind them and filled their glasses with iced water, their cups with coffee.

'Like entering a team in the Birdathon. That was your idea, wasn't it?'

'Sure.' She looked up at him. Her face was freckled and there were crumbs around her mouth. 'Mick was looking forward to it, being part of the old team again.'

'I think the Birdathon should be cancelled,' George said slowly. 'Or if that's not possible at least the Oaklands team should pull out. What do you think? Should the race be scratched?'

'Heck no! Let it go ahead. As a memorial to Mick if you like. He would have liked that.'

'You've heard there's been another murder?'

'Yes.' She gave a sudden and wicked smile. 'Mary Ann's going to need as much good publicity as she can get after two murders within spitting distance of the new reserve. And I've got a financial stake in the project being a success. Maybe I should take part myself.'

Despite himself he admired her refusal to pretend at a grief she did not feel.

'I don't think that would be a good idea,' he said.

'Maybe not.' She got up and walked into the café to find the restroom. As soon as she had disappeared through the door he stooped and looked in the shiny carrier bags under the table. In one there was a parcel, already gift wrapped. On the label she had written: 'For Paul, all my love, Mom.' In the other there was a dress which even he could tell Laurie would never wear. So she had not been lying about the shopping. He wondered if she had been equally truthful during the rest of the conversation.

Laurie made her way back to the table. She smiled at a young waiter, who watched her until she sat down.

'Tell me about your children,' George said. 'How old are they?'

'Paul's sixteen. Laura's fourteen.'

'Laura's named after you?'

'Yes. That's right.'

'And Paul?'

'Mick chose that. He was very keen. I think perhaps it was a family name.'

'He had a close friend called Paul Butterworth,' George said.

'Did he?' It seemed to mean nothing to her. 'Perhaps that was it then. Funny though. I don't think he ever mentioned him.'

'Did he talk about any of his friends?'

'Only Rob and Ollie, and not them much.'

'He had a girlfriend, you know, when he was at school. He wrote to her while he was at university.'

'Did he?' She seemed surprised, impressed. 'He never said.'

'Her name was Nell. Helen.'

She shook her head. She wasn't much interested in what Mick had done before he met her. A child skated past them. He was alone, frowning with concentration, his hands clasped behind his back.

'I used to bring my kids here,' Laurie said. 'They won't come now. They think they're too old.'

'You told me Michael's parents wouldn't come to your wedding.'

'That's right.' She looked away from the skating boy. It was not a question she had been expecting.

'They were never invited,' George said. 'My wife's spoken to them. They didn't find out about it until afterwards.'

'Mick told me he'd asked them.'

'But you're not surprised he didn't?'

She shrugged. 'Look, I never found out what was going on in that family. I gave Mick the chance to talk about it but he didn't want to. That was all right by me. I wouldn't have wanted him prying into the things that went on under our roof when I was a kid.' She shivered slightly. 'I asked them to the funeral.'

'I know. They won't come.'

She shrugged again. She didn't care.

'Can I ask about something that happened when you first went to High Island with Mick and the others?'

She nodded.

'The night before you left Oaklands there was a storm. The electricity was off. You were talking in the boys' room, playing a truth game. When they asked which of the three you liked best, why did you choose Mick?'

She didn't ask how he knew about that evening or pretend not to remember, but she took a long time to answer. He had to prompt her:

'You did say that you could have had whichever one you chose.'

'That's right.'

'So why Mick?'

She turned away from the ice rink and looked at him, suddenly serious.

'You want the truth? Like in the game?'

'Of course.'

'I thought he was damaged goods,' she said. 'I recognized the feeling. But that was only part of it. I knew I could make whatever I wanted out of him. After years of being bossed around I saw he was someone who'd do just what I told him.'

'And did you get what you expected?'

'Oh, yes,' she said. 'Pretty much.'

Chapter Twenty-Eight

Julia arrived at the car just on time, hurrying. She was breathless and her arms were full of packages. But there was none of the elation of the serious shopper who's just had a fix. His remark about Bristol had worried her. George was pleased about that.

On the freeway he tuned the car radio into a classical music station so he would not have to talk to her. Occasionally he thought she was about to start a conversation, to ask him perhaps what Molly was doing in Bristol, but she did not find the courage and when they arrived at the hotel she scurried off, hardly making time to thank him for the lift. He presumed she had gone to find Oliver.

Mary Ann was waiting for him in the lobby. She knew he had been to see Laurie. She took him into the small lounge where the same old man slept soundly in his chair.

'She won't sue,' George said.

'Are you sure?'

'I don't think she ever intended to. Perhaps you misjudged her. She loves this place, too, and wanted to be a part of it.'

She shot him a glance, embarrassed.

'I'm not sure I can share it,' she said. It had been a difficult admission for her to make. He thought she would be no good at playing the truth game.

'Your wife phoned,' Mary Ann said, glad to change the subject. 'She asked you to call her back. She's in the same place in Devon. Use the phone in my flat. Joe Benson seems to have taken up permanent residence in the office.'

So he sat in comfort on the white sofa, and in the background there was the noise from the kitchen next door, banging pans and the occasional scream of a temperamental chef.

He had to wait while the pub landlord fetched Molly from her room. She sounded tired.

'Well,' she said. 'It was just as you thought.'

'Was it!' There was a quiet satisfaction that he had worked the thing out but he was not sure how far it helped clear Rob from suspicion.

'It wasn't easy to get in,' she said.

'How did you manage it?' He was prepared to let her share some of the glory.

'I had to get her address first and that wasn't easy without drawing too much attention to myself. Her phone's ex-directory. I think other people have been trying to trace her. Her old friends at the BBC were very cagey.'

'Debts?' he asked.

'It looks like it but they've all been cleared now.'

'So?'

'So I thought of Nigel.' Nigel was an old birding friend of George's who was a sound recordist in the BBC's natural history unit. 'He'd been to a party in her flat. He knew it was in Redlands but he couldn't remember the address. We drove up and down for about an hour before he recognized it. We found a chatty neighbour who confirmed it. Unluckily there was no obvious way in. No key under the door-mat. Nothing like that. No alarm system though and only a Yale lock on the kitchen door. When I met Sally for lunch she told me she didn't bother much about security.'

The tiredness had gone and her voice was excited. So, George thought, Molly had been breaking and entering, too.

'I had to persuade Nigel to be look-out for me but he wasn't very keen. I don't blame him and he did let me sleep at his place. The area where Sally lives is rather arty. I thought there'd be lots of late-night people and it would be best to try to get in early in the morning.

'I parked in a street nearby and walked. It was still dark. No one was about. There's a back alley between the houses. It's just wide enough for one car to get through. The houses are terraced. There are no gardens at the back, just paved yards and then a high wall. Most have a wooden door in the wall which backs into the alley. Sally's did, but the door was bolted. Twenty years ago I'd probably have been able to climb the wall but I didn't think I'd manage it now. Luckily the bolt was rotten. It took one shove and it opened. It seemed to make an enormous racket but no one took any notice. Her flat's on the ground floor. According to the neighbour the people upstairs were on holiday. Then there was just the kitchen door to get past.'

'And how did you manage that?' he asked, playing along, thinking that one day he'd tell her his story of breaking into the Brownscombe Associates' office.

'Not with a credit card,' she said firmly. 'I don't believe that's as easy as people make out.' In her career as a social worker she had specialized for a period in work with juvenile offenders. She had picked up a lot. 'What you need is the nylon binding tape used by industry to secure large parcels.'

'And you just happened to have some with you?'

'It wasn't that easy actually. I had to raid a skip at a big do-it-yourself store close to Nigel's flat.'

She chuckled and he wondered what was wrong with them both. It was so undignified this grasping after sensation. That was for the young. Perhaps they should give up the agency and settle for a contented and uneventful retirement like Connie and Russell May. But he couldn't imagine himself playing bowls.

'Was the technique as effective as you'd been led to believe?'

'Eventually, though it took a lot longer than I'd expected to get the door open. I suppose my fingers are stiffer than the lads.'

'But you *did* get into the flat.' He interrupted her to move the conversation along. He hoped Mary Ann wouldn't add this telephone call to his bill. Rob Earl's employer would have a fit.

'Of course.' She paused, savouring the moment. 'It was a real sense of achievement when I felt the lock move. I suppose that's ridiculous. The door opened into a small kitchen. The door had a glass pane so I didn't risk the light. I had a torch. Then there was a living-room. The curtains were drawn so I was able to put on a desk lamp, and have a proper look round. I think Sally Adamson must have been brought up with expensive tastes.'

Oh, quite, George thought, remembering the bags full of designer shopping. Julia would have seen to that. And Oliver would have indulged them.

'It wasn't a room I'd feel comfortable in. It wasn't at all the sort of place you'd expect a young person to have. Not a scrap of student woodchip wallpaper, no breeze-block bookshelves. Sally has a leather sofa and state-of-the-art music system. Furniture for making an impression.'

George thought he had been very patient. He had let Molly ramble on for long enough.

'I'm not interested in her interior design.'

'Except that she'd spent more on the place than she could afford. The kitchen was full of electrical gadgets. And all bought on credit. I found the agreements in a ghastly reproduction mahogany desk.'

'Ah,' he said, thinking: at last. 'And what else did you find?'

'In the same desk a typed list of names. I think it must have been used for the mailshot. I recognized some of the people we *know* received information and a begging letter from the Wildlife Partnership. Others were familiar through your work with Green Scenes. Sally would have had access to the names of interested people through the BBC. They must have had a contacts file.'

'There was no proof though? The list wasn't headed Wildlife Partnership?'

'It wasn't headed anything. I made a note of some of the names. We could check that they'd been targeted.'

'That's still not proof. She could always claim a coincidence, say that she'd kept the list after using it for work.'

'Well she could,' Molly said, 'if it wasn't for the invoice.'

'What invoice?'

'I found a bill from a local printer's. It was for three hundred colour brochures. There's no record that the bill has ever been paid.'

'You'll have to check with the printer. See if he kept a copy.'

188

'There's no need for that.' Her voice was infuriatingly smug. 'In the same file there's a draft which he sent originally for Miss Adamson's approval. It was definitely the brochure which Cecily received.'

That's it then, he thought. That's enough.

'Why did she add her own name to the list of supporters?' he asked. 'We'd never have traced her without that.'

'Pride I suppose. She liked to think she was a celebrity. Or a perverse sense of humour. You'll have to admit that it must have taken nerve. The dressing up. The Texan accent. Making herself older, more impressive. Hiring Jason and renting the office. There was something flamboyant and stylish about the whole plan. I don't think she only did it for the money. She could have gone to mummy and daddy if that was all it was about. They'd have paid her debtors, wouldn't they?'

'Oliver certainly. Like a shot.'

'I think it might have started as an elaborate hoax,' Molly said hopefully. 'To prove to herself that she could carry it off. After the television series ended and there was no prospect of other work she needed to believe she was still good at her job. She met Laurie Brownscombe at the party her father took her to. Perhaps she just started off practising the accent. As an actress might. And wondering if she could convince people that she was Texan. She'd try a phone call to test the voice. And then she'd think about the appearance. You notice there was no attempt to impersonate Laurie. In the bedroom I found a blonde wig and the clothes Jason described the woman who'd employed him as wearing. She'd created a fictional character and she needed a vehicle for her. Laurie had talked to her about the Wildlife Partnership. The fraud grew from there.'

'Hmm!' George was sceptical. 'I think it more likely that the conversation with Laurie gave her the idea for an easy way of making money and the fancy dress came later. So that if the fraud was discovered it could never be traced back to her.'

'I suppose you're right.' There was a pause. 'I liked her. When I met her for lunch that day I really liked her. But it was a mean and horrible thing to do. I wonder how many people responded to the letter. Then there was Jason. She'd convinced him that he had a proper job and one day he'd fly off to Houston. Now he's back on the dole. Why do you think she sacked him and closed down the operation in such a hurry? Because we'd started poking around?'

'I think it was all over before that. Don't forget Cecily phoned the office number demanding to speak to the person in charge. Jason would have told her that a woman was making a fuss. Sally's bright enough to quit while she's still ahead.'

'What will you do about it? I can hardly go to the police. They'd want to know how I got into the flat.'

'I'm not sure that I'll do anything yet. Did you find evidence that Oliver and Julia knew what she was up to?'

'Nothing.'

'They certainly know now.' George remembered the argument he'd overheard in Boy Scout Wood on his first afternoon in High Island, the woman standing in the Cathedral screaming out her jealousy. He'd thought Oliver had a lover. Instead it seemed Julia had spent her marriage competing with her daughter for his affection. 'Julia blames Oliver for getting Sally involved in it, but I can't believe he took any profit. Perhaps Sally asked his advice, hypothetically, about how you'd go about setting up a new wildlife charity, and he was too besotted to see what she was up to. Perhaps she got frightened when Cecily started making a fuss and she ran to daddy for help. I'd say that was more likely.'

'Like a spoilt kid.'

'Which is what she is. And now the parents have papered over their differences to cover up for her.'

In the kitchen next to Mary Ann's flat the noise was increasing to a crescendo. Soon the first dinners would be served. There was a crash of broken crockery and a stream of oaths. It seemed that the tension and excitability which had affected the guests had afflicted the hotel staff too.

'Can this have anything to do with Michael's murder?' Molly asked.

'Would the Adamsons go as far as murder to protect their only daughter, if Michael had found out about the British fraud and Sally was behind it? Is that what you mean?'

'It provides a motive of a sort. And parents do desperate and irrational things when their children are involved.' She stopped suddenly, realizing how like a social worker she sounded.

George did not answer. He was pleased that the case was less muddled but he still thought it had all started much longer ago, before the chance meeting of Laurie and Sally at a party in London, perhaps even before the stormy night in High Island when four young people played the truth game by candle light.

'I was wondering if I might join you,' Molly said. 'After three days in the West Country I could do with some sunshine.'

'I'm afraid not,' he said, quite seriously. 'I'd like you to find Michael's friend, Paul Butterworth. His name's cropped up in a different context. And there's a girl who seems to have disappeared altogether.'

So, Molly thought. Here I am, taking instructions again.

Chapter Twenty-Nine

The search of the grounds continued at first light on the following day. Areas of woodland and garden were taped off and residents were confined to the house, so it was impossible to pretend that everything was normal. Some escaped in the mini bus with Rob to the Anahuac refuge. Others seemed afraid of missing something and sat on the veranda watching the searching policemen through binoculars. They were quarrelsome and overwrought. There was bickering, odd outbursts of temper followed by shaken apologies.

'Why don't they go home?' George asked Rob at breakfast. Rob had been surprised by the question. His depression had lifted and he seemed to be thriving on the frenzy.

'No one will want to leave before the bird race!' he said.

And when George canvassed opinion, it seemed that Rob was right. Even the frail and the timid were curious to see how the race would turn out. The shared danger had made them passionate supporters of the Oaklands team. They wanted to be there to cheer them on.

Only George thought the bird race should be cancelled and he found it hard to explain why he felt so strongly about it. Partly there was distaste. He suspected that visitors would be attracted into the area not to support the competing teams but to see where the murders had been committed. He imagined them waiting, almost hoping for more violence. Partly there was a practical problem. The bird race was scheduled for the following day. How could the sheriff's men complete a proper search of the grounds if they were bring trampled by birdwatchers, keen to catch a glimpse of Swainson's warbler? How could the crowd be controlled?

He took his concerns to Benson, who swept him off in his constable's car to the Gulfway Motel for coffee. There were a few truck drivers having a late breakfast, some birders stocking up before the next attack on Boy Scout Wood, but after Benson had had a quiet word with Miss Lily and slipped a couple of bills across the counter, their plates were taken and they were hurried away. She locked the door behind them. As before, Benson and George had the place to themselves.

Benson was sympathetic but unmoved.

'Hey, George! This is the States! If we were to shut down an area for a week every time there was a murder the country would go bust. I told you. The birders mean big bucks in this town. If I try to stop the event I'll have a riot on my hands. I mean it's advertised. They'll turn up anyway. What do you want me to do? Set up road blocks? It's not possible.' He narrowed his eyes. 'Unless there's something you haven't told me. Unless you think there'll be a risk to the public. Have you any evidence of that?'

'No,' George said. 'I've no evidence.' Only a feeling, he thought, and Benson would laugh at that. I would if I were in his shoes.

'Then we have to convince people that it's business as usual. That there's no need to panic and they can visit High Island.'

'Your friend in the gas station told you that did he?' George muttered. Benson pretended not to hear.

'Tell me,' the constable said, leaning forward across the table. 'How are your investigations proceeding? What can you tell me?'

'The fraud I was telling you about,' George said, 'concerning a non-profit organization called the Wildlife Partnership. Brownscombe Associates had nothing to do with that. Its scope was limited to Britain. The name was used. That was all.'

'I passed the information you gave me about that to the sheriff's department. They checked it out. They thought the Brownscombe business was legitimate, too. But thanks anyway. It might have led to something.' He waved at Miss Lily to bring more coffee, ordered a slice of pie. 'Anything else?'

'Laurie Brownscombe thought she should have had a stake in the Oaklands Hotel. Her grandmother was a partner in the place.'

He looked at Benson steadily. 'But you were brought up here. You'll know all about that.'

Benson laughed. 'I remember those old ladies. They used to come to church dressed from head to toe in black. They had the sweetest singing voices you ever heard.'

'You didn't tell me.'

'No. I didn't. I take my work here seriously. It's not my place to divulge confidential information to a private investigator. You'll have to accept that, George. All the information goes one way.' He laughed again. 'But I knew you'd find out anyways. If you were as good as I thought you were.'

'You don't think it's relevant to the murder?'

'That Laurie Brownscombe's as jealous as hell of her cousin? No. I've known Mary Ann Cleary since she was a kid. She wouldn't murder anyone. She'll fight like a tiger for that place but she's not the sort to stab a man in the back. If it was the other way round I might be persuaded. I went to High School with Laurie's father. He was never any good. By that time the sisters were too old for much heavy work around Oaklands, but he wouldn't lift a finger. He was always in some bar drinking, even then. Elsie did it all. She could have gone away to college. She was clever enough to get a scholarship. But she stayed on to look after the old ladies, keeping the hotel open somehow.'

'Where's Laurie's father now?'

'In jail. I checked. Where he spent most of his life. But you don't want to hear my stories about the old times, George. Once you get me started we'll be sat here drinking coffee all day. Believe me, you can forget about Mary Ann Cleary. The motive for this killing doesn't go back that far.'

'I'm not sure.'

'What do you mean?'

'I think it's too much of a coincidence that Michael was killed two days after meeting up with friends he'd not seen for twenty years.'

'You think there was a grievance that's been festering away over all that time?'

'Something like that.'

'You find out what it is then, George, and we've got our murderer.' But he spoke as if he didn't really believe it. He stood up and called Lily back into the restaurant so he could pay.

'Can I drive you back to the Oaklands Hotel?' George shook his head. He was glad to be away from the place for a few hours. He sat where he was. Benson drove off and Lily opened the door to admit the group of birders who'd been waiting impatiently outside. While he drank the rest of his coffee he listened to them talking. They were discussing their strategy for the next day's bird race. They might have been planning a military operation in unfriendly territory. At last he could stand no more and he began to walk slowly back to the hotel.

He took an indirect route past the post office and Joe Faggard's museum. The sun was shining but there was still a blustery wind from the sea. On the James Taylor High School sports field a baseball match was being played. After the rain the field was a startling green. A gaggle of teenage girls in brightly coloured clothes waved and cheered. Connie May was there, watching the game through the high wire mesh fence. When she saw George she turned away from the leaping teenagers and they walked the rest of the way together.

'You didn't go with the others to Anahuac,' he said. 'I thought you liked to stay close to Russell.'

'No. I couldn't face it today. All the chat's getting on my nerves. To tell you the truth, Mr Palmer-Jones, I won't be sorry to be home. Russell's very keen on the bird race but it doesn't seem right to me.'

'That's rather the way I feel too.'

'But they say you're going to be a member of the team.'

'Do they?'

'I'd be glad if you would. You could keep an eye on Russell for me.' She smiled but he thought she meant it. He didn't know what to say.

'Well?' she said more brightly. 'Did you find out who Esme Lovegrove was chatting up that lunch time before she died?'

'No. Not yet.' Then he thought that was one aspect of the case he hadn't properly followed up. There were still questions to ask about the appointment Esme had made. He had been distracted by the Adamsons and the Wildlife Partnership. For the first time he thought he could see a way forward.

Chapter Thirty

George caught up with Oliver and Julia in their room, just before lunch. He couldn't dismiss them altogether. They had a motive for Michael's murder. He suspected they had been hiding out there, hoping to avoid him. When he knocked on the door there was a silence, as if they were debating whether it was practical to pretend they weren't in. They must have decided that he couldn't be fooled because a voice called out, 'Just a minute,' and the door was opened by Oliver.

'Ah, George. What can I do for you?'

'You might let me in.' George spoke mildly but he had his foot by the door. He'd had enough of being messed about by them.

'I don't know. Julia has a migraine. Perhaps we should talk somewhere else.'

'I think Julia will want to hear what I have to say.'

'Let him in Oliver.' Julia was resigned but not unwell. 'We've done all we can.'

Oliver stood aside and George walked into the room. Julia was sitting in an easy chair next to the long window which must once have been the door on to the veranda. Mary Ann had stood outside it, listening to a group of young people revealing their secrets, telling the story of their lives.

'You'll have come about Sally,' Julia said. 'Is that it, Mr Palmer-Jones?'

She was wearing a dress he had not seen before, a purchase, he supposed, from the Galleria. Her hair was pinned elaborately away from her face. She was not so concerned about her daughter that she had let herself go.

Oliver looked crumpled and grey. He turned to his wife, as if to warn her not to speak, but she went on impatiently. 'It's no good Ollie. She's not a child any more. You can't take the blame for what she's done.' She looked up at George. 'Our daughter's a manipulative woman, Mr Palmer-Jones. She can twist Oliver round her little finger. She always has done.' She might have been talking about a stranger. 'I'd like to point out that I had no part in this mess. I was furious when I found out that he covered up for her.'

'I didn't,' he said. 'No. Not exactly that.'

'What, exactly, did you do?' George asked.

'She came to me a couple of months ago,' he said. 'Not home. To my office in London.'

'She wouldn't come home!' Julia spat. 'She wanted sympathy. Not home truths.' Oliver ignored his wife's outburst. He had heard it all before, so her words had no meaning. He sat on the edge of the bed. Neither of them thought to offer George a seat and he stood just inside the door, leaning back against it.

'I've never seen her so upset,' Oliver said. 'Not even when she lost her job with the BBC. She was terrified. Really. In floods of tears.'

'She's an actress,' Julia said. 'She was putting it on.'

'Eventually I calmed her down and she told me what happened. An unfortunate prank which had got out of hand. Obviously that's what it was.'

'How much money did she make by this prank?' George asked.

'I'm not sure.' Oliver was defensive. 'Not exactly.'

'But presumably there is a list of donors and donations so the money can be returned? As a lawyer you'd have asked her that?'

'Of course. She's unfortunately vague. You know, George, I think she was very depressed at that time. She had a sort of breakdown.'

Not too depressed, George thought, to dream up the 'prank'.

'If she continues to be unfortunately vague,' he said, 'we'll have to ask the police to look into her bank account and trace all the incomings and outgoings. I suppose she did start a bank account in the name of Wildlife Partnership UK'.

Oliver nodded sadly.

'And if anyone had checked they'd have discovered that the Wildlife Partnership was a perfectly respectable non-profit organization which had done a lot of good work in Central and South America. They'd assume that Sally's charity was part of the same outfit.'

'I don't think,' Oliver said, 'that anyone actually checked. It's a minefield, charity law. Very few people understand it.'

'But Sally would have understood more than most because she'd grown up with it.'

'I suppose she must.'

'And why was she so upset when she came to see you? I take it that she hadn't had a sudden crisis of conscience?'

There was a silence. Oliver considered lying, looked at Julia, then thought better of it.

'No,' he said. 'But she was frightened.' 'Because Cecily Jessop had phoned the Bristol office threatening police action, lawsuits and other unimaginable torments if the Wildlife Partnership turned out to be a fraud?'

Oliver nodded.

'Instead,' George said grimly, 'she consulted me. What did you advise Sally to do?'

'To close down the operation immediately, of course.' It was Oliver the lawyer, the upright citizen.

'Oh, of course! But perhaps you could be a little more specific. You didn't advise her to return the money to the subscribers or to pass it on to the Wildlife Partnership in Houston?'

'That possibility was considered.'

'And then discounted?'

Oliver had been staring at the floor. He looked up. 'She's my only daughter, George. What could I do? If the fraud had been discovered she'd have been ruined. I couldn't take the risk. I advised her how to cover her tracks. I told her to stay in character and fold up the operation as if it were legitimate.'

'And to keep the money.'

'The money wasn't the question!' Oliver was becoming irritable. 'I would willingly have repaid that. But how could she give it back without implicating herself in the fraud? I hoped the fuss would just die away.'

You can't know Lady Cecily Jessop, George thought.

'Then of course,' Oliver went on persuasively, an obvious afterthought, 'in a couple of years' time when it had all been forgotten we would have made a substantial donation to the Wildlife Partnership.'

'Anonymously,' George said, not believing a word.

'Well yes. Anonymously.' He twisted his wedding ring around his finger.

From the chair by the window Julia had been watching them. She's trying to work out what I intend to do, George thought. Still leaning against the door he swivelled to face her.

'When did you find out what Sally had been up to?'

She shrugged. 'The same day. After she'd confessed to Oliver and asked for his help. I could tell he was upset when he came home from work. I guessed it was something to do with Sally. She's the only person he cares that much about. He never sees these friends he's supposed to be close to. He had to cross the Atlantic to do that.'

'And you supported him in his aim to help Sally?'

She shrugged again.

Oliver stood up. His voice was shrill, melodramatic. 'But you weren't concerned about Sally, were you, Julia? You weren't worried that she might actually have to go to prison? No, George. All Julia was bothered about was what people in the village would say if the thing got into the newspapers. That's why she didn't want me to confide in you. If it weren't for her I'd have spoken out sooner.'

'Don't be pathetic, Oliver,' Julia said. 'You're making yourself ridiculous.'

Oliver sat on the bed.

'Weren't you a little concerned about coming here and meeting the Brownscombes who represented the real Wildlife Partnership?' George asked.

'Ah,' Julia said. 'Well Oliver didn't actually tell me about that bit, did you, darling? He told me that Sally had got the idea from an American woman she had met at a party. He didn't tell me that it was quite a particular American, the wife of a bosom pal. He didn't tell me that we'd arranged to spend a week with her on the Upper Texan coast. I didn't realize *that* until Laurie started talking about it at dinner the first night here, and even then it took me a long time to catch on. I was listening to be polite, as one does at dinner parties, but not with any real interest. Then I heard the name and it all came together. That's what Oliver and I were "discussing" when you found us in Boy Scout Wood. I mean fraud is one thing. Quite respectable in certain circumstances. Especially if shares are involved. But murder is quite another.'

'Well really!' Oliver blustered contrived indignation. 'You can't think that Mick's murder could have had anything to do with that other business. I'm sorry George, but if that's what you think you must be losing your judgement.'

Julia looked at him with a malicious smile. George thought she was probably enjoying herself. She spoke slowly.

'Rather a coincidence though, isn't it darling? I don't know what you boys had discussed that first night when you came back to the hotel in Houston worse for wear after the Mexican meal. Perhaps you got all chummy and confessional. Perhaps you admitted to Michael that Sally had been using the Wildlife Partnership name to pay for her smart flat in Bristol. What did you expect him to say, Oliver? "Don't worry, old pal. Don't think about it. We're all friends together after all." But perhaps he didn't say that. After twenty years the friendship might have worn a bit thin. Did he threaten to go to the authorities, darling? Is that why you stabbed him in the back with a chisel?'

'I don't think,' George interrupted quietly, 'that the murder weapon has been found yet.'

She laughed. 'Don't worry. It's not inside knowledge. Just what everyone's been saying. And I'm only joking, George, about Oliver. He wouldn't have the nerve. Not even for Sally, would you, my love? Besides, he couldn't stand by and let Rob Earl be accused of the murder. He's far too much of a gentleman.'

They both looked at Oliver. He seemed on the verge of tears and struggled to speak.

'I didn't tell Michael about Sally. Please believe me. I wouldn't.'

There was a moment of silence, then George continued as if Oliver hadn't spoken:

'Talking about confessions, do you remember your last night at Oaklands? You played a truth game.'

'So we did. How do you know about that?'

George did not answer the question.

'Laurie asked you what was the wickedest thing you'd ever done. What did you tell her?'

There was a pause. 'I don't know.' It was the old Oliver, charming and in control, as if in talking about that night he was reliving his youth. 'I really can't remember. It was nothing too heinous I'm sure. Rob was the exciting one.'

'What *did* the others say?'

'Come on George! It was twenty years ago. And other people's sins have never held much interest for me. I doubt if Michael said very much at all. He went through a silent phase when we travelled through America. Sometimes we forgot he was there.'

'He spoke about crashing his father's car. Does that jog your memory?'

'Did he? Of course he *was* speaking by then. We'd met Laurie. She brought him back to life. But it doesn't help me remember what crime I admitted to. It must have been something extremely boring and unremarkable.'

I wonder, George thought, if Mick would have remembered.

'What will you do now?' George addressed the question to both of them. He found it hard to believe that they could continue their life together, after such antagonism, but perhaps they had devised ways of surviving these skirmishes.

'I want to go home,' Julia said. She stretched her arms above her head.

'Honestly, Ollie, I don't think I can stand it here any longer. You're the lawyer. Surely you can persuade the sheriff to let us go. There might be seats on the flight this evening.'

'Oh, no,' Oliver said. 'That's quite out of the question. Tomorrow's the bird race.'

Then George thought that madness had overtaken them all.

Chapter Thirty-One

They found it just as they were planning to give up the search for the evening – a small patch of freshly dug earth, the size of a pet's grave. It was covered with twigs, impossible to see unless you bent down close. It was under the live oaks at the edge of the garden, in the woodland which Mary Ann intended for a wildlife refuge.

Then they had to bring lights because the lieutenant wanted to come from Galveston and by the time he arrived it was nearly dark. Benson heard about the find at home. He stood like a big grizzly, silhouetted against the floodlights, glaring down at them. They crouched, moving the soil and the leaf mould with small trowels, archaeologists on a dig, looking for buried treasure.

First out of the hole came a short-handled shovel which had been used to dig the pit and also, it turned out later, to hit the back of Esme Lovegrove's skull hard enough to kill her. Then there was a plastic carrier bag. It had come from Gatwick airport's duty free shop and would have held a bottle of spirits – it was too big for perfume or even for packets of cigarettes. Now it contained a chisel with a sharp point and a fat wooden handle, a wood carver's chisel said Benson, who knew about tools. Lovely and old and just right for the job.

'For sticking through a victim's ribs?' said one of the officers but nobody laughed and Benson did not consider that worth answering.

All this George saw from the edge of the gathering. He stood apart from the officers like an uncertain guest at a funeral. He had spent the afternoon sitting on the veranda, listening to the conversations going on around him, asking questions. Esme Lovegrove had been much on his mind.

He had even sought an audience with Joan, the sister. He had offered to go up to her room but she had come to him. They had taken tea together, sitting side by side on an uncomfortable wrought iron bench, and had chatted for half an hour before tiredness or the medication she'd been prescribed had overtaken her.

He had begun to feel a little cold – there was still a cool breeze in the evenings, a remnant of the storm – and was about to go to the bar before preparing for dinner when he recognized the excitement of the officers searching the wood. He sauntered over and stood unobtrusively, watching, tolerated because they knew he was a friend of Benson's. He saw the exhumation of the shovel and the carrier bag. Although the lieutenant was there it was Benson who carried the bag right under the floodlight and opened it, a fist through each handle. He did not see inside but he knew what it contained because Benson described it, lovingly: 'A wood carver's chisel.' And immediately that triggered a memory of his visit to Laurie's house.

It meant nothing to Mary Ann. She was sure it had not been taken from Oaklands. It was the sort of thing a craftsman would own. For as long as she could remember Oaklands Hotel had been run by women and they had no time for wood carving. It was old enough to have belonged to her grandfather but she did not remember seeing it around as a child. Wouldn't it have come as part of a set?

This was what she had told the detective. She repeated the conversation to George when she invited him to her flat after dinner for coffee and brandy.

'Wouldn't it have come as part of a set?' she said again, asking George's advice.

'I think it would.'

He was more interested in the shovel. That must have come from the hotel. He asked her about it.

'Sure. I recognized that. It's been here for ever. I mixed mud pies with it when I was a kid. But I haven't seen it for years. It'll have been in the storeroom with all the other junk.'

Then George said he would have to go.

'That's fine George,' Mary Ann said. 'We're real busy. It's the Birdathon reception tomorrow night. I'll be in the kitchen until dawn.'

'That's still taking place?' he thought the discovery of the murder weapon might have made a difference.

'Mr Benson said it should. It's too late to cancel, he said.'

'I bet he did.'

'I asked Miss Lovegrove if she'd mind. She had no objections. Really, George, she wanted the race to go ahead.' Mary Ann paused. 'And I spoke to Laurie. She's agreed to come over tomorrow night to present the trophy to the winning team. I thought it was time we patched things up.'

'A nice gesture,' George said bitterly. He still considered the bird race an appalling idea.

'Yeah!' Mary Ann said, pleased. 'I thought it was.'

The rest of the bird race team was in the bar, planning its strategy for the following day assisted by the birdwatchers in Rob's group. George saw them from the door but he did not go in. He spent the evening prowling round Oaklands Hotel.

He began outside in the paved yard beyond the kitchen where the residents parked their cars. He crossed the yard and looked up at the house trying to place the window which had been lit on the night of Esme's murder. Through the uncurtained windows of the kitchen he saw that a chef was still working, presumably preparing the next night's feast. He was chopping, hitting the palm of his hand on the wooden handle of a wedge shaped knife, a knife which would have been a more effective weapon than a wood carver's chisel. Mary Ann was there too, and a couple of women stacking a dishwasher but outside it was dark and no one saw him.

The old stables which formed two sides of the yard had been turned into storerooms. The doors were unlocked, there was nothing of value inside. The shovel would have been here with the car spares, a rusting lawn mower, and the piles of cans and bottles waiting for recycling. The storeroom had an electric light, a neon tube which flickered and left the corners in shadow. When George switched it on he had left the door open and a rectangle of light would have been visible from the kitchen, but the people there were so engrossed in their work that they did not notice. Would they have seen a visitor, crossing the yard in daylight, poking around the storeroom? Probably not.

Inside, everyone was in the bar. Even the sleepy old man had deserted his seat in the lounge to watch the preparation for the bird race. It was something special to focus on. They needed that. And a few beers. From the bar came shouts and bursts of laughter. George ignored the noise and continued his tour of the hotel. He walked through the restaurant where the tables were already set for breakfast. He stood for a moment at reception. A pale young man was answering the phone. George hoped briefly that it might be Molly with news which could finish the matter tonight, but in Britain it was four in the morning. If she had news she would have called before. He climbed the stairs and wandered round the corridors, finding his bearings, occasionally bumping into a couple of chambermaids who were turning down the beds. Eventually he talked to them though they would not stop work. He stood in bedroom doorways while they changed damp towels, rinsed out cups, replaced sachets of coffee and sugar with the speed and mechanical efficiency of robots.

Then he let them move on down the corridor while he considered what he had learned and what he should do with the information. He could not face talking to the stone-faced sergeant or the deputies who had been left in charge of the taped off area where the murder weapon had been found. Joe Benson had gone home. George had learned from Mary Ann that Benson had married just a year ago. They had all thought he was a confirmed bachelor, then he had married a Mexican girl a third of his age. There was a baby. Before the murders Joe Benson's romance had been the talk of High Island. It would be easy enough to find out where they lived and George did not even think Joe would mind the intrusion. The constable had invited him home sometime for a beer. He probably wanted to show off his lovely wife and baby. But what would George say to him? I know who killed these people but I've no idea why. Better to let Benson spend the evening with his family in peace.

The bar was quieter. People had started to drift away to bed. Rob, Oliver and Russell May sat at one table. They had enjoyed being the centre of attention. Russell looked every now and again at his wife who was sitting with other women from the party, clasping her orange juice, apparently as proud as punch of him.

'George!' Rob said. 'We could have done with you here. Where have you been?'

Trying to save your skin, George thought. He said nothing.

'The essence of a bird race is in the planning,' Oliver said primly. 'Especially when we're working in such a small area.'

'I'm sure I can safely leave that to you.'

'We need to be at the Bolivar Ferry at dawn, George. That's where we intend to start. Meet for breakfast in the restaurant an hour before that. Mary Ann will leave out cereal and thermos flasks of coffee.'

'I'll be there.' Because although the thought of the race depressed him he felt, like Connie, that they needed looking after. Playing nurse-maid to a bunch of birders, he thought: Has it come to this?

Chapter Thirty-Two

It took Molly longer than she had expected to trace Paul Butterworth. His name was not in the telephone directory. She thought he had probably been a young teacher when he had befriended Mick Brownscombe more than twenty years before. It was possible he was still working in the area. Even if he had changed schools someone might remember him, have an address for him.

She parked in the town centre and enquired at the public library.

'The Grammar School? Well it's comprehensive now, but it's still there.' The librarian was elderly. She had views on the demise of the grammar schools. Molly interrupted and asked for directions. The librarian was offended and gave them, sniffily.

There was a walk through a Victorian park along the River Taw. The tide was out leaving expanses of glutinous mud. In the park the daffodils had been battered by the heavy rain. The school was at the end of a lane of substantial houses with large gardens.

Molly had timed her visit carefully. Ten forty-five. She had thought that would be break-time. All the teachers would be in the staffroom and she might be offered coffee. But when she arrived the playground was empty and she wondered if these days they worked straight through until lunch.

The first building she came to was red brick mock medieval. It had cloisters and quadrangles. She walked round, trying to find a way in. All the classrooms were empty. In some, chairs had been set upon desks. She swore under her breath. She should have realized the school would be closed for Easter. Paul Butterworth, even if he still worked there, might have rented a *gite* in France or be birdwatching in Nepal. She presumed he was still interested in birds. She hoped so. It would make things easier. There would be less to explain.

'Can I help you?' It was a small woman dressed in a tweed skirt and suede boots. She approached Molly carefully across the playground. As if, Molly thought, I'm about to attack her. She probably thinks I'm one of the mentally ill let out unsupervised into the community. It's my clothes. I should have tidied up.

'Can I help you?' the woman said again.

'I'm trying to trace a member of staff,' Molly said. 'For an old boy.'

Her voice, educated and southern, must have reassured the woman. She came closer.

'I'm afraid there's no one here,' she said. 'It's the holidays. I've only come in to open the head's mail.'

'You're a secretary?' This was better than Molly could have hoped for. In her experience secretaries knew far more about what was going on in a school than the teaching staff.

'The head teacher's secretary.' This was obviously a position of status.

'Then perhaps you could help me. Does Mr Butterworth still teach at the school? I believe he's a biologist.'

The woman looked at her. 'I'm afraid I couldn't pass on information about any of our staff,' she said piously.

Trust me, Molly thought, to get one who can hold her tongue.

'Then I'd like to speak to the head,' she said.

'She's away!' The woman's tone was almost gleeful. 'In Tuscany. We're not expecting her back until the day before term starts. It won't give us a lot of time, I'm afraid, to get things straight.' Her disapproval at the head's lack of consideration was compensated for by her delight at Molly's inconvenience. 'If you tell me what it's about. . .'

'No,' Molly said. 'I'd prefer to talk to Mr Butterworth.'

She found a scrap of paper in her anorak pocket. On it she wrote her name and the phone number of the pub where she was staying.

'If Mr Butterworth does work here you'll have access to his

home number. Perhaps you could telephone him. Tell him that I was asking for him. It's about Michael Brownscombe, an old boy of the school. I'll write that name down too. If he's prepared to meet me I'll be at that number. I'm only in the area for another day. I think he would be very interested to see me and he would be disappointed if you didn't give him the opportunity.'

She turned and walked away, ignoring the twittering questions of the woman in the suede boots. She drove back to the pub, though she would have enjoyed the chance to explore the town. The landlord was surprised to see her so soon.

'Nose to the grindstone, is it?' he asked.

He still seemed to believe the fiction that she was writing a book.

Butterworth phoned in the evening, just as she was giving up hope. He spoke softly but without accent. He was very nervous and she wondered how he faced a classroom of children.

'Mrs Tiddy said you were trying to trace me.' Before she had a chance to reply he added: 'I can't tell you anything about Michael. I've not seen him for years. I don't know where he is, even.' There was a panic in his voice.

'I know where he is.'

'Well then. You don't need my help to hound him.'

'It's not a question of hounding. I've news about Michael. I'd like to see you.'

'I'm sorry. It's not convenient.'

She spoke quickly before he could replace the receiver. 'My husband's George Palmer-Jones. If you're a birdwatcher you'll have heard of him.'

There was a pause.

'Of course.'

'May I visit you. This is really very awkward over the phone.'

He made up his mind very quickly, took a deep breath. She thought he was not used to committing himself to anything.

'Tomorrow then,' he said. 'But not too early. I care for my mother. She needs my help in the mornings.' Then briskly he gave her details of how to find him.

He lived in the Taw valley, seven or eight miles inland from

Barnstaple. There was a lane with overgrown hedgerows, late catkins and primroses. Where five-bar gates blocked gaps in the hedge she had a view over water meadows to the river, to grey herons standing one-legged in the water and buzzards sailing over beech woods. The sun was shining.

It was a white stucco house with a grey slate roof, not very big or even very old, only impressive because of the garden. It stood side on to the lane. There was a white gate with enough of a lay-by beside it for her to park and still just allow room for a vehicle to pass. The garden was terraced, not tidy but already full of colour. There were no other houses. The sounds were of farmland; lambs and lapwings and the distant hum of a tractor.

She walked through the gate to the front door. There was no reply to her knock and she thought he had lost his nerve and run away. Then he came hurrying around the house to greet her. She thought she had been right and he must just have qualified when he knew Michael. He had the sort of ageless face which hardly changes between adolescence and senility, but the shock of fair hair hanging over his forehead made him seem young to her. He was wearing cord trousers and a thick, checked shirt. In his hand he carried a plaid rug.

'Come down,' he said, without introducing himself. 'I was just settling mother out of the wind. She likes to be out and the rain's kept her indoors for days. The sun's pleasant but this breeze is still very cool.' The voice was concerned.

Molly followed him down stone steps to a path through a shrubbery.

'She's blind,' he said. 'Almost entirely now. Diabetes. Nothing they can do. We have help during term time but in the holidays I like to spend as much time as I can with her.'

They came to a paved terrace cut into the slope of the hill, sheltered on three sides. In the centre there was a pond with irises and marigolds. To the side of the pond stood a large frog roughly carved from stone. It was two feet high and grinning.

Butterworth saw Molly looking at it. 'Fun isn't it?' he said. 'It was given to me by a pupil. We like it, don't we, Mother? The frog.'

'Very much.'

He gave all his attention to his mother. She wasn't much older than Molly. Certainly she was a great deal more elegant. Her white hair was immaculately cut and styled. She wore tailored trousers and a thick mohair jacket. Her face was made up. Molly caught herself wondering if Paul put on the make up for her and why the idea shocked her. Mrs Butterworth sat very upright on a wooden garden chair and allowed her son to tuck the rug around her.

'I created this garden, Mrs Palmer-Jones,' she said. 'I don't need to see it to enjoy it. Paul can't give it the time it deserves but he keeps on top of it.'

'I try,' he said. He fussed around her like a hair stylist round a favourite customer.

So he's told her about me, Molly thought. At least she knows my name.

'You mustn't bully Paul, Mrs Palmer-Jones. He's always been a frail boy. He has trouble with his nerves. He takes after his father.' She stared unseeing over the garden. 'My husband killed himself when Paul was three years old.'

She spoke in a matter-of-fact tone but it was a startling revelation to make to a stranger.

'I hope I never bully anyone, Mrs Butterworth,' Molly said quietly. Paul's mother smiled.

'Nor do I,' she said. 'But I like people to know how things stand.' She stretched out her hand and touched Paul's arm. 'Take Mrs Palmer-Jones into the house,' she said. 'She won't want me to hear what she has to say. Make her coffee. You can bring me some later.'

'We won't be long,' he said. He was reluctant to leave her.

'Go on. Be as long as you like.'

They sat in a conservatory to talk. The house itself was shabby and unloved. The coffee he made was strong and good and Molly thought he would be skilled at practical things. She wondered again how he coped with teaching. She asked him if he enjoyed it. It was as good a way as any to introduce the subject of Michael Brownscombe's death.

'I hate it,' he said passionately. 'I survive from one holiday to the next. The sixth form aren't too bad. They're interested and they want to work. And the young ones are all right. When they first arrive they're keen because it's all new to them. The rest is a nightmare. But I have to stick at it to keep this place up. Father left us the house but no money. Mother struggled to stay on when he died. She couldn't bear to leave and nor could I.'

'Tell me about Michael Brownscombe,' she said. 'Was he one of the keen ones?'

'Michael was one of the angels.' He smiled. 'From my point of view. Quiet. Well behaved. Some of the teachers thought that was unnatural. He was in the fifth form when I arrived at the school. Sixteen. I was twenty-two. I'd just finished my post-graduate teaching certificate. This was my first job.'

'You introduced him to birdwatching?'

'Not exactly. He was already interested.' It seemed not to occur to him to ask why she wanted to know these things. She thought he probably had little ordinary social contact with other adults. 'I wanted to make a good impression at the school. It was the only way I could see of staying in this house. So I formed a natural history society. To show that I was prepared to make an effort. That although I wasn't much good at rugby I was willing to give up my Saturday mornings. It didn't last long. A few boys and girls came along at the start. We went out locally and I remember I took them in a mini bus to Dawlish Warren. We entered a team in the County Bird Race. Then it just petered out. I suppose I didn't inspire them.'

'But you still took Michael out?'

'Yes. He was a real enthusiast.'

'Was there anyone else?'

'What do you mean?' He looked at her warily.

'Did anyone else come birdwatching with you?'

'No!' The denial seemed too vehement. 'Just Michael and me. And he couldn't come every weekend. His parents were in the holiday business and he was expected to work, especially in the summer. He was young. He had his own life to lead. But I suppose we became good friends. I don't think any of the other teachers knew. I didn't ask him to keep it secret. There was nothing to hide. Not what you might think. I was rather ashamed that I couldn't make friends of my own age. I suppose it seemed pathetic that I had to turn for company to one of the boys.'

'You kept in touch when he went away to university?'

'In the holidays, yes. And we wrote. I was pleased that he'd made friends. He told me about their birdwatching trips.' He paused. 'I suppose I was jealous. I had a hellish time at university. But mother started to be ill at around that time. I had plenty to keep me occupied.'

'Did he tell you he was going to America?'

'I heard that he was going.' The answer seemed deliberately vague. 'What is all this about?' he asked. 'Have you got a message for me from Michael? You said your husband knew him.'

'Michael's dead,' she said. 'He was murdered. At High Island, in Texas.'

'So,' he said calmly. 'After all this time.' He stood up and looked out of the smeared glass down the garden, then turned to face her. 'I suppose I should understand it. My mother still hates my father. And he died more than forty years ago.'

Chapter Thirty-Three

The rules of the bird race were simple. Each team had four members. Three of the four had to see a bird for it to count. The object was to collect as many species as possible in twenty-four hours. All birds had to be seen on or from the Bolivar peninsula.

The I10 marked the boundary.

When the Oaklands team arrived at the Bolivar ferry it was still dark. The lights of Galveston were reflected in the bay. The team was using Oliver's hire car. Oliver seemed altogether more cheerful, quite boyish, as if, in revealing his involvement with Sally's fraud, the slate was wiped clean. He thinks he's charmed me into believing him, George thought. As he would have done in the old days.

Rob was hanging out of the car window and smoking, the murders forgotten. Nothing was as important as winning the bird race. He muttered into the darkness: 'You'd think the storm would have brought something in. This must be the best place to start.' Nobody answered or took any notice of him. The muttering was a nervous habit like the chain-smoking. He could not stand the tension of waiting.

Russell sat in the back with George. Two old men together. Nothing had been said but they knew it needed someone with sharper, younger eyes to be in front to spot chance wanted species by the side of the road. Russell seemed to have lost something of the previous evening's excitement. He's worn out, George thought. Like me. He's looked forward to this trip for so long, now he doesn't have the energy to enjoy it.

George wondered what Molly was doing. He had phoned her before leaving the hotel. In England it would have been late morning.

The landlord recognized the voice before George identified himself. 'She's still out,' he said. 'Went away first thing and I've not seen her since.'

George had felt let down.

It began to get light and they got out of the car. They identified birds on call before: they could see them properly. Hundreds of laughing gulls were roosting on the old pier sheds. Then the sun shone and they could start the race properly. George took notes and counted up the running total. Adult Franklin's gull going north. Brown pelican. And just as they had decided that they had ticked off everything they could expect to see at the ferry there was a juvenile magnificent frigate bird. Huge. A seven-foot wingspan and a forked swallow's tail. Ferocious, like some throw-back from Jurassic times, Oliver said. It had been blown from the Caribbean by the three days of storm. No one could have predicted it.

That set the tone of the day. It was like a dream. Wherever they went they saw all the species they expected to get, and more. George had never known a day's birding like it. The birds Rob had staked out on his day of planning were waiting for them. The willet was still displaying on the post by the side of the road leading to the Flats. A solitary sandpiper was still in the ditch. As the day wore on and their score increased they stopped being surprised by their luck and took it for granted. When they bumped into competing teams who complained about birds they had missed they had to control their glee.

'You always miss a few,' they said. Though that day they missed nothing.

'Well,' George said to Russell, 'it's not much like the old Devon Wildlife Trust Bird Race.'

'No.' Russell shook his head as if he could not quite take it in. He tried to find words to explain how he was feeling but there was no time. They had to get back into the car and drive on to Anahuac. Rob was worried that they were running behind schedule.

They reached the Anahuac Wildlife Refuge at eleven o'clock. It was airless and hot. A heat haze stretched over the marsh to the horizon. By the visitors' centre there was a public telephone and George called Molly again.

'Sorry mate,' the landlord said. 'She's still out.'

For the first time George was concerned. Perhaps he had misjudged the facts of the case and she was in danger. What information could a teacher have which would take all day to pass on?

As he turned away from the phone to return to the car he flushed a large brown moth of a bird which had been lying horizontally along the low branch of a shrubbery tree. Its dead leaf camouflage would have made it impossible to see if it had not moved.

'Chuck Will's widow!' he shouted.

But there was no one to hear him. The others were in the toilet block, and he had to drag them out. Russell hopped out of the cubicle with his trousers round his ankles like a child in a sack race. But they got it. And it fluttered away over the marsh so the carload of birders who pulled up behind them had a brief, tantalizing, untickable view.

At Anahuac, Rob Earl organized a rail pull. He had prepared the rope in advance. It was coiled in the boot of the car, with the packs of sandwiches and the flasks of cold drink. The rope was twenty yards long, strung every six feet with an old square detergent bottle filled with sand. He gave one end to Oliver and the other to George and made them walk across the wet meadow dragging the rope between them.

'It's brilliant!' he said. His face was red with heat and excitement. 'There's nothing like it for flushing out rails.' He turned to Oliver. 'If only we'd thought of a trick like this when we were here the first time. There wouldn't have been so much sitting round the Oaklands Hotel, moaning and waiting for the wind to change.'

Oliver did not reply.

'Isn't it cheating?' George resisted the euphoria. There was the nagging worry about Molly, the unfinished business, the dilemma of what to tell Benson.

'Nothing against it in the rules.'

'All the same.'

'Oh, come on George. Don't be boring. Not today. Today we're making history!'

And that was how he saw it. It was as important to him as that.

They walked slowly, tugging the rope through the marsh grass. George suddenly found the situation ridiculous. What was he doing here, up to his ankles in mud? These were boy's games and he should have grown out of them. He watched the Sora rails which had been skulking in the vegetation fly out into the open. They had short wings and an ungainly, awkward flight which took them only a few yards before they scuttled back into the marsh again. Then he saw a flash of white which made him forget his ethical misgivings. It was the wing of a tiny yellow rail, the bird which Rob must have been after all the time. George felt a rush of adrenaline and yelled with the rest of them. He was still just as much a boy as they were.

Rob was triumphant. 'There you are George. What did I tell you? Wasn't that worth it?'

And George admitted that he supposed it was.

In the afternoon they returned to High Island, to the Audubon sanctuaries. Again Rob had left nothing to chance. He had briefed one of his party, the retired doctor from Inverness, to go round the reserves in the morning and the man was at Boy Scout waiting for them, eager to report what had been seen.

They sat at Purkey's Pond to eat lunch, adding species to the list all the time, feeling like celebrities as people from the Oaklands Hotel turned up to cheer them on.

Connie May was with them. She had been at the sanctuary entrance when they arrived. Perhaps she had been there all morning looking out for the hire car. She beamed.

'I hear you've been doing ever so well,' she said. She sat next to her husband, unwrapped his sandwiches, poured him a drink. Like a mother flushed with pleasure at her child's achievements.

Even Julia Adamson came to Boy Scout Wood. Her face was hidden by large round sun-glasses so George could not tell what she made of them all or why she was there. Perhaps she had come to pass on information because he overheard her say to Oliver:

'The merry widow's arrived at Oaklands. They're making a fuss of her of course. You can tell she's loving every minute. She can hardly be grieving for Michael, can she?'

Oliver said: 'And I suppose you'd grieve for me?'

The thought of Laurie at Oaklands made George more anxious. He was taking a risk. He should have passed on his suspicions, however tenuous, to Benson. There would at least be a shared responsibility then. He was desperate to talk to Molly but it seemed that the day had a momentum of its own. He could not control it. There was no time to get to a phone.

Rob moved them on. To Smith Oaks. To the Oilfield Ponds. And as night began to fall, back to the coast, to the town of Gilchrist, close to where they had started. In the dusk, black crowned night heron drifted over their heads. As they drove back to the hotel they completed their list with a barn owl which they saw in the headlights hunting along the roadside.

George, who had spent the day expecting a disaster, was relieved. It was over. He could take charge of events again.

'This is it then,' Rob said. 'Glory awaits us.'

They knew they had won. Even cautious George was sure of that.

The others walked ahead of him into the house, their arms round each other's shoulders, swaying like drunken football fans after an away win.

Rob turned back. 'Come on, George! We did it! Don't be such a cold fish!'

George shook his head. The day had been an escape. Nothing had been resolved. With a sudden panic he pushed past them into the hotel.

Chapter Thirty-Four

Molly must have been waiting for his call because the phone was lifted after the first ring.

She spoke. He listened in silence.

'Well,' she said at last. 'What will you do?'

'It's not proof.'

'You could get proof. If you wanted to.'

He didn't answer.

'Do you want to?' she demanded.

He was still thinking about that when she said, 'I'm going to bed. And in the morning I'm driving home.'

'I'll come home tomorrow,' he said. 'Whatever happens.'

He replaced the phone. Somewhere there was an answering click. A door being shut. Or opened. He was in Mary Ann's flat. He had asked to use the phone there. The rest of the hotel was a madhouse. Even from here he could make out the strains of the country band Mary Ann had hired for the night, cheers, singing. And footsteps. He could hear footsteps on the polished wood floor. He had not locked the door behind him. He turned round, startled, although he had been half expecting her. In her hand was a kitchen knife.

'Not a chisel then, this time,' he said.

'I want to talk to you.' Her voice was urgent. She waved the knife in front of him.

'Of course not,' he went on as if she hadn't spoken. 'The chisel was only meant for him, wasn't it? It was special. Why was that?' He knew already.

'Because of Helen,' she said. 'He killed our Helen.'

'Little Nell.'

'That was his name for her,' she spat back angrily. 'We never called her that.'

'She was an artist,' he said.

'She was brilliant! She could have gone to Art School and made a living at it. All the teachers said that.'

'It was her chisel? She used it to make her carvings?'

Connie May nodded.

'When did you find out?' she said.

'About Helen? Just now. My wife's been talking to Paul Butterworth. I should have guessed, shouldn't I, when I saw you at the High School watching the girls.'

'She was their age when she died.'

'Why don't you tell me about it?'

'That's why I'm here,' she cried. 'Not to hurt you. To tell you. I had to make you listen. Too many people have walked away while I've tried to explain.'

She sat next to him on the sofa with the point of the knife against his chest so he could feel it pricking him through the thin material of his shirt. She had been a school cook. She was confident with knives. He supposed he would be able to overpower her if he had to but he hoped he wouldn't have to try.

'Helen was a school-friend of Mick Brownscombe's wasn't she?' he prompted.

She nodded. 'We were pleased as punch when she got to the Grammar. She was never what you'd call brainy. But a worker. A tryer. And good with her hands.'

'Younger than Mick?'

She nodded again. 'She met him at that club Mr Butterworth started for the kiddies. She'd always been fond of animals. We didn't think there'd be any harm in it.'

'The school entered a team in the County Trust Bird Race,' George said.

'How did you know about that?'

'I found a winner's certificate among Mick Brownscombe's belongings. He'd kept it. Their friendship must have meant a lot to him.'

And that was how I first knew it was you, he thought. That among other things. Russell organized the bird races for the Devon Trust. He must have known Michael, must have recognized him as Wilf Brownscombe's son but he claimed never to have met him. He could have told me today. I gave him the chance. But still he said nothing.

'It meant a lot to Helen,' Connie May said. 'She waited for him all the time he was at college.'

'He kept one of her wood carvings,' George said. 'He brought it with him when he left Britain.'

'When he ran away!' she said.

They sat for a moment without speaking. Outside in the garden fireworks were being let off. There were shouts and screams.

'What happened that night?' George asked.

'He'd been drinking,' she said. 'Working in some bar his father owned.'

And you've never had a drink since, George thought.

'Helen spent the evening there. It was the only way she could get to see him. Wilf never gave him time off. The last bus home was at ten-thirty. She left the bar and walked into the village. It was raining, cold, the end of the season. He told her to wait and he'd drive her home when the bar closed but she was a sensible girl and she said she'd get the bus. He didn't like that. He followed her. In his father's car.'

George imagined the narrow Devon lane with its overgrown hedgerows, the boy driving frantically after the girl, hoping to make his peace with her before the bus took her away.

'He skidded,' Connie said. 'Crashed into her.' She turned her head away but the point of the knife was still at his chest.

'What did he do?'

'Left her. Went back to the bar. Phoned an ambulance. And phoned his father Wilf Brownscombe. Just the man to fix anything. By the time the police arrived to find out what had happened there were half a dozen witnesses to swear that Mick Brownscombe had never left the bar all evening.'

'Why are you so sure that he had?'

223

'Russell was a special constable. He had friends who were policemen. He knew what was going on. If anyone had tried hard enough there'd have been forensic evidence to link that car to the accident. But Wilf Brownscombe had money and influence and he knew too much about some very senior police officers. You don't only get corruption in the city, Mr Palmer-Jones. No one tried very hard.'

And it *had* happened, George thought. Just as Connie had described. Mick admitted it. On High Island in the middle of a storm he told the others how he had crashed his father's car when he was drunk. He couldn't admit to it all. That was too terrible a secret even for the truth game. But Laurie had realized there was more to be told. She'd seen him as damaged goods and that she could do what she liked with him.

'We tried to get justice,' Connie went on. 'We wrote to the papers and the chief constable. The letters weren't printed. Russell was sacked from his job as a special because they said he was too emotionally involved. Then Michael suddenly flew off to America. His dad hadn't liked the idea before. He'd been dead set against it. But suddenly the trip had his blessing and Michael flew away to enjoy the holiday of a lifetime.'

No, George thought, remembering what Oliver had said about the trip, Michael didn't enjoy it. He hardly knew where he was. It was only when he came to High Island and met Laurie that he considered any future for himself. And then he grasped the chance. He was desperate. He hated his father for saving him from prosecution. He should have been grateful but he hated him. He couldn't go home.

'Everyone forgot about it,' Connie said. 'Even some of our friends forgot that we'd ever had a daughter and when people asked us we'd say: "No. No children." You don't want to have to explain.'

'But of course you didn't forget.'

'We wanted justice,' she cried. 'That was all that kept us going. We'd lost our only daughter.'

As Sally was the Adamsons' only daughter and Oliver would have done anything for her.

She took a deep breath and tried to calm herself. 'We knew Michael would have told Mr Butterworth what he'd done,' she said. 'They were that close. He would have had to tell someone and there was no one else he could confide in. If Butterworth had come out into the open, made a public statement that would have been enough. We could have left it alone.'

'But he wouldn't?'

'We saw him several times but we couldn't persuade him. I suppose it was a sort of loyalty.'

'Why did you leave it so long before trying to find Michael?'

She looked at him as if he were a fool.

'Because we couldn't afford it. Until Russell was made redundant.'

'You knew he was in Houston?'

'Oh, yes,' Connie said bitterly. 'We found out that much. We knew he'd set up in business for himself and was doing very nicely thank you.'

'So you booked on this trip.'

'We'd been planning it for years.'

'There were no friends out here working for British Gas, were there? You thought you would hire a car and go to Houston to find Michael. But there was no need. Michael came to you.'

'Yes,' she said. 'He came to us.'

'Did you mean to kill him?'

'No! We wanted to talk to him. To show him how much he'd hurt us.'

'But you brought the chisel with you.'

'To remind him. Of what had been. Of the waste.'

'Why then was he killed?'

She didn't answer and he changed tack, said conversationally: 'You shouldn't have made up that story about overhearing Esme Lovegrove. I was in the lounge the lunchtime of the day she died. She saw you burying the chisel and you had to kill her. You made up the story to save yourself.'

She looked at him with growing horror.

'Not me,' she said, so quietly that it was almost a whisper. 'Is that why you think I'm here?' She looked at the knife, threw it away from her onto the floor. That was to make you listen. I had to make you understand why he did it. Why do you think I asked you to stay with him all day? So that it couldn't happen again!'

'Where is he now?' George asked.

'Quite safe. With Rob and Mr Adamson. Everyone's making a fuss of them for winning the race. I wanted him to have that.'

'Russell killed Michael and Esme Lovegrove?'

She paused, then nodded. 'Michael Brownscombe didn't recognize us at first. We'd followed him down that narrow trail. It was raining. No one else was about. We thought we'd lose him and Russell shouted after him. We'd been talking to him earlier about bird watching in Devon and he didn't have a clue who we were. You'd think he'd remember, even after twenty years. So Russell shouted. He turned round and then he did know us. Perhaps he had all along and he'd just been pretending. But he wouldn't stop and talk. He turned his back on us and carried on along the trail. Russell lost his temper then. He picked up one of those metal poles and ran after him. He hit him. He's never been a violent man and I wasn't expecting it. I couldn't stop him. Then he rolled him off the track and stuck the chisel in his back. It was to remind him of Helen, Russell said. As if Michael would know. He must have been unconscious. Russell can't have known what he was doing. After all those years of brooding ... that's what I came here to explain. And perhaps he was right. Perhaps that's what Brownscombe deserved.'

'And Esme? Did she deserve it?'

'No. She was just a stupid woman. Russell went off on his own to bury the chisel. I thought they might search our rooms. I wanted to go with him but he wouldn't have me involved. He found the plastic bag in the dustbin and the shovel in that shed by the car-park. Esme saw him go into the woods from her bedroom window and followed him. To chat him up. I suppose she thought it was exciting going after a married man. He lashed out at her with the shovel. He came running up to our room in tears. I'm surprised nobody saw him. He didn't know what to do. He wanted to hide her body but I said no, that wouldn't be fair. To leave her sister not knowing, wondering. We had to wait for Helen to die. She was on a life-support machine for three weeks. All the time we were hoping she might pull through. I told him to put the body where someone would find it.'

She stopped for breath and looked directly at him. 'I had to find you this evening to tell you. I waited until you were on your own. Russell's not himself. He might do something silly again.'

'Why didn't you tell me the night he killed Esme? Why the story about her arranging to meet someone?'

'Because of the bird race. He so much wanted to take part in that.'

From the stable yard there came a noise: one voice, yelling. It was too early for the revellers to be returning to their cars and this was different from the good-natured taunts in the bar. George could not make out the words but the tone was sharp, deadly serious.

Connie recognized it immediately.

'That's him,' she said.

George ran out of the flat and along the corridor past the kitchen to the back door. Connie sat for a moment, frozen, then she followed.

Two figures stood in the stable yard. Laurie Brownscombe was spot-lit by a security lamp. She must have been on her way to her car. Russell May was closer to the out-house, in shadow. Laurie was turned towards him with a puzzled expression on her face, not scared in the least.

'I'm sorry. Did you want to speak to me?'

'I want to speak to you lady. Tell me. Did you know you were sheltering a murderer for twenty years?'

He moved out of the shadows towards her. Laurie edged away from him towards her car.

'Don't turn your back on me,' Russell shouted, petulant as a child. 'Don't you dare do that!' Then, still like a playground bully: 'I'm bigger than you. And I've got a gun.'

'Has he?' George demanded in a whisper to Connie.

'Of course not.'

But George thought it was not impossible. He had seen all the news reports about how easy it was to buy firearms in the States. Russell was angry enough and convincing enough to get away with it.

Laurie stood very still, her hands flat palmed towards him.

'He was going to marry my daughter,' Russell said. 'Not you. Not some stuck-up American. There'd have been children. My grandchildren.'

He moved towards her. George inched forward too. Still he was not in a position to see whether Russell May was holding a weapon.

Suddenly there was an explosion of noise. A shout followed by a gunshot. The sound was so intense that George turned his head away. When he looked back at first the scene seemed unchanged. Laurie Brownscombe still stood, her hands ahead of her. The noise had not attracted attention from the hotel. To the people inside it was just one more firecracker.

Then he realized that Connie was screaming and he saw Russell May lying on his back in the yard. Joe Benson, stiff-armed with a gun in his hand moved into the spotlight.

George walked towards him.

'He said he was armed.' Benson's voice was gentle, almost apologetic. 'I couldn't take the chance.'

'No.' And wasn't it better, George thought, to end like this, than with a squalid court case and years in a Texan jail? 'No,' he said again. 'You couldn't take the chance.'

'What did he mean about his daughter? About Laurie having taken her place?'

'I'll explain it all to you later. Over a beer.'

Benson lowered his gun and put his hand on George's shoulder. In the distance they heard drunken singing. 'Rule Britannia' and 'Land of Hope and Glory.' Rob and Oliver were celebrating.